Charming

Charming

Jade Linwood

SOLARIS

First published 2023 by Solaris
an imprint of Rebellion Publishing Ltd,
Riverside House, Osney Mead,
Oxford, OX2 0ES, UK

www.solarisbooks.com

ISBN: 978-1-78618-846-5

10 9 8 7 6 5 4 3 2 1

A CIP catalogue record for this book is available from the
British Library.

Designed & typeset by Rebellion Publishing

Printed in Denmark

To all those princesses
who realised
that they could rescue themselves

The Palace of Sleep

NCE UPON A time, in a land far away...
There is a palace. It is as much fort as palace, though splendid, in a square, frowning sort of way, its towers muscular and business-like. The formal grounds are perfectly groomed, although, strangely, not one gardener can be seen.

The lake, in its marble bed, lies utterly still, a perfect mirror of a clear blue sky dotted with white clouds. The actual sky is dove grey, raining in a soft and constant drizzle, of which no single drop mars the lake's surface, nor bends a blade of the perfectly scythed grass.

Not one bird sings, not one bee buzzes, not one insect darts through the unmoving air. And even in the open, the scents of leaf and grass and water are strangely muted, like things smelled in a dream.

All around the edges of the grounds is a huge hedge of briars, as tall as a clocktower, set thick and close and twisted. Its trunks are gnarled and furrowed and as wide as a man's thigh, its stems gleaming red and writhing like the veins of a giant. Its thorns are mahogany daggers, and its leaves bristle with grey, jabbing spines. This hedge of briars never flowers, nor fruits; and that is just as well, for its berries, however large and juicy and gleaming, would surely be poisonous.

A little way outside the briar hedge, near a clearing, two fellows crouch in some bushes. One of them does not need to put much effort into it: being short and oddly shaped, he is what you might call 'pre-crouched.' This is Roland, something between a valet and an accomplice.

The other is so tall that, despite his best efforts, his slightly damp golden locks are visible above the top of the foliage, like the nest of a particularly fussy and well-groomed bird.

This is Jean-Marc Charming Arundel, more generally known as Prince Charming.

He has all the expected attributes. Well, many of them, at any rate.

He is certainly very handsome.

"WHY THE EVER-LOVING *Goose* are there ogres?" the Prince muttered, glowering through the bushes. He did a good glower. Like most expressions, it only made him more handsome. If the man ever caught a cold, he would blow his nose appealingly.

Roland blowing his nose, on the other hand, was something to inspire nausea in people fifty feet away. He snorted (imagine, if you will, the sound of a frog drowning in yoghurt).

"They probably thought the palace was empty," Roland said. "That's their thing. They're like them little crabs, whatsit, hermit jobbies. Ogres can't build, they don't have the brains or the patience, but they find an abandoned palace, fort—even a mill, in a pinch—and they're in like rats down a sewer. Big, hairy, tusky, stinky rats. Saw the palace, but couldn't get past the briars."

"Stinky is right." Charming wrinkled his nose.

"I know. Nothing else 'round here smells hardly at all, 'snot natural. But them? They pong, all right."

"Look who's talking." Charming sighed, then turned back to his study. "I can see two adults and two youngsters, sitting around what I sincerely hope is the corpse of a pig, and not some local tragedy."

Roland sniffed. "Yep. Pig. *This* time."

"I'm amazed even you can smell anything other than ogre."

"The important thing is they don't smell *us*."

The ogres, were, indeed, pungent; a bloody, dank, cheesy reek. They had long tusks, and long, sharp, extremely dirty nails on both hands and feet. They also looked as though their skin was somewhat too big for them, sagging around their middles and joints. Even the young ones were twice Charming's height—the adults were as tall as oak trees. Each had by their side a crude club, little more than a tree branch with most of the bark knocked off by use, stained here and there with old blood. They were not above striking each other with them as they fought over the meal.

Charming stared up through the drizzle at the towers of the ducal palace, just visible over the briar hedge. "I hope it's worth it."

"So do I," Roland said. "It's a bit risky, this. I mean, apart from ogres, which we didn't know about, there's the what you might call 'interested bystanders.' Which, I might remind you, we did. Know about. 'Cause I told you. And you listened about as much as you normally do."

"Judging by the state of the place, the interested bystanders have *lost* interest," Charming said.

"It's possible," Roland admitted. "They do that. And then they remember things. And one day they turn up on your doorstep reminding you about some bargain great-grandpa made of a summer evening, which you're now responsible for, ta very much."

"I'll cross that particular troll-guarded bridge should it appear in front of me. Hold on, they're getting up, they must have finished. Shall we get on?"

"Don't say I didn't warn you," Roland muttered.

"You didn't warn me about the ogres," the Prince said with a grin, and slipped from the bushes with his usual lithe grace to sneak up on the big male. Grumbling, Roland followed.

Charming hacked through the big male's hamstrings and, as the roaring ogre toppled forward, leapt up his back like a startled deer and sprang over his head, taking out the big female on his way past with a well-timed stroke to the throat. The ogres' two offspring stood side by side, gaping, as they struggled to catch up with events.

Roland, who was finishing off the big male with an efficient dagger into his ear, was promptly drenched with the female's blood—which, like everything else about them, stank. It was the aroma of a butcher's stall which had crashed into a cheesemonger, then been abandoned in the hot sun for at least a week.

"Oh, very nice," Roland shouted. "Thank you *so* much."

"Oh, stop complaining," the Prince replied, as he jauntily dodged the descending club of one of the younger ogres. "I'm doing all the hard work." He nipped around and poked the ogre in the bum, causing him to turn clumsily but at high speed and whack his nearby brother across the head with his club, felling him like a tree. "Timbeeerrrr!"

Roland dodged the falling ogre, just. "Showy," he said. "Always so bloody *showy*."

It takes more than a single blow from a club to knock out an ogre, but once he was on all fours, blearily shaking his head, it was easy enough for Roland to put his dagger through his eye, nipping out of the way as the giant collapsed. "See," he said to the corpse. "No need for all that palaver, is there?"

The corpse, unsurprisingly, failed to respond. Charming was dodging about in front of the remaining ogre, which kept whacking his club at where the Prince had just been.

"Finish the blasted thing off, will you?" Roland snarled. "I want to get this stink off me."

"Do you really... oops! ...think... oho, will you, eh? ...anyone will notice? I mean, you're not the... wahey! ...most fragrant of creatures, Roland."

"That's *my* stink," Roland said. "I *worked* on that. It's my whatsit, signature perfume. *Some* people find it very appealing."

"How extremely odd of them. Oh, all right, I suppose we should get on." Charming looked around, leapt up a nearby tree like a leopard, and holding on with his left hand stabbed the ogre through the flabby chest.

It took a moment for the beast to realise he was dead, looking down at the sword, frowning. Then he pitched backwards, taking Charming's sword with him.

"Bother. Stuck on a rib." Charming dropped out of the tree—right onto the last ogre, which neither of them had noticed, fast asleep in the bushes below.

His entire family being slaughtered had not wakened him from his stuffed slumber, but a pair of scratched and battered leather boots and six feet of muscular Prince landing on his privates did the job.

He bolted upright, roaring, projecting the Prince through the air, to land on his back, inches from the briar hedge. And a long way from Roland, or his sword.

Charming had had the breath knocked right out of him, and for a moment could only stare at the approaching ogre. Roland was scurrying towards him, but the beast was closer, and there was nowhere to go. The briars were an impenetrable wall. The ogre raised his club.

Charming managed to turn himself over and scoot out of the way with inches to spare. Slam! Down came the club, where his legs had been seconds before, as Charming's feet shot up in the air and slapped down into the mud, hauling him upright. Slam! The club shattered a rock, sending fragments whistling around Charming, one of them ripping through his sleeve. Charming leapt over the club as it came down again and grabbed the ogre's forearm, digging his fingers into the wiry hair, and clinging on as the club swept back into the air.

The ogre held his club aloft, scowling, looking for the annoying creature that had been *just there* a moment ago.

Charming held on with all his might, trying not to breathe in, his boots dangling just above the ogre's shoulder. His foot brushed the ogre's ear, and the creature shook his head.

Charming closed his eyes for a moment, then opened them and let go, springing off the ogre's shoulder and landing in a nearby tree.

The ogre worked out where he was just as Roland sliced

through his ankle tendon. He flailed towards the Prince, hampered by his newly-crippled leg. Roland threw the Prince his sword, and he caught it, and, dispensing with the flourish, got the ogre through the throat.

This time Charming was the one who got drenched.

He sat back in the crook of the tree, and looked down at himself, trying not to gag. "That's *never* going to come out, is it?" he said. "Now, normally I might say, showing up bearing the evidence of a hard-won fight always goes down well. But I think the stench is likely to make things come up, not go down. I suppose there's the river?"

"If I *might* point out to Your Highness," Roland said, "that river comes *out* of the city. You en't going to get any cleaner bathing in that. There's a spring, just the other side of the briars."

"Oh, for a proper hot bath, and lithe and willing maidens with warm towels," the Prince said, descending from the tree.

Roland collected his pack beast. It was a bony, ugly creature with capacious saddlebags and a permanently disgruntled expression, and was generally referred to, should anyone ask, as '*mostly* donkey.'

"No lithe maidens for you in there," Roland said. "Or just the one."

"True," said Charming. "But I'm sure I'll cope."

Our heroes, or our hero-and-a-bit, started towards the hedge of briars.

ROLAND PULLED A small double-headed axe from his pack. Charming eyed it suspiciously, and looked at the massive, tangled wall of spines and trunks. "Are you *sure* that's going to get through?"

Roland shrugged. "That wizard's usually reliable. For a wizard. I mean, you *could* try with that pretty sword of yours, but I don't fancy your chances."

"It just looks so small."

"Size isn't everything," Roland smirked, and swung. The blade gleamed flatly as a snake's eye. When the edge hit them, the briar stems parted with somehow unsettling ease, as though they were hardly there at all, though they gave off a thick, bitter smell, like the taste of woodsmoke. There was a low rushing sound, though there was no wind. Green dust sprayed from the cut.

Roland swung again.

"Can you make it any higher?" Charming complained, scrambling along in a back-wrenching stoop and trying not to impale himself on thorns.

"My arms are only so long. You want to try? This isn't as easy as it looks."

"The axe won't work for me, will it? That's what the wizard said. Needs your 'special qualities,' Roland."

Roland muttered something obscene, but kept swinging. A single rowan tree, slender and flower-crowned, appeared as the briars thinned; Roland glared at it and gave it a wide berth. "What is it with you and rowans?" Charming said. Roland did not answer.

By the time they emerged by the spring-fed pool in the palace grounds, there was little left of Charming's shirt. He whisked off the remnants along with the rest of his clothes, placed the scuffed boots carefully close to hand on the bank, and plunged into the cold water with a gasp. "Soap?" he prompted.

Roland threw him a bar of soap and clambered in more slowly, retaining his under-things, which consisted of baggy drawers and a pair of extremely thick socks whose original colour could only be guessed at, and only by the brave.

Charming scrubbed soap through his blood-drenched hair. "Oh, this is going to *ruin* the condition. I wonder if there's any almond oil in that palace. I suppose an avocado might be too much to ask for."

"Given the palace's been bespelled since before they started importing them, probably, yes."

"I shall just have to make do." Charming emerged from the pool, looking rather too much like a piece of classical statuary for anybody's good. His hair, despite the soap, was quickly drying to a leonine mane, if a little fluffier than usual. Roland produced clean clothes from his saddlebags, and they made their way towards the palace.

Now its entire frontage was visible, it was obvious that, despite its manicured grounds, the palace had been built for withstanding armies. It stood on a hill commanding a sweeping view down into the valley. The city of Caraggia, some way upriver, was a picturesque tumble of warm red domes, austerely imposing civic architecture and crowded streets, through which the river curved, gleaming in the sun. A wide carriageway swept down from the gates of the palace towards the city, until the briars blocked it. The air at least did not smell of ogre, though it did lack the scents that a damp summer day should have. Instead of the sweet green of wet growing things, it smelled like an old, empty barn, where hay had been stored long ago; it smelled of dust and the long-gone ghosts of a thousand tiny meadow flowers.

"Well, will you look at that," Charming said. "The grass looks as though it was just scythed yesterday."

"Stasis," Roland said.

"Whosis?"

"Stasis. Everything within the bounds of the briars has been in stasis—as in, not growing, or dying, or changing. Interesting spell. Nasty in the wrong hands. Or just the stupid hands. It's all in the wording. I knew a wizard, once, tried to use it to make himself immortal."

"Didn't it work?"

"Oh, it worked, all right," Roland said, with a deeply unpleasant grin. "He's probably still there, in that box."

Charming gave him a sideways look.

"You remember what I told you?" Roland said, as they neared the great iron gates. Two guards stood grasping their spears.

"Of course I remember. You are *sure*? It's a long way to the next one."

"Told you. It's all in the wording."

The guards remained staring straight ahead.

Roland put his hand to the gates, which swung aside with a deep groan.

They walked through the inner courtyard, observed only by statues, most of them high-nosed men in heavy robes; one, presumably the Duke, depicted in armour, on a rearing horse, his sword aloft. Roland tied up the beast, and they approached the inner doors. "Ready?" Roland asked.

The inner doors opened with a groan so dramatic it could have been scored for a dozen shrieking violins.

PICTURE THE SCENE. The main reception hall of the ducal palace. Without, a fortress. Within, a floor of red and white tiles laid in intricate geometric patterns, high windows spilling a tranquil silver light across the room. It smells of the memories of perfume: musk, amber, civet.

Every wall is rich with frescoes, depicting military triumphs and various interactions (only the friendly ones, of course) with the Good Folk, in the stiff but colourful style of a bygone age.

And these unmoving crowds, frozen in time, are reflected in the room itself. A young man bows over a lady's hand, one toe pointed before him; he wears a long, full robe in deep blue embroidered with gold, its sleeves brushing the floor. The lady wears a voluminous green gown, the wide sleeves trimmed with dark fur. She looks down on the man's bent head with an expression of faint distaste, from beneath an elaborately plaited hairstyle topped with a jewelled net. A young dog is caught in mid-pounce at a cat, which, judging by its puffed fur and snarl, had no desire to make friends, and has not mellowed over the years. A servant bears a jug of wine, and is in the act of surreptitiously wiping his mouth on his sleeve. The whole room is like some giant, complex game of chess. Even Charming, known for his poise, stands for a moment, dumbstruck.

As for those frozen in the hall—did they once have lives, hopes, loved ones? Homes of their own now rotted to dust, gardens all overgrown, families left waiting beyond the Palace walls, for whom great-great-grandma is little more than a rumour?

But they are almost all, even the best-dressed of them, servants. Most of the rest left before the fateful birthday, knowing what was about to befall those who stayed. And who cares about servants' stories? Apart from the Good Folk. They sometimes show an interest in servants; and if you're very clever and *extremely* lucky, you might even survive it.

And *there* is the Lady Bella. Born to wealth and power

and loving parents, gifted with wit, beauty, grace, poise, and song. Lucky, lucky Lady Bella—if you forget the curse and the hundred years of sleep, you might believe nothing bad could ever happen to her.

In her long sleep, she has sometimes dreamed. Most of her dreams are gentle, and full of laughter and music and sunlight. But now and then, she dreams of her christening. A warm, bright place. Happy gabble, friendly faces bending above her, smiling.

A sudden change in temperature. A chilly gloom, a spreading quiet. A single face, not friendly at all, with flat, unblinking eyes.

As a baby, she used to scream, which is the only power babies have. In her dream, she is robbed even of that, clutched in unbreakable silence.

The face draws closer, the eyes penetrating and cold, and then it smiles.

And there the dream ends, with a smile, and silence.

"I DON'T KNOW whether I'm more disconcerted by the people or the clothes," Charming whispered. "Look at those robes! How did anyone *move* in them?"

"They're aristocracy, like you. They have other people to move for them," Roland said. He did not whisper, and his voice grated on the silence.

"But why are they here?" Charming peered at the necklace around the lady's neck.

"Got to make sure their Dukeships had a proper functioning palace to wake up to. I *told* you all this, but you were too busy making sheep's eyes at that tumbler."

"Oh, yes, the tumbler." Charming gave a reminiscent sigh. "*Astonishingly* flexible."

"You keep going on like that, and even a lass who's been literally locked up asleep for a hundred years isn't going to fall for your charms. And that necklace is paste."

"Really?"

"Really. Come on, or the hundred years'll be up before we get there."

Research is a valuable thing. If you're looking to wake someone who's under a spell, it's worth doing some digging into the conditions of the spell she's under.

The basics had remained reasonably accurate: A daughter is finally born to a long-childless couple. One of the Good Folk doesn't get invited to the christening, takes offence, turns up anyway and curses the child to die on her twentieth birthday. One of her sisters turns the curse aside so she only goes to sleep. Briars grow up all around the castle, etc. etc.

This, however, is where the shift happens. "She'll wake up in precisely one hundred years, and by the way, there'll be a prince there, who is the very picture of love," gets turned, over the years, into: "She'll wake up at true love's kiss, which will be provided by the brave and noble prince who risked his life to find her."

It's a fine example of romanticisation. It makes a better story, especially if you're trying to persuade teenage girls that having no life at all until a man comes along is a perfectly acceptable fate.

Not to mention that the Good Folk are extremely precise with language and can use it to tie you into knots that would make a sailor cry. Also, staying out of their interpersonal quarrels is really a *very* good idea. (Seriously, why *else* would someone not invite a Very Powerful Fay to the Christening, when this is obviously an all-round Bad Idea? Because another Very Powerful

Fay persuaded them not to, that's why. As to the reasons they might have done such a thing...

Well, that's another story.)

CHARMING AND ROLAND passed down winding corridors, where here and there servants had been caught mid-bustle. Portraits adorned the walls, many of them showing the same young woman, from a round-faced, wide-eyed baby in her mother's arms, to a young girl perched on a plump and glossy pony to a young woman playing the lute. In every picture she smiled and grew more beautiful, and in every one she was surrounded by adoring faces.

Eventually our heroes arrived at the bedchamber of the Lady Bella Lucia dei' Sogni. Where the rest of the palace smelled ancient and unused, this room had a little freshness, a hint of spring flowers. It was draped in dark blue silk, embroidered with maroon fleurs-de-lis. A maid slept in the chair by the bed, her hands folded in her lap.

The lady herself lay under a silk coverlet, the reverse of the draperies: blue fleurs-de-lis on a maroon background. The colours might have been specifically chosen to flatter her rich olive skin, but in truth she would be beautiful in a hessian sack. Masses of dark curls cascaded over the pillows, softer and glossier than the silk.

Charming gave a soft whistle. "She's actually as pretty as her portraits. Prettier. How often does that happen?"

"Hmph," said Roland. "You watch yourself. It's not just the Good Folk, you're looking at some seriously powerful would-be in-laws, here."

"It'll be fine," Charming said. "Trust me."

A subtle shiver went through the room. The draperies stirred. Roland sniffed the air. "Right, it's time."

Charming got down on one knee, next to the bed. It might have been sheer luck that a shaft of sunlight fell through a gap in the curtains just then, transforming his hair into a corona of gold and making the blue of his eyes glimmer like sapphires.

The air rippled. The hair on Charming's neck stood on end as magic rushed over his skin.

The Woken Princess

HE LADY BELLA yawned as prettily as a kitten, stretched, and opened her wide, dark eyes. "Oh!" she said. "Good morrow. Thou must be the Prince."

For a moment, Charming only smiled. Then he coughed, and shook his head. "And you must be the most beautiful creature I've ever seen," he stumbled. "I'm sorry, I'm a little overwhelmed. I had a whole speech and everything."

She laughed, and turned her gaze to Roland. "Hail. Thou wert not in the spell."

Roland rubbed his nose. "No, well," he said. His usual truculence seemed to have retreated, to be replaced with something that looked almost like shyness. "I'm his... valet."

"I trow you look after him very well," she said, looking over at the Prince. "He appears as though you do, certain."

To the astonishment of the Prince, something that

might almost have been a blush appeared beneath the layer of grime that Roland had managed to reacquire between the pond and the palace.

The maid coughed. "Excuse me," she said. She moved between Charming and the bed, folding her arms and radiating protectiveness from every inch of her tiny frame. "*Sirrahs,* th'art in Milady's bedchamber, I know 'twas in the spell but 'tis still improper."

"Ah, yes, of course," Charming said. "My apologies." He rose to his feet, put his hand on his heart, and bowed. "Milady."

"Sir." She held out her hand. "Your name, if you will."

"Prince Charming." He smiled reassuringly at the maid. "I do have documentation."

Bella laughed again, delightfully. "'Twas in the spell," she said. "Thou couldst not be other than a true Prince." A small, perfect frown formed between her sculpted brows. "Your speech... This is how they speak in your home? I must learn."

"In my home we speak another tongue," Charming said. "Here, I believe you will find the change is merely the passage of time. No doubt you will learn the new ways easily, but I find your speech enchanting; do not change it entirely, I beg you!"

The maid coughed again, a little more firmly.

The Prince smiled, and bowed over the small, lovely hand held out to him; then he and Roland left the room.

They were greeted by a slightly dazed-looking crowd of courtiers, led by a tall, beak-nosed man in a long red robe. Sharp eyes took them both in, and a somewhat frigid smile was accompanied by a flourishing bow. "My Lord Prince? I am His Excellency's steward. You are come most timely, and of course I doubt not thou art indeed the promised Prince, but, a thousand apologies, I must ask... you have proof?" He held out his hand.

Charming gestured to Roland, who whipped a roll of papers bound with scarlet ribbon out of his backpack. "I also have my seal," he said, drawing the heavy ring from his finger. "I hope that will prove sufficient."

The steward bowed. "You understand, we must protect the interests of both Her Grace and of the city. Meanwhile you and your... man... will wish to refresh yourselves after your ordeal. A room awaits you."

They were led to a richly tapestried chamber with a fire crackling in the hearth and a bottle of wine on the table. Roland sniffed the wine and took a slug.

"You might use a glass," Charming protested. "I don't want any now."

"Fussy," Roland said. "Anyway, it might have been poisoned."

"Why would they poison me?"

"Point," Roland said. "They only just met you. Give them time."

"You're very mean," Charming said.

"Well, *yes*," Roland said, his voice dripping with so much sarcasm it almost burned a hole in the marble flooring. "Sure you don't want some? Excellent vintage, been cellared properly, too."

"No, thank you."

Around them the palace creaked awake, with the sounds of hurrying footsteps and doors opening and closing, and exclamations of surprise and wonder and annoyance. A yowl and a pained yelp suggested the cat and dog had not resolved their differences. The windlass in the courtyard groaned with strain, as gallon after gallon of water was drawn from the well and hauled to stables and bedrooms and the vast and echoing kitchens.

"Why're they washing everything?" Roland mused. "'Sall been in stasis, there isn't even any *dust*."

"Because people like a wash when they wake up," Charming said. He considered Roland a moment. "Most people, anyway." He stared out of the window, drumming his fingers on the sill.

"Nerves?" Roland said.

"Certainly not."

At length, a servant appeared to usher them into the ducal presence.

They entered a room only slightly less vast than the entrance hall, with tall, mullioned windows giving a view over the grounds. The brief flicker of sun had withdrawn, and a soft rain was now drifting down. Groundspeople with axes were already hard at work clearing the dying briars from the carriageway that led down to the city.

At the far end of the room, on tall chairs of glossy dark wood upholstered in burgundy velvet, on a high oak dais richly carved with fleurs-de-lis and snarling lions, sat the Duke and Duchess dei' Sogni. Behind them hung a tapestry depicting a hunt, riders and hounds gaining on a tiring stag that stumbled among exquisitely depicted wildflowers. They were a handsome couple, if not to the preternatural degree that their daughter enjoyed; both beginning to grey at the temples, both with the aura of people whose orders were obeyed, by most, without question.

Charming went down on one knee. Roland, with a grunt, did likewise.

"You are most welcome," the Duke said. "Please rise, sirrah." He glanced towards the door, as did the Duchess.

"Your Excellencies," Charming said.

"You have already met our daughter," said the Duke.

"I have, Your Excellency—I hope you will forgive my intrusion, but it seemed wise to follow instructions to the letter. To risk such a jewel for some trifling error..." He shuddered.

There might have been a glimmer of tears in the Duke's eyes, though no one would dare remark on it. "A jewel indeed she is," he said. "The most precious of all."

"It took me but a moment's speech with her to learn as much," Charming said. "And I hardly dare hope I may be worthy."

"You *appear* so much what one would wish," the Duchess said, "that I wonder if mayhap the Good Folk visited thee likewise."

"You flatter me, Your Excellency," Charming said. "I owe my looks, such as they are, to nothing but a fortunate family line. And it is obvious to me"—he bowed—"that the Good Folk alone were not responsible for the Lady Bella's beauty."

The Duchess acknowledged the compliment with a modest tilt of the head, but was immediately distracted when Lady Bella appeared, dressed now in green and gold, smiling and running towards her parents with her arms outstretched. The Duchess's expression melted into a genuine smile. "Bella! My lambkin! Art well? Art famished?"

"Bella! My dove!"

The two stern rulers were gone, replaced by a mere mother and father, as the Duke and Duchess all but scrambled from the dais in their haste to embrace their daughter.

There followed a great deal of hugging, and exclamation, and conviction that Bella had grown (not possible, in stasis, but parents will be parents), and more tears. Charming and Roland stood back while all this went on, and the Duchess stroked her daughter's hair and the Duke called for feasting, and the ringing of bells, and the drawing up of marriage papers, and Bella laughed, and blushed like the most perfect and rare of roses, and Charming just kept smiling.

THE BLARE OF a herald's trumpet cut through the general bustle. "Oh, hello," muttered Roland, looking out of the window.

"Ah, surely the good townspeople have come to rejoice with us!" the Duke said. He, too, glanced out of the window—and frowned.

Three large, stately coaches trundled up the carriageway. Before them rode heralds dressed in scarlet and white, flying banners bearing a gold lion on a white field.

"Your Excellency?" said the Captain of the Guard, a man who still had the look of someone who was not sure if he was awake, but was doing his best.

"Open the gates," the Duke said, "but be vigilant." The sentimental father was gone. Here, again, was the man who had successfully wrested control of a city from his rivals, defended its borders at the head of his troops, and had lent so much money to so many rulers that he could, should the occasion arise, have taken entire provinces as interest payments.

"If I may, Your Excellency?" Charming said. "I believe I know who these people are."

"Careful," Roland muttered.

"Thou dost?" the Duke said.

"While you were... indisposed," Charming said, "without the care of your guiding hand, the city found itself in some little confusion and trouble. The good people decided to form a council... what are they called, Roland?"

"The Serenissima."

"Ah, yes. The Serenissima. To handle the daily running of the city's affairs."

"Did they so," the Duke said thoughtfully. "I trow I left most clear instructions."

"Ah, but even Your Excellency could not foresee every eventuality," said Charming. "The times have been tumultuous. I believe they have been most careful in defending the city's interests."

"Have they," the Duke said.

"And they have a great deal of support," Charming said, "both within and without the city. Of course, it is Your Excellency's choice, but allowing them to retain some of their power may help avoid"—he glanced significantly at Bella—"problems for anyone in the future."

Their Excellencies exchanged a look. "It is a consideration," the Duchess said.

"Come, Papa," said Bella. "Let us have no frowns, on such a happy day! Why, 'tis my birthday, is it not?"

"Indeed," said the Duke, helpless not to smile at his daughter. "Tell me, child, art thou twenty, or one hundred and twenty? If 'tis the latter, why, I fear the Prince will find thee a little too old for him!"

"Oh, *Papa*." Bella kissed him on the cheek and took his arm, and beamed a smile of surpassing joy and loveliness.

The representatives of the Serenissima entered together, and were dressed alike, in a style similar to the Prince's: the men in fitted doublets and narrow breeches tucked into high boots, the women in equally close-fitted jackets, with long skirts in place of breeches. The colours were sombre, the doublets adorned only with a few lines of bronze braid.

Though slightly damp from the rain, they looked, among the antique splendour of the ducal court, like people on serious business.

They bowed.

"Your Excellencies," said a smooth, plump fellow. "We heard the bells, and made haste to come and give our congratulations on this most happy occasion." His gaze kept slipping away from the Duke and Duchess towards Bella, as though he could not be quite sure she was real, and had to keep checking.

"If 'tis indeed congratulations you bring," the Duke said, "truly the occasion is happy."

"Why, Your Excellency, what else could it be? Forgive me, I am Agnolo Baldovinetti, guildmaster of the Bankers' Guild and elected spokesman for the Serenissima, these good people you see here with me."

"And thou hast come to return to me the rightful rule of my city?" the Duke said.

The words, pointed as a spear, met the gazes of the Serenissima with an almost audible clang.

"Now, Papa," Bella said. "These good people have come hither, in all this rain, and have been offered no morsel of meat nor cup of wine, what will they make of our hospitality?" She smiled brilliantly, causing answering smiles to break over the faces of the Serenissima, and anyone else in range, like the crashing surf. "A feast is e'en now being prepared, and there will be plenty for all. Will you not dine with us?"

"Bella," the Duke said, with an attempt at fatherly

authority, "'tis not yet your place to take part in these discussions."

"But Papa, you yourself said that I must learn the arts of diplomacy, and how to host great occasions. Besides," she said, "I could not bear for anyone to feel slighted, or unheard, on such a day."

Charming bowed. "As the man fortunate enough to be named your future king, I could not agree more. I would also wish to learn more of how your city has become so astonishingly wealthy..."

There was a guttural cough, from somewhere behind him, but no one was looking at Roland. With few exceptions, anyone who wasn't gazing adoringly at Bella was gazing adoringly at Charming.

"...and influential," Charming went on. "Indeed, your Excellency, your own coinage, the carre, is not only still in circulation—it is now the only coin accepted without question in every single place that I have travelled! Isn't that astonishing?"

"Is't so indeed?" said the Duke. He had not, precisely, defrosted; but the ice had thinned a fraction.

The Duchess clapped her hands. "Set places for our guests," she called.

Bella laughed with pleasure. "Now," she said, taking Senor Baldovinetti's arm. "Good sir, will you explain to me what the Serenissima does? I am, as you know, a little behind the times!"

The most powerful man in the country, with the (possible) exception of the Duke, beamed down at her. He patted her hand in a fatherly way, and began to explain, in elaborate—indeed, tedious—detail, how splendidly he managed the current running of a great city. Bella hung fascinated on every word.

The palace had been well stocked when the spell took hold, and the tables were so laden the timber could barely be seen. "Look at that marchpane!" the head of the Bakers' and Confectioners' Guild gasped. The cake in question was a perfect recreation of the palace, so incredibly detailed that there were even tiny flickers of silver in the blue paste waters of the lake, to represent fish. "I *must* speak to their confectioner," the guildmistress declared, with a determined glint. "I want to find out where they got that blue."

Below the salt, the table was extremely crowded, except immediately around Roland—hungry as everyone was, sitting near him tended to dim the appetite. Roland seemed not to notice. He ate hugely, drank vastly, listened to everyone's conversations, and said little but 'pass the bread,' and 'giz some more of that stuff in the green dish.'

At the meal, Baldovinetti, a man who had been nimbly negotiating the snake-pit of Caraggian politics for thirty years, found himself, by Bella's design, seated next to the Duke's steward. The steward was fanatically devoted to the interests of the Family, and as wary and venomous as a mamba.

Bella, in passing, said, "Oh, Senor Baldovinetti, our steward has a most wonderful device, for viewing objects in the night sky!"

Senor Baldovinetti, a passionate amateur astrologer, turned to the steward with astonishment, and the two were soon deep in discussion of the movement of planets.

Bella, after a brief conversation with the head of the Bakers' and Confectioners' Guild, rousted out the lanky, grey-haired palace confectioner and introduced them. "Our confectioner has grandchildren, too," Bella said.

"The most adorable twins."

An immediate sympathy passed between the two grandparents. "Little devils," the confectioner said, with resounding fondness. "And once they get into the sugar there's no stopping them. The mess two four-year-olds can make of a kitchen..."

The guildmistress groaned in sympathy. "Flour!" she said. "It wasn't even very *much* flour..."

"I wonder if..." The confectioner glanced out of the window. "But no. It's been too long."

The guildmistress patted his arm. "I'm sure your family will welcome you," she said.

Next, Bella introduced the head of the Vintner's Guild to the Duke's cellarer. The guildsman was delighted to discover—not to mention sample—some vintages that had been thought lost, and which, unlike everything else, had been allowed to age. (The Good Folk have a lot of respect for the particular magic of wine, and seldom interfere with it.) It was decided between them that a new vintage, from the ducal estate's own vines, could be produced and marketed to the pleasure and profit of all. It would, of course, be named after the happy couple...

For all her concern with making sure everyone had a pleasant party, Bella frequently found her gaze drawn to Charming. He seemed to know when she looked at him, and would give her a loving smile, and a nod of approval. When she managed to get the head of the Embroiderers talking to Papa about the creation of a slightly more modern and even more splendid set of livery for the palace servants, he gave her a little, private thumbs-up.

Charming himself, meanwhile, drew out the head of the Armourers' Guild on the subject of the latest fashion in plate mail and the complexities of a good pauldron,

Jade Linwood

and ended up with an offer of a complete suit of armour for himself and any mount he wished. A brief discussion of the difficulties of keeping harness in good condition with the head of the Leatherworkers resulted in a new set for the Mostly Donkey. Chatter with the guildmaster of the Butchers ended with the presentation of a selection of the best preserved meats, which Roland eyed with great approval.

Charming flirted outrageously with the guildmistress of the Bakers and Confectioners, who laughed, fanned herself, and gave him her secret recipe for rum cake.

He even, by some unknown alchemy, managed to win a genuine smile from the steward, to the astonishment of those who witnessed this marvel.

The guildmaster of the Entertainers, a man with a mane of hair almost as impressive as Charming's own, watched him work the room, and sighed. "Imagine *that* stuck in the palace, charming the boring nobility," he confided to his friend. "He'd *slaughter* 'em on stage. Such a waste."

When, full of food and wine and good feelings, the representatives of the Serenissima took their leave, Senor Baldovinetti and the Duke shook hands. "I look forward to seeing Your Grace at our next meeting," Baldovinetti said. "We will benefit greatly from your wisdom and judgement. Your Grace has the weight of history at your back."

"And I will no doubt benefit from thy introduction to these new times," the Duke said. "So much hath changed! And, in truth, not all for the worse," he said, with a glance at the women of the Serenissima.

Bella, blithely unaware that she had achieved the kind of diplomatic outcome that usually takes months of wrangling and bitter compromise, was only pleased that everyone seemed to have enjoyed themselves.

As THEY READIED themselves for sleep, the Duke found his wife seated at her dressing-table, staring not into, but through, her mirror.

"An interesting day," he said. "And remarkably successful, I trow."

"Indeed," said the Duchess. She turned to look at her husband. "I fear for our daughter," she said.

"Ah, now, what megrim is this, my dove? Think'st thou the Serenissima will rise against her? Why, they were clay in her hands."

"I know." The Duchess rubbed her own hands together, as though they were cold. "But she is so young and so untried in the world... and the world, my love, is but seldom a kindly place."

The Duke put his hands on her shoulders. "And our daughter has such gifts as she needs to make her way in this harsh world, doth she not?"

"But the Prince..."

"Did you not see how he watched over our little Bella with a most loving attention?" the Duke replied. "Whenever I looked, he was close, though never crowding, seeming ready at any moment to protect her from hurt or insult."

"As though any would dare, here in our very palace," Her Grace pointed out. "But he hath indeed the capacity to please. If he can pull a smile from the steward—I swear I had not thought the man's face could stretch to one."

"And he *is* the chosen of the Good Folk," the Duke said.

"Indeed, he is," the Duchess said.

The Duke's grip tightened for a moment.

The Duchess patted his hand. "You are right, it is but a foolish megrim," she said. "Now, my love, it is time for bed."

"It seems strange to sleep again so soon," said the Duke.

"Oh, *sleep*," said the Duchess, "sleep I have had enough of for now."

"Oh?" said the Duke. "*Oh*."

LUCKY LADY BELLA, awaking on her wedding day! What could be more perfect? Early, as was once her habit, to the smell of baking bread, the first clean brilliant sunshine and the birds singing their little hearts out. But then, how could it be otherwise? She blinked, and stretched, and smiled, and shook out that glorious hair with a gesture as unconscious as it was graceful. She was awake! And she would be awake all day! What could be more delightful? Unable to stay one more moment she bounded out of bed, threw a robe on over her nightgown, and splashed her face with water from the ewer.

The sounds of the morning—the creak of the windlass from the well in the courtyard, the chatter of the maids and serving-men, the sound of the soldiers drilling on the parade-ground, all were wonderful to her.

And somewhere in the palace was her betrothed. That was the most wonderful of all.

Sweet, smitten Lady Bella. She thought of his face, and his hair, and his smile, and his broad shoulders, and the way he had watched her as she spoke to the Serenissima. Sometimes people spoke of the Good Folk in such a *careful* way, as though they were not to be trusted. But—despite the unfortunate misunderstanding about her christening, and she was *certain* that if people had only explained, and been reasonable, it could all have been sorted out—they had given her such wonderful gifts, and the best of them was surely the Prince! Was he not the most perfect, kind creature? His every action had been courteous, gentle, and—there was no other word for it—*charming*. His name was so apt it made her laugh.

She rang for the maid, and pored over gowns with her. Splendid enough for one's betrothed, but not so splendid it would put to shame someone with nothing to wear but what his man carried with him. Such a strange, funny little fellow, that Roland. She must talk to him; he would know things that his master, however wonderful, would not. Servants always did. And his life, accompanying so brave a prince—how strange and adventurous it must have been!

Bella asked the maid to dress her hair simply, in the style she had seen one of the younger ladies of the Serenissima wear.

"Well, 'tis very *modern*," the maid said, having done her best. "But still, thou look'st the picture of beauty, Milady. E'en more than always." The maid beamed. "Love is the best cosmetic, they say."

"Oh, Lucia. I'm to be married! Is't not wonderful and strange?" Bella had the new way of speaking almost pat already, such things came easily to her, but Charming had asked her not to lose all of her old speech, and it was easier for those around her, who did not have her facility with language, if she did not change all at once.

Lucia nodded, and sniffed. "Oh, Milady!"

"Don't cry! Please don't."

"No, Milady."

"I know 'tis a great change, but is not life change?" Bella bounded to her feet, and spun around. "Let us go, I must greet my Prince!"

But before she could reach the door, it opened. The Duchess stood there.

Bella had never seen her with quite that look on her face. Whatever circumstances the troubled world of courtly politics threw at them, Mama had always breathed in, lifted her chin and prepared to Deal With It. Whatever this was, it had shaken her to her iron core.

"Mama?"

"Oh, my treasure, my little sparrow..."

The Duke appeared at her shoulder, his face rigid, his eyes incandescent.

"Mama, what is it? Papa?"

"He is gone, my sweeting," the Duchess said.

"Who... what meanest thou?"

"Your Prince. His man. His beast. Gone."

"Aye," said the Duke. "And a good portion of my treasury withal!"

"Treasury?" Bella said. She did not understand. What had the treasury to do with anything? The Prince was gone?

The Duke snarled. "He begged for advice on how he might best secure his own treasury, and, being a fool, I showed him all I did, and come the dawn the captain finds the guards drugged, the doors open, and all that might be easily carried and easily sold, gone!"

This made no sense. Bella had woken in a world where everything was as it was meant to be, and now... *nothing* was as it was meant to be.

There must be some mistake, some misunderstanding.

People were so ready to assume the worst.

"Mayhap 'twas thieves?" Bella said, striving to keep her voice light and steady. "Perhaps... perhaps he tried to stop them, and they forced him to go with them..."

"A pedlar on the road saw him and his man pass by," the Duke said, "in the small hours, with their beast full laden, laughing as they went. Laughing!"

"L... laughing?" Bella found that she was no longer standing, but seated on her bed, as though some string had been holding her upright, and was suddenly cut. Her insides felt grey and cold and numb, but somewhere there was pain waiting, she could feel it, ready to cut her through the heart.

"Husband," the Duchess said sharply, "hast not orders to give, and pursuit to arrange?"

"Aye, aye. Fear not, Bella my lamb, we will have him soon, and he will pay for the insult to you and to this house!" The Duke swept away, feet thundering on the tiles as he strode.

"Mama?" Bella said, and even to herself her voice sounded strange, and thin, and very young.

The Duchess opened her arms, and Bella dived into them, as though she could hide there. There her confusion and shock broke into horrible, painful, gut-wrenching tears; the first she had wept since her christening.

The Prince and His Servant

HE MAIN ROAD leading out of Caraggia continues along the coast, but branching off it, winding through the heavily forested hills, are dozens of smaller cartways and footpaths. They lead to forester's cottages, charcoal burner's huts, and perhaps here and there a place occupied by someone who is neither. Keep an eye on the smoke. If the smoke from a chimney (or perhaps the hole in the roof of a cave) is any colour other than grey or white, it's usually wise to keep your distance, unless you come with appropriate gifts, a great many precautions, and a very polite tongue in your head.

TRAVELLING ONE OF these lesser-known tracks were Prince Charming, Roland, and the Mostly Donkey. Already surprisingly far behind them, the city of Caraggia glimmered like a half-forgotten dream.

Roland, gnawing on a cold sausage while leading the

Mostly Donkey, kept a sharp eye on the surrounding trees. Along with his other oddities, Roland had a strange, uneven gait—not precisely a limp, more as though his limbs, while working perfectly efficiently, were not constructed the same way as those of, for example, Prince Charming.

The Prince strolled along as though he were born to walk the roads, though better dressed and better nourished than most people who live such a life. He sang a jolly tune with extremely rude lyrics. He seemed entirely at ease, at least until the Mostly Donkey let out a screeching complaint that echoed through the landscape, outraging Charming's ears and sending birds scolding into the sky.

"Goose almighty," yelled Charming, clamping his hands over his ears. "Can you shut that beast up? It's going to draw attention, bawling like that."

"Attention from whom, d'you think?" Roland said. "We're not exactly in the middle of the city here. You could probably murder an entire village and no one'd notice till tax time."

"Are you *sure* it isn't overladen?"

"What, feeling sorry for it, are we? You want to carry some of the gold, maybe, Your Highness?"

Charming glanced at the beast uneasily. "I just don't want it to collapse out here in the middle of nowhere, before we can deal with the stuff."

"It won't," Roland said. "It's stronger than it looks. Like me."

"It would have to be." Charming glanced over his shoulder, and sighed.

"Now what's the matter?"

"She really was *exceptionally* pretty," Charming said.

"And terribly sweet."

"Naïve, you mean."

"And what's wrong with that? And *so* rich. So truly, astonishingly, eye-wateringly rich. The treasury wasn't a hundredth of it. In other circumstances, I think it would almost be worth staying for the actual marriage."

"You'd get itchy feet in a week."

"Well, yes..." Charming shrugged. "But I'd have time to make some arrangements. Get more of the loot *and* enjoy some delightful company—and a little luxury."

"Oh, yes, that'd go very well, that would," Roland said. "This, this is just theft, and an insult. A false marriage, and all that entails? That'd be the sort of thing they'd go to war over."

"With whom, precisely?" Charming said. "One of the nations mentioned on my papers, which doesn't actually exist? Ooh, I know, they could trace the seal ring to... let's see, that useful little woman you found whose shop moves around all the time."

"They'd put a *lot* more effort into finding you. You've been lucky so far, and yes, you've got help, *including* me, but I'd advise you, my Lord Prince, not to get too bloody cocky. That's when things go wrong." He shot Charming a glance of mingled resentment and resignation. "I speak as one who knows." He bit down on his sausage.

"What *is* that revolting object?"

"Mallegato. Blood sausage. Got raisins and pine nuts and..." Roland mused as he chewed, staring at the trees. "Lemon. And something else. I'll get it in a bit. Pity I didn't get the recipe."

"I got you one for rum cake."

"When am I going to have time—or a decent kitchen— to make rum cake?"

"When would you make repulsive sausages, then? Don't be so grumpy. It's a lovely morning, we pulled it off, and we're headed for... hmm, Macqreux. Ooh, *yummy*. Best seafood anywhere, Macqreux. Good wine, too. Not as good as home, but not bad."

"Bit heavy-handed with the thyme," Roland said. "Not *everything* needs a load of thyme in it."

"I'm sure we can find something that will please your refined palate, Roland."

"Just *saying*."

The Mostly Donkey made a noise like a dying accordion.

"Absolutely," Roland said. "Couldn't agree more."

"I'm sure the beast has most worthy opinions on gourmet cuisine," Charming said. "You only talk to that thing when you're peeved at me."

"If that was the case I'd only ever talk to the beast, Your Highness."

"Are you *ever* going to treat me with anything resembling the respect due to my station?"

Roland gave a sort of grinding chuckle, in which the words 'fat chance' might have been discerned by the keen-eared.

Caraggia faded behind them. Ahead, silver and shimmering, was the first blue glimpse of sea.

Three Ladies and a Wedding
(The First Part)

HE GREAT SEAPORT of Beria is a very busy, very pungent place. Forty different types of cheese compete with the day's trade in fish, the dung-and-lanolin of a great many sheep, roasting malt from the brewhouses, and throngs of people—from the heavily perfumed to the ripely unwashed.

Splendid ancient houses and splendid new houses are crammed together along the river down to the sea. This day the place is even busier than usual: the tall round towers, with their conical tops, are reflected only in fragments around the mass of boats that jostle on the waterways. The sun shines on silk and velvet, towering headdresses and extravagant hats, flashing rings and full purses. Merchants and pickpockets alike are having an extremely profitable time, and even the poor are getting a bit of the action, as free wheels of cheese and thick woollen hose are handed out in the squares.

The source of all this splendour is a wedding. The son of a powerful merchant house (thanks to their fine dairy herds and expert cheesemakers) is to be wed to the daughter of an equally powerful house, whose riches come from the fleece of the pampered sheep that roam their many fields.

Everyone of any possible significance is here, because even though the tragedy that befell the Duke dei' Sogni was a long time ago, people still keenly remember what happens if you miss the wrong someone off the invitation list.

Thus, three influential women, strangers to each other (and, to be fair, to the bride and groom, but such is the nature of high society weddings) are seated at the same table.

Among the merriment and toasts to the happy couple and more than a few ribald jokes about the wedding night, though they join in the toasts and make the minimum of polite conversation with their neighbours, the three women seem somewhat subdued.

"THIS WAS A mistake," said the Lady Bella Lucia, staring into her untouched glass as yet another toast to the happy couple echoed around the tables. "I thought this would be a good way to... reintroduce myself? But I was wrong."

"To come back into society after a long absence is hard," said Doctor Emilia Rapunzel. "Believe me, I know this." She was a striking woman with sharp hazel eyes, a hawkish profile and long-fingered, restless hands with faint chemical stains on the fingertips. Her hair was confined under a handsome but close-fitting headdress that allowed not a single strand to escape. She had something of the air of a much-admired but slightly terrifying headmistress. "But you do not enjoy it?"

"I travelled for some time, after..." Lady Bella

hesitated. "My parents were convinced it would do me good. Mama thought I needed to learn a little more of the world. And I think they hoped, perhaps, I would meet someone. Everyone I met was very kind... but after a year or two, it was simply too much. So I went home. But they worried, and then I felt I was being a coward, so..." She waved her hand at the surrounding merriment. "But I really shouldn't have picked a *wedding*."

"Ah."

"Oh," said Princess Marie Blanche de Neige. "I know how *that* feels." She had the strong shoulders and lean musculature of someone who spends a great deal of time on horseback, close-cropped curls that gleamed like bronze, full lips, and eyes so very dark they tempted observers to look closely into them—were they deep brown? Or truly black? However closely one looked, they remained largely unreadable.

"And everyone *knows*," Bella said. "And *talks* about it, or—worse—very carefully *doesn't* talk about it."

"*I* don't know," Doctor Rapunzel said. "I have not been much in society myself, until recently."

"Oh, well, you're bound to hear soon enough." Bella gave a brief rendition of her fleeting, ill-fated engagement to a certain Prince. Those who had been there might have been puzzled as to how little the actions of the Prince himself were mentioned, and how frequently the possibility of robbers, kidnappers, and other external forces came into play, but the gist was clear enough.

Marie Blanche looked her up and down and said, "Whatever else he was, he was certainly a fool."

Bella ducked her head, and blushed.

"Hear that bird?" Marie Blanche said.

From a nearby tree, decorated with bunting and strung

with nuts and dried berries, cascaded a string of merry trills.

The other two women tilted their heads to the sound. "Yes?"

"'I'm here, I'm strong, I'm pretty, come and make strong, pretty babies with me,' that's what he's saying," said Marie Blanche. "That's all there is to it, for birds. *Most* birds. They're generally straightforward, though they do like to gossip. People, on the other hand..."

Lady Bella leaned forward. "Something happened to you, too?"

Marie Blanche shrugged. "*I* was a fool."

"I'm sure you weren't," Lady Bella said. "You know the language of birds! You must be clever."

"These days I generally prefer the conversation— and the company—of birds, or beasts, to people." She blinked, realising what she'd just said. "My apologies, I didn't mean..."

Doctor Rapunzel smiled. "*I* generally prefer books," she said. "Though even they are not without their treacheries."

"Oh, dear," Lady Bella said. She allowed the hovering server to pour a bare inch of wine into her glass, and leaned her head on her hand, smiling sadly at Princess Marie Blanche. "Well at least *your* story hasn't spread as far as mine, or not so that I've heard. I don't suppose you want to talk about it? Sometimes it helps."

Perhaps it was her wide, direct gaze, or the sympathy of her tone, but something about Lady Bella encouraged confidences. The generous servings of wine may also have played a part. In any case, for the first time, Princess Marie Blanche found herself talking about the strange turn her life had taken.

"Do you know the Chateau Hivernal?" she began...

The Lonely Princess

HE CHATEAU HIVERNAL is tucked in the centre of verdant, prosperous Macqreux. All around are fields of lavender, now in full bloom under the rich gold sun, infusing the landscape with a purple mist and the air with soothing, sleepy perfume. Within the fields are the gardens of the estate, laid out in geometric symmetry. Even the carrots and cabbages of the kitchen gardens grow in smart, obedient rows, protected and framed by neat, low hedges.

At the heart of all this orderly comfort lies the Chateau itself, of honeyed stone that deepens in colour with the sunset. Long green shutters on the many windows reflect the formal lines of the hedges, and the plumes of the white marble fountains dance with their reflections in the windowpanes.

There is a castle, too, which is very splendid, but the Chateau is so much more comfortable, and closer to the town and the best doctors. That is why they are staying here: so that Queen Katherina, Princess Marie Blanche de Neige's step-mama, may be easier in the later stages of her pregnancy.

Marie Blanche glances up at the window of Queen Katherina's room, smooths down her hair, and hurries to wash away the last traces of the stables.

SEVEN YEARS HAD passed since Marie Blanche's mother Queen Lisabèu died in childbed. She and the King had been a love match, and while the Queen was alive, Marie Blanche had been kept warm in the circle of their affection. But when Lisabèu died, she seemed to take the greater part of the King to the grave with her.

Marie Blanche herself was but fourteen years old, and her mother's absence gripped her bones like winter cold. Trying to warm both her and him, she comforted her father as best she could. She coaxed him to eat, played the lute for him (badly—she hated the lute, but her mother had played), asked him to ride out with her; all to no avail. He would eat a mouthful or two before speaking of how Lisabèu had enjoyed some dish or other, or how if she had eaten more of this or less of that she might have lived. He would stare at the wall as Marie Blanche played and pat her arm partway through a piece and say she lacked her mother's touch, and perhaps should try the flûte à bec instead. He would not ride out, however fine the weather, but would only retreat to his book-room, where he kept his favourite portrait of the Queen.

Princess Marie Blanche, with no one to take much notice of her doings, began to slip away from her tutors and her maids to spend time in the kennels, the stables, and the mews.

The great fierce hunting dogs, sensing her trouble—

and, too, missing the Queen who had loved them so well, and the King who never hunted any more—would lick her hands and put their heads in her lap. Her horse carried her gently, until she grew impatient and angry at the world and everything in it, then he would gallop with her, far away from the court, leaving her groom behind, so that she might cry her heart out in peace.

The hawks, having no notion of sympathy, only watched her with their bright cold eyes; but training them, and flying them, and seeing them take their prey, still gave her something she needed.

Sometimes, she went to her mother's tomb. In each season she laid on it something the Queen had loved: a bunch of primroses, a yellow rose; a sweet pear, or a plump partridge. She would talk of this or that, quietly, while one of the dogs rested at her side, and remember things her mother had said to her, and the scent of her, and the touch of her hand.

The King, meanwhile, seemed almost to forget he *had* a daughter, or indeed a kingdom. He stayed in his book-room, and barely spoke even to his ministers.

The machinery of palaces and kingdoms is heavy and complicated, and depending on the individuals who make up its parts, may roll along for some time without a guiding hand, but soon, a cog will loosen here, or a joint seize there.

Ambitions and rivalries among the lords and ministers that had long been reined in by the King's hand and by the weight of custom begin to bubble up, ready to spill over and make a mess.

Land disputes that required the King's decision went unresolved. Negotiations over mining rights with the dwarven clans hung in the balance, and though the clan leaders sympathised with the King's grief, there was work to be done and it could not wait forever. The captain of the western border patrol was retiring, no successor had been chosen, and the countries that bordered Macqreux began to look at its rich fields and fat veins of metal, and lick their lips.

ONE DAY MARIE Blanche, on her way to the stables, saw Captain Formarch of the Western Border Patrol sitting in the audience chamber, patiently awaiting the King's notice. He had taught her to use a sword, but since then he had grown stooped and grey, faster than the years seemed to account for.

He was rubbing and pulling at his fingers, and she noticed that they were pallid with cold and swollen with the joint evil.

"Why, Captain Formarch, it is very good to see you."

"Your Highness!" The captain got to his feet with a little difficulty, and bowed.

"Have you been waiting long?"

"Oh, no, Your Highness," he said, but something told her that was mere politeness.

There was no fire in the great marble fireplace, and the chamber was like a room carved from ice. Marie Blanche noticed, too, that there were cobwebs in the corners of the walls, and the green paint of the shutters was faded and cracked.

The captain had grown grey in the service of the kingdom, and had many old wounds to trouble him. He should not be sitting all day in a cold, unswept chamber, in the middle of winter.

Something Marie Blanche's mother had said returned

to her, in that icy room: *When you are not sure what to do, set your hands to what is in front of them.*

Marie Blanche sent for someone to light the fire, and someone else to heat soup and mull wine, and while these things were being done, she said, "What did you want of the King? If you will tell me, I will speak to him." Though how much good it would do, she didn't know.

The captain looked at her under his bushy white brows. "I wished to discuss my successor, Your Highness. Though I'm willing to go on as long as I can, I'm not who's needed, in these uncertain times. Someone younger, whose joints don't creak, and whose mind don't creak neither. There's new ways of doing things now, and I'm too old to learn 'em and not nimble enough to do 'em if I could. I've someone in mind, if you'd lean into the King's ear." He paused, and made as though to pull at his fingers again, but stopped himself.

"And what else?"

"Your Highness shouldn't be troubled with such things."

"Captain, remember what you said to me when you were teaching me the sword?"

"I probably said a great deal, Your Highness. I hope some of it was useful."

"You said, the small movements matter." Marie Blanche looked at the fireplace, and frowned. "Small movements, and small gaps, are where trouble gets in. Remember?"

"Hah! Fancy you remembering that. True enough, and it's not that small a thing that troubles me, truth be told. It's the supplies, Your Highness. Food for men and beasts both. Not been regular nor as much as it needs to be, not for months."

"I see," said Marie Blanche.

She knew the King would not want to be bothered. She could give him the captain's recommendation for a successor, and he would say, as he had to any question of late, 'yes, yes,' or 'no, no' or 'someone will see to it,' and wave it away, which was all very well, but feeding thousands of troops and beasts was undoubtedly more complicated and could not be solved with yes, yes, or no, no. And as to someone seeing to it... well, it appeared that someone would have to, and that someone would have to be Marie Blanche.

So the Princess, not yet fifteen, began to take up the role that would one day have been her brother's, had he not died in the birthing-chamber along with her mother.

She sent the captain away fed and warmed, and with his recommendation for his successor confirmed. She sent a message to that effect to the major-general of the army, sealed with her father's seal, and if the major-general wondered who had actually sealed the document, he was rather too relieved to question it.

Then Marie Blanche began to ask questions about the supplies. On getting answers that were incomplete and confusing, she asked more questions. Since she had no one to fuss over her and tell her that princesses did not behave this way, she went out of the palace, accompanied only by her groom, and questioned not just captains but the common soldiery, and the camp cooks, and the drivers of supply carts, and the girls who gutted fish in the market.

And when she had answers to all her questions, she went to her rooms and thought for a long time. Then she spoke to certain of the ministers, and told them what she had discovered, and then she summoned the quartermaster.

The quartermaster, when he was told the Princess required his presence, smiled to himself. He dressed in his most expensive robes (and *very* expensive they were) and a large and impressive hat. He presented, he thought, a solid, fatherly figure, a figure that any young girl might turn to for advice and help now her own father had abandoned himself to grief. Such a fatherly figure might, perhaps, one day guide the military spending of an entire kingdom, and gain a great deal of power and influence thereby.

He entered the audience chamber stomach first, nose tilted at the right angle for looking down.

There, instead of a child in a regal gown and a coronet too heavy for her, he found a young huntress, with a great black-feathered gyrfalcon at her wrist, and a massive boarhound to either side of her throne.

This, thought the quartermaster, was inappropriate; what if she dressed this way to greet some foreign dignitary? How badly she needed a guiding hand! Not to mention the way the dogs and the gyrfalcon were looking at him in a most discomfiting fashion. Such animals should not be permitted in the throne room.

One of the dogs growled. Suddenly, despite his embroidered velvet collar, the quartermaster's neck felt cold and strangely vulnerable.

"Your Highness," he said, and bowed. "I hope I find you well this morning."

"Quartermaster." Her tone was cool, almost indifferent. Probably, the quartermaster told himself, she was merely bored, and had only been persuaded by one of the court to speak with him, in the hopes of bringing her to a sense of her duties—perhaps even by that interfering old fool of a captain.

"It seems as though you would rather be hunting this morning," he said, gesturing at her clothing, and the beasts, and smiling.

"Oh, I am hunting now."

"Now, Your Highness? I'm afraid I don't follow."

"I am hunting a thief," she said.

For the first time, he looked at her face, properly.

Those dark, dark eyes were as clear and cold as the gyrfalcon's, and her smile showed teeth.

The quartermaster's hands went as chilly as his throat, and he summoned his best expression of innocence, which he had not expected to need, and which sat stiffly on his face. "Why, who would dare steal from Your Highness?" he said.

"Not from me, but from my father, and from the kingdom," she said. "By the law, an act of treason."

"Treason? But I... there is a mistake... someone has turned Your Highness' mind against me..."

"I had not accused anyone, yet; and yet you assume I meant you?"

The cold reached down the quartermaster's throat, and froze any words that he might have found there.

Marie Blanche rang the small bell that rested at her right hand. Then through one door came the royal auditor, who laid on the table a number of heavy leather-bound books, and looked at the quartermaster over the top of her spectacles.

And through another door came several guards, who merely stood there, looking to the Princess, and not looking at the quartermaster at all.

"I do not wish one of my first acts in my father's name to be a bloody one," said Marie Blanche. "I offer you exile, *if* you return what you have stolen. I suggest you accept it."

The quartermaster recovered his voice, and stammered and protested a little more, but being a man who knew the value of self-preservation as well as a pound of corn, he eventually accepted the offer.

Marie Blanche had him escorted away by the guards, in the company of the royal auditor, and collapsed back into her chair, and hugged her dogs, and shook for quite half an hour as they licked her hands and whined.

Not all of the money was gone. Some of it had been spent on a fine new house in the best part of the city. Marie Blanche gave it to Captain Formarch, so that he might live out his retirement in comfort.

Next, she began a round of visits to the heads of the dwarven clans, starting with Hethotain Strongthew, the head of the Oakapple Clan.

MARIE BLANCHE RODE out to the clan's village, accompanied by her groom, the Royal Geologist, the Royal Auditor, the Registrar of Lands and two guards. There had been some argument about this, and strong representations made that there should be a great many more guards. Marie Blanche stated that she was going to negotiate, not invade, and if anyone gave her any more trouble about it, she would simply go alone.

She then gave the cold unblinking stare that, unbeknownst to her questioners, she had learned from her gyrfalcon.

The story of the quartermaster had got around.

No one gave her any more trouble about it.

THE PRINCESS AND her escort came to a halt in a clearing at the base of a great terraced hill of reddish stone, where—along the paths cut into the rock—the arched doorways of the dwarven houses could be seen. In front of them was a single great door, carved all over with oakleaves, their edges inlaid with gleaming bronze. The air smelled of earth and metal.

The last time Marie Blanche had been here, Papa had drunk brandy and laughed with Hethotain Strongthew, and Mama had been enchanted by her gift of a bouquet of stone flowers, delicately carved from quartz and jasper and carnelian, and possibly even more enchanted by the little dwarven girl who had handed it to her with great solemnity. Those flowers still stood in the window of Mama's solar.

Marie Blanche blinked, and breathed in hard, and held up her head. Without so much as the rustle of a single leaf, a fox as big as the largest wild boar emerged from the trees, and sat and watched them, curling its great fluffy tail neatly around its paws.

The horses snuffed, and shuffled, and eyed the fox suspiciously. The groom looked stolidly ahead. The geologist, the auditor and the registrar looked to Marie Blanche. "Um," said the registrar, who spent rather more time looking at maps which had *here be monsters* in the corners than was probably good for him.

Marie Blanche soothed her mount, and said, "Wait. And remember, we are guests."

The doors opened, and out came Hethotain Strongthew, with two other dwarves (behind her a great many more could be seen, grinning and shoving and peering to get a look at the visitors).

Hethotain was gnarled and scarred from years of mining (dwarven rulers work alongside their clans, or they don't remain rulers for long). She had long plaits woven with threads of gold and bronze, and finely embroidered clothes of soft leather. She bowed. "Princess Marie Blanche," she said. "It's a pleasure to see you again." She glanced at the trees, where the sparrows were gossiping loudly, raised an eyebrow (her brows were also threaded with gold and bronze, which made her look at once regal and oddly antique, like an ancient mask), and said, "You're most welcome. Please allow us to stable your horses. And don't mind that one." She jerked a thumb at the fox. "She's just nosey. Like others I could mention," she said, somewhat more loudly.

Some of the faces behind her withdrew, though the rest remained as unabashedly curious as ever.

The Princess and her people were led—with great courtesy, and under intense scrutiny—through smoothly polished stone corridors into a room furnished with low (at least by human standards) benches, plump with cushions; equally low tables inlaid with gleaming tiles of polished stone in intricate patterns; and many softly glowing lamps carved from agate and quartz.

They settled themselves among the cushions—apart from the registrar, who insisted on perching on the very edge of a bench, with his legs bent, as though he might need to leap up suddenly.

Refreshments were brought: little seeded honeycakes and bowls of creamy curd, jugs of small beer and of sweet yellow apple juice. One jug, heavily chased and jewelled and whose contents sent a waft of alcohol clear across the room, was waved back to the kitchens by Hethotain.

"So," Hethotain said. "Did your father send you to negotiate for him?"

"Papa still finds himself indisposed," Marie Blanche said, carefully. "I am his representative, for now."

"I see."

That seemed to be enough to allow negotiations to go ahead.

Marie Blanche kept herself very upright, despite the comfort of the cushions, and when she did not understand something (which was frequently), she asked. Hethotain explained, and the auditor scribbled, and the registrar poked at things on his maps, and the geologist got quite excited.

When things had been sorted out to everyone's satisfaction, documents were signed and hands were shaken, and the elaborate jug reappeared. Hethotain sighed. "I told you to take that away."

"But... traditionally..." said the dwarf holding the jug, "I mean, we *always*..."

"I am not giving a child the hundred-year-old stone brandy," Hethotain said. "Tradition or no. Forgive me, Your Highness."

Marie Blanche, whose eyes were watering from the vapours wafting from the jug, said, "If I am old enough to negotiate mining rights, I think I am old enough to drink a very little brandy. Does it still count if it's watered?"

"I'm sure it will," said Hethotain, glaring at the jug-holder, who shuffled and dropped their gaze.

Even well-watered, a sip of the brandy was strong enough to take Marie Blanche's breath away, but she managed, by clenching her jaw very hard indeed, not to cough.

Hethotain knocked back her own glass with a flourish. "Well, that's done," she said. "I hope His Majesty will be pleased. I have another proposal for Your Highness."

"Yes?"

"The sparrows were discussing your arrival. They seem quite taken with you. It struck me that it might be useful for someone in your... position"—she looked at Marie Blanche under glimmering brows—"to have extra sources of information. I can teach you the languages of birds, if you wish to know them. Those that visit this country, at least."

Though Marie Blanche was still ignorant of many things, she knew, if only from the faces of those around her, that this was an extraordinary offer.

"Why, I would be most grateful," she said.

Over the following months, Marie Blanche spent some time with Hethotain. She discovered that the Oakapple Clan were notorious among the other clans for their stone brandy, their taste for luxurious living, and their bronzework.

When either of them had time, Hethotain taught Marie Blanche the tongues of birds, and took her hunting in the fringes of the Oldest Forest, where there were many strange and dangerous beasts and rumours of even darker things.

One morning, Marie Blanche was struggling with a complex and extremely dull dispute between two neighbouring lords, who were both in the habit of writing very long and rambling letters detailing the petty irritations that each had visited on the other. It was a beautiful day and the windows were open. Outside, the sparrows were chattering, and she knew the language well enough that she could hear fragments of conversation. It was a little distracting, since even though most of the conversation was about where the fattest seeds were to be found, and whose nest was extremely shabby, and who thought far too well of themselves for lining theirs only with the finest wool, it was still rather more interesting than the letters.

Regretfully, she had just got up to close the window, when a flurry of newcomers arrived. "*...a terrible noise...*" they chattered, all excited. "*...the trees shook so my cousin's nest fell to the ground! ...a great cloud of dust, near the fox queen's den, and all the dwarves running about...*"

The mine. *Hethotain.* Marie Blanche ran from the room, calling for her horse, and for all those skilled in doctoring and strong of back to follow her, with water and bandages and rope and anything else that might be needful after a cave-in. The royal geologist flung himself on his overfed, underused pony and urged it alongside her, his fear of strange beasts quite forgotten.

The day being windless, a plume of dust was still visible over the trees, and Marie Blanche made for it.

She found several dozen dwarves gathered around the mine entrance, grim and dust-streaked. They turned as she arrived.

A dwarf with reddish plaits just visible under the dust said, "Your Highness?"

"It's Thogath, isn't it? What can we do?" Marie Blanche said.

"How did you...? Never mind. We've ten trapped below, we're shoring up ready to try and dig them out now."

"Direct my people as you wish," Marie Blanche said. She looked everywhere, but could not see Hethotain.

"She's down there," Thogath said quietly. "We were breaking a new seam. The clan leader always goes in for a new seam."

Marie Blanche swallowed.

Hammering and creaking and shouts and dust, a

sudden rumble; everyone still—waiting—then moving again. *Set your hands to what is in front of them.* Marie Blanche, seeing a gap in a line, grabbed a rope, hauled. Lifted a sledgehammer—or tried—but it was a dwarven hammer, and her muscles, strong as they were for a human girl, weren't made for it. So she handed around water, sent the geologist and the blacksmith in to help, and set her hands to what was in front of them, thinking, trying not to think, *Hethotain.*

Her eyes were gritty with dust, her tongue coated with it. She took a mouthful of water, spat.

"They're through, they're through!"

She looked around, blinking.

An anxious, muttering stillness, tension in the bodies around the opening.

A stretcher. Her throat tightened.

The dwarf on the stretcher was grey-faced and clenched with pain, young—not Hethotain. Borne away to where bandages and salves and splints were lined up on trestles.

More figures emerging, coughing and limping. None of them Hethotain.

Another stretcher. The face covered. A moan from the crowd. Marie Blanche clutched the water jug to her, feeling its handle digging into her palm.

The plait swinging down over the edge, black, unadorned with metal. *Not Hethotain.*

Finally, finally, there she was, leaning on another dwarf, both of them so coated with dust they looked like people of stone or clay.

All the strength went out of Marie Blanche's legs, and she found herself kneeling on the ground, while someone buzzed around her head like a concerned fly.

"I'm well enough, I'm well, look to the injured," she

said, when she had her voice back, embarrassed, pushing herself back to her feet. The dwarf hovering over her, she realised, was of the Polecat Clan. Looking around, she saw more of them—when had they arrived? She had not even noticed.

Later, much later, when the sun was setting, and the most urgent of the shoring up was done, and those who could be helped had been helped, Hethotain came and found Marie Blanche. "So," she said. "Your Highness."

"You're not hurt?"

"I was lucky. How'd you know?"

"I heard," Marie Blanche said. "The sparrows."

"Well," Hethotain said. "Well."

"I'm so sorry."

Hethotain sighed. "One we couldn't reach. It's said her spirit will stay in the mine, to watch and warn and guide."

"That doesn't seem fair," Marie Blanche said, looking around at the last of the bright day, the sun sinking in a flurry of ruby and gold, the birds chattering excitedly about all the great happenings as they settled for the night.

"No, it doesn't. Your Highness, we're most grateful for your help today."

"I hope it was of use."

"It was. And I'd like to return the favour."

"There's no need."

"There is," Hethotain said, the sunset drawing fiery lines along the gold and bronze woven into her hair and brows, bright among the dust. "When a cave-in happens, all the clans come to help, even if they're at odds."

"Oh, I saw the Polecat Clan here."

"Yes. Awkward bastards, but they turn up, it's what we

do. So. If you are ever in dire need, there is a phrase in the language of the peregrine falcon, that will bring you the help of any dwarven clan, wherever you are."

And Hethotain taught her the phrase, that sounds like nothing so much as a deal of clatter and screeching to the untrained ear, that means, *Noble bird, in time of need I stand, I summon thee in the name of the Oakapple Clan.*

THE DAYS WENT on, and Marie Blanche had less time for hunting, and none for friends. The girls of her own age she had ridden with, and danced with, and embroidered with, were still riding, and dancing, and embroidering, and even betrothing, while Marie Blanche was negotiating, and administering, and adjudicating. She learned everything she could from everyone who would teach her, and gained the respect of many—and the fear of some.

She still had the kitchens make her father's favourite dishes, and sometimes he ate more than two mouthfuls. Over these meals she would tell him what she had been about that day, and sometimes he said, "Oh," and sometimes, "Indeed," and sometimes, "Well." After a little while he always pushed away from the table and went back to his book-room. Only if she spoke of the upkeep of her mother's tomb or her annual memorial ceremony, would he say more than, "Someone will see to it." So Marie Blanche set her hands to what was in front of them, and saw to it herself as best she could.

But there were those who would not negotiate with a mere girl-child. In the spring, a meeting was due to discuss trade routes and tolls with two of their neighbouring countries, Teviens and Matrecourt, and their rulers would speak with no one but the King himself, even though (after a great deal of solemnity, and the writing of heavy documents, and hurrying back and forth of ministers, and little from the King but a nod and a sigh) Marie Blanche had been officially declared his heir.

So Marie Blanche racked her brains. She read through the letters about the trade routes again. She went to her mother's tomb, and sat there for some time in the chilly sunlight, looking at the tomb and the names and titles on it. *Set your hands to what is in front of them.*

Then she went to the Registrar of Lands, and spent some time with him.

Finally, with papers in her hand, she went to the King's book-room. She stood outside the door for a moment, with her hand pressed to her stomach. Then she reached back and shook her hair loose, letting it hang straight as it had when she was a little girl and no one expected her to know anything about trade routes and borders.

Then she knocked, and opened the door.

The King's robe was stained, and his beard untrimmed. The chamber was cold but somehow stuffy, and books and papers were piled on every surface, the papers mostly silvery with dust. Only the portrait of the Queen was free of dust, looking down, smiling, perfect, unchanging.

Marie Blanche thought of how the three of them used to sit here, with Papa sometimes reading out a particularly wise or amusing passage, and Mama looking up from her own book or her embroidery frame to smile, and Marie Blanche on a cushion at their feet, a puppy nestled at her knees, and everything bright and warm.

"Yes?" The King pushed his book aside, but his gaze drifted back to it as though drawn on a thread.

"The King of Teviens and the Duke of Matrecourt are talking of trade routes."

"What of it? My ministers will see to it."

"Is not Mama's parents' chateau on the border of Matrecourt?"

The King sighed. "Yes, a most pretty place, your mother had a great fondness for it. We spent a summer there, surely you remember? Someone fell in the horse-trough. How your Mama laughed! No one had a laugh like my Lisabèu..."

"Yes, Papa, I remember. But now here is some dispute about the estate, and which side of the border it falls. If it cannot be resolved, the chateau may be the centre of some trouble, perhaps even bloodshed. Mama would hate that."

Marie Blanche rather hated herself, at that moment.

"What?" said the King. "No. It must be a place of tranquillity, as Lisabèu would have wished. What is to be done?"

"The ministers say it is only a place. If it is sold off and the estate broken up, everything will be easily solved."

"Absolutely not!" The King stood up, and it was suddenly painfully clear how his robe hung loose about his spare frame.

"They will not listen to me," Marie Blanche said, tugging on her hair, a habit she had long since broken.

"Then they must listen to *me*." He called for his chamber groom, and his barber. He summoned the Registrar of Lands, and rounded up his trusted advisers.

Marie Blanche slipped silently away. She had already made the arrangements for the journey, and all that was left was to charge the servants who would travel with the King to make sure he ate adequately.

And so on a day of cold winds and clouds tumbling across the sky, the King left his palace for the first time since his wife died, though even at the last moment he looked longingly from the window of his carriage, not at his daughter, but at the window of his book-room.

Marie Blanche got back to work, and worried, and waited, and watched every day for a messenger.

ON A DAY of wild winds and flying leaves and rain and mud, a messenger finally arrived, huddled and dripping on a muddied horse, bearing a note in the King's own hand:

My dearest daughter,
    How glad I am that I came on this trip! The negotiations have been most successful, and I have wonderful news!
    I will tell you in person when I return.
    Your loving Father

It was as though the letter came from the man he had been. Even his signature seemed to have regained some strength and flourish. Marie Blanche felt a lightening of her heart, and her shoulders lifted a little, as though some invisible burden had grown slightly less heavy.

Papa came home from his trip a changed man. He strode instead of drifting, his footsteps loud and confident as they had once been, when he had sometimes caught his wife or his daughter or both into his arms and spun them about for sheer joy. His face was once more bright and his eyes sharp. His glooms and grief had disappeared as if by magic.

The news he brought, of course, was that Marie Blanche was to have a step-mama.

"I know that it seems very sudden," he said. "But

you will see. No one could ever be my Lisabèu, but Katherina... well. She is a wonderful woman, though she has not had an easy life. I know you will be kind."

He looked so happy, for the first time in so long. What was she to do but smile and declare that she was eager to meet his new love?

As to Marie Blanche, she barely knew how to feel. Her mother, indeed, could not be replaced, but it would be something to have an actual person to take one's troubles to, instead of a tombstone. And oh, it would be good to have time to hunt, or ride out just to see the sunrise, and practise her swordplay, and walk in the hills for no reason but to listen to the birdsong and watch for the shy martens to emerge from their burrows.

If she felt a little anxious that Papa would not quite like some of the things his daughter had done while he was indisposed, or that he would perhaps not understand the delicacy of some of the relationships she had built, she told herself not to be foolish, and to simply be grateful that Papa was back to his old self, and ruling as he had before. And indeed, the King seemed happy enough with everything, except that the palace and grounds were a little down at heel, and everything must be trimmed, and polished, and painted, and made splendid for his bride-to-be.

Marie Blanche stood for a long time in Mama's solar, where she had read, and embroidered, and talked with her friends. The little bouquet of stone flowers was still on the windowsill, sunlight waking rich colours in the translucent petals. Marie Blanche ran her finger over it, then picked it up, and took it away to her own rooms. The new Queen would never know it had been there, and would not miss it.

The Princess and the Stepmother

ARIE BLANCHE WAITED on the steps of the palace on the day her new step-mama was to arrive. A smile was fixed to her lips, and the gown her maid had chosen, encumbering as it was, at least helped hold her upright. She cared little for clothes—she preferred what she could best ride in, generally breeches—but for this guest, she must wear a gown.

The servants were all in their best: the men in red doublets and black hose, the women in red gowns and white aprons, as had been Mama's fancy. The horses in the stables were groomed to a shine. The weeds had all been pulled from the gardens, the grass scythed, every last drooping flower or browning leaf whisked away. It was a morning of sun and cloud, the light darting sudden and sharp across the land before hiding away again.

The first Marie Blanche saw of her step-mama was the flash of sunlight catching the paintwork of the brand-new carriage, with the royal crest painted on the door. It was drawn by four glossy chestnut horses, and accompanied by two heralds riding before it with red pennants fluttering in the breeze, half a dozen outriders with spears and breastplates shining silver, and behind them all an old, heavy, lumbering wagon drawn by oxen and covered in black cloth.

A woman stepped from the carriage into another fleeting shaft of sunlight. It deepened the crimson of her gown, made brilliant the ermine that trimmed it, gleamed from the gold roses that embroidered her deep blue underskirt. It shone on wings of black hair framed by a stiffly moulded headdress in a crimson that matched her gown. It lit a face as pale and perfectly carved as any of the marble statues in the gardens, and flashed in the great ruby on her finger, and the rubies that hung from her ears.

"Katherina!" The King ran down the steps to her, took her hand and turned to face his daughter.

"Marie Blanche, this is Katherina, who will be my queen and your step-mama. Katherina, this is my darling girl, Marie Blanche. She has been handling things so well while I was not myself, that I am tempted to abdicate in her favour, so I may spend all my time with you!"

"You would soon be bored, I am sure!" Katherina said, smiling.

Set your hands to what is in front of them. "You are most welcome," said Marie Blanche, and she curtseyed.

"Oh, I hope we are not to be quite so formal?" said Katherina. She gestured at the palace and the legions of servants, then at herself, with a rueful smile. "I am not used to all of this," she said. "Everything I have about me is your father's gifts, but for that poor old wagon and my few little bits and pieces. I am sure to make so many mistakes! I hope you will be kind, and show me how I am to go on."

She took Marie Blanche's hands—callused from riding and other work—in her own, soft and smooth and cool. The ruby flared in the sunlight, red as blood. She smelled of some rich, strange scent, with a faint hint of something metallic.

"I cannot replace your dear mother, but I promise I will treat you as my own mother did me!"

And indeed, perhaps she did.

THE CHANGES CAME slowly, and there was always a good reason for them. The red of the servants' livery was replaced with blue, because the old livery was beginning to look worn, and the blue cloth was more hard-wearing. Red was gently removed from Marie Blanche's wardrobe, because it was not the most flattering of colours for her. "You have no mother to tell you these things, and poor substitute as I am, I will do my best to guide you," Katherina said, smiling. Soon Katherina was the only one in the palace who wore red, and it must be said it suited her very well indeed.

Papa put on a little weight again, though never quite as much as before. He sent all over the kingdom, and beyond, for whatever his queen might fancy, and sat up all night planning entertainments for her. Marie Blanche worried, and still took over where she could, for Papa often looked tired. And she, too, wished to please her step-mama, who had made him happy again, and who tried so hard to improve their lives. Certainly there was no more worrying about unlit fireplaces or unswept rooms, for the palace ran so smoothly and the servants were so quiet about their work, it was almost as though fires lit themselves and brooms swept untended.

Servants moved away, or were pensioned off, or dismissed, and new servants arrived—perhaps more frequently than used to be the case, but surely that was only the way of things.

Some things did not change. Papa would rather spend time with his new queen than ride out for days to speak with the dwarven clans, or the local landowners, or deal with small disputes. So Marie Blanche continued to do so.

"I suppose it is the way you do things here," Katherina said, as Marie Blanche dressed in breeches for yet another expedition to inspect a copper mine, or accepted a drink from the flask of a huge, bush-bearded local lord (who almost certainly had giants' blood in him), after the successful pursuit of a man-eating bear, or any of the dozen other things which had over the last few years become as natural to the young princess as breathing. "I am merely a provincial, and no doubt seem very crude and silly with my old-fashioned ways!"

"Of course not, Step-Mama," said Marie Blanche.

"It is only that I fear these habits of yours may spoil your prospects for a good marriage. What if your prince should come, and find you drinking with commoners, or in breeches that smell of the stable and all bloodied from the hunt?" Step-Mama smoothed her own stylish skirts, with her white and clean-nailed hands. "My only concern is your future, my dearest."

It did occur to Marie Blanche, fleetingly, that the sort of man who would have no objection to these things would be the best kind of husband, but he was not here, and Step-Mama was. So she scrubbed at her short fingernails until they bled, and never entered Step-Mama's rooms without changing out of her outdoor clothes.

Still, somehow, Step-Mama always found a missed speck

of dirt or a rogue straw from the stables, and she would sigh, and smile sadly, and say that no doubt she was being foolish to fuss so, but it was only out of love.

Marie Blanche would leave the Queen's rooms with a catch in her throat and a cold sensation in her stomach. She would ride out to see the sun rise, or walk in the hills to watch for the shy martens, and sometimes even see their little kits playing, but these things did not bring her the peace she hoped for. She felt lonely most of the time, despite living surrounded by people. She told herself she must be feeling grief for her mama, even now, after all this time, and that she must just learn to live with it.

One spring, when she was visiting Hethotain to confirm some new arrangements for the transport of ores (which did not really require confirmation, but Marie Blanche somehow found herself taking every chance to be away for a few days), Hethotain asked, as she always did, after the King and Queen. "They are well, and send their warmest greetings," said Marie Blanche, as she always did. But for once, she did not leave it there. "Step-Mama worries over me a great deal," she said. "I don't think I am the stepdaughter she expected."

"Not everyone's stepdaughter has run a kingdom before she reached the age of twenty," Hethotain said.

Marie Blanche laughed a little. "True. She said she would need to ask me how to go on, but despite what her life has been, she runs the household as though born to it!"

"What has her life been?" Hethotain said.

"Oh, she does not speak of it, but Papa told me it had not been easy. Perhaps that is why she frets over me so. Poor Step-Mama."

Hethotain said, "Hmm," and frowned under her bushy brows and stared into her cup, and stroked the head of the great fox queen, swollen heavy with kits, who lay at her side, grinning and panting and staring at Marie Blanche with her bright gold eyes. After some time Hethotain looked up and said, "Listen to the little swallows—those with the blue heads, from Matrecourt—when they fly in from the north over the next month. Their accent is different. You may find their speech interesting." And that was all she would say.

So Marie Blanche took her notebook to the lake and listened to the swallows when they flew in from Matrecourt to swoop above the water gathering midges.

They chattered about twenty dozen things, as swallows do. And one of the things they chattered about was someone they called the Red Queen, and how she, like they, had migrated south, but seemed to be *staying* in the south, instead of going home in the summer like a sensible creature.

Marie Blanche was amused, and wondered if they could mean Step-Mama, who came from Matrecourt—though of course she had not been a queen, back then.

Oh, how grand her nest, the swallows chattered. *How bright her plumage.*

She is like a cuckoo-bird, said one. *Never her own nest, always another's!*

Indeed, indeed, chirped a second.

Marie Blanche frowned.

The silly sparrows take seed from her hands, said another. I *wouldn't*.

That's what comes to birds that spend half their time grubbing on the ground, said the first, with the contempt of a bird that spends the greater part of its life never coming to earth at all.

Marie Blanche put her notebook away and rode home,

wondering what she had heard, and if it meant anything, and whether she should tell Papa.

But that very day, Queen Katherina announced her pregnancy, and Marie Blanche squashed her worries and buried them deep. Step-Mama was good and loving and made Papa happy, and a child would make him even happier, and swallows were notoriously vain and superior birds. What did they know of anything?

ONE AUTUMN DAY, when the lavender had all been harvested and grey clouds chased their shadows over fields of browning stubble, and the air smelled of smoke and rain, Marie Blanche returned from a ride, made sure to wash away any traces of mud, and went to Queen Katharina's rooms.

She found Step-Mama sitting gloomily in front of the mirror she had brought with her from her home. It was an ugly great thing, with an overly elaborate frame, and the glass somewhat cloudy, but Marie Blanche understood that having something familiar, in a strange place, could be a comfort.

"Step-Mama, are you well?"

"Oh, my dear," Queen Katharina said, resting one hand on her belly, which was barely swollen yet. "I swear this child is the *fussiest* creature. If I eat one thing it does not like, it makes me miserable. Not a single morsel can I stomach, in three days!"

"Poor Step-Mama. You must eat, or the baby won't grow!"

"So true, so true. There is one thing that might help, but it is too much trouble, and dangerous to get besides."

"Tell Papa, and I am sure it can be got for you!"

Queen Katharina shook her head, and dabbed at her eyes. "Oh, no. Your poor father grows weary of my whims and needs. I am sure *your* mother was not such a demanding, troublesome wife when she carried you!"

"Tell *me*," said Marie Blanche, "I will get it for you, whatever it is!"

"No, no, it is too dangerous! I must suffer. I only fear for the child." Queen Katharina put her hand on her belly again, sighed, and gave a brave, trembling smile.

That smile was, by now, so very familiar—the smile of a woman beset but striving to remain cheerful—and it filled Marie Blanche with an equally familiar guilt. She would do anything to make Step-Mama feel better.

So she begged and pleaded, and finally, reluctantly, Step-Mama told her that the one thing that would cure her endless sickness was a rare white mushroom, that grew only in the depths of the Oldest Forest, at the foot of the Howling Mountain.

"But you must not go," she said. "It is too much to ask of you."

"Not at all," Marie Blanche said. In fact, the thought of leaving the chateau for several days made her heart feel lighter, until it was immediately weighted down again with guilt. How could she be happy to leave poor Step-Mama, when she was so ill, and poor Papa, who was so worried about her?

"The King won't like it," Step-Mama said. "It's dangerous, that far into the Oldest Forest, even for so good a huntress as you."

"Don't worry, Step-Mama," Marie Blanche said. "I'll talk him round."

Step-Mama demurred and protested some more, but eventually, turning her hands out helplessly, she gave in.

"If you insist on going," Queen Katherina said, "there is one other thing. The mushroom—it's only to help sickness, but some people think it's for evil spells. If anyone finds out that you're looking for it... Oh, I'd hate for any bad rumours to start up about you! How will you keep it secret? Your groom, your guards—people gossip so! No, no, I can't have it. I can't risk your reputation."

"I shall tell everyone I am going to negotiate with the Oakapple Clan, which I need to do in any case, and I shall take no escort," said Marie Blanche. It would be a little unusual, but she had ridden out alone before, though never so far. And her old groom, like so many of the other servants, had retired now. The new one she scarcely knew, so leaving him behind was no great hardship.

"You are far too good to me," Queen Katharina said. "I shall pack your supplies with my own hands." The Queen drew Marie Blanche into a warm, perfumed hug. Marie Blanche clung to her for a moment, breathing in her scent, and then went to see the King.

The King had been a big, bearded, roaring man. That was how she remembered him, swinging her up onto his shoulder and laughing, spinning Mama around in the dance and lifting her off her feet. But in the last years, he had lost substance, even after his marriage to Step-Mama; he seemed a little collapsed in on himself, like furniture that needed restuffing. He was staring at—or through—some papers on his desk.

"Papa, I need to leave for a little while."

"Leave? Where are you going?" The King rubbed his eyes. "I need you here, my dear. I find my duties lie heavily on me these days."

"The Oakapple Clan want to open up a new seam that will run beneath the royal lands. It would be a courtesy if

I myself were to go and speak to them. Besides, last time I was there Hethotain promised to teach me more of the speech of blackbirds."

"Well," said the King, "if you must go. But I don't know what blackbirds can have to say to anything."

"I shall be as quick as I can, Papa, and if the blackbirds say anything interesting I shall be sure to tell you about it."

He reached out his hands to her, and she saw that they had developed a faint tremor, which had never been there before. "Have you told your step-mama? I don't want her to worry."

"Oh, she knows, and is quite happy. Don't trouble yourself, Papa."

"Be careful, then, my dear." His clasp felt cold and dry. "Send my warmest greetings to Hethotain." His old self reappeared for a moment, sharp and clear. "Don't let the planned works encroach on Polecat Clan territory; that sort of trouble we *don't* need. And"—he winked— "don't let her give you any of that brandy of theirs until *after* the negotiations."

"Hah, I know better than that."

"I know you do. And hurry back."

"I will." She embraced him, and made for her rooms to pack.

Queen Katherina, true to her promise, put together food for Marie Blanche with her own hands, including an apple so glossy and perfect that it looked almost too good to eat.

Marie Blanche travelled for many days, feeling her shoulders stretch and open as she rode past the empty fields, watching the rooks circle and call crude jokes to each other. Her stomach became more settled the further she went from the Chateau. All around her the country readied for winter, the barns groaning with corn and the haylofts sweet with stored summer grasses, the liquid gold of cider in barrels and the paler—and many times more precious—gold of lavender oil.

At the Oakapple Clan holdings, Hethotain greeted her with warmth, and a steady look. She made commonplace enquiries after the health of the King and Queen, to which Marie Blanche gave commonplace answers.

The negotiations went well, and were accompanied by so much good food that the apple remained uneaten in Marie Blanche's saddlebag. Hethotain taught her the basics of the speech of blackbirds, which is very different in grammar and emphasis from that of sparrows. (Sparrows gossip constantly, but with patience, useful information can be gleaned among the chaff. Blackbirds chatter less, but say more, when they are not having shrieking hysterics about the presence of a hawk, or a shadow that might be a hawk, or the rumour of a hawk, or a sudden unexpected twig that briefly reminded them of a hawk.)

The fox queen's kits were now each the size of a well-grown hound, and they played about Marie Blanche's feet and licked her fingers.

The negotiations concluded, she mounted up and pointed her horse's head towards the Oldest Forest. Hethotain asked her if she wanted help with whatever she was hunting, but Marie Blanche waved the suggestion away. "I don't think what I hunt will be a very difficult prey," she smiled. She was about to make a joke about monstrous man-eating mushrooms, but remembered what Step-Mama had said, and closed her mouth on it, waved farewell, and rode on.

Even just at the fringes of the Oldest Forest, the trees were large and impressive, despite the loss of the leaves which now lay at their feet, red and gold and smelling of spices.

Deer tracks wandered among the trees. As Marie Blanche rode further in, the paths grew wider, and the bark of the trees was scored here and there with the marks of great claws.

All this was nothing new, for she had often hunted this far into the Oldest Forest. But she saw no sign of the white mushrooms that Step-Mama needed, and so she went deeper.

The trees became massive, their bark thick and wrinkled. They seemed, out of the corner of the eye, full of grimacing faces that disappeared as soon as you looked at them directly. At first the carpet of fallen leaves gave everything a warming golden glow, but as she rode on, the branches laced more thickly overhead, and the leaves were fewer, or had rotted faster, and there was more undergrowth, clutching and tricksy to a horse's feet, and even at noon it was always a green and whispering dusk.

Her horse, a gelding normally so well behaved he seemed half-asleep, was uneasy, his nostrils wide and his ears twitching. She soothed him and carried on, deeper and deeper into the forest.

After two days she was almost at the foot of the Howling Mountain, and her food was nearly gone, except the apple, which she had kept till last. It was still glossy and perfect.

Marie Blanche took it out of the saddlebag. How it gleamed, even in the forest's gloom! How kind Step-Mama was! She took a bite, then spotted a fine fat rabbit.

A rabbit is better eating than an apple, no matter how glossy and perfect.

Marie Blanche cast the rest of the apple aside, and took aim... and fell from her horse, with her bow still clasped in her hand.

MARIE BLANCHE WAS woken by a forceful jab beneath her ribs, and the unpleasant sensation of a piece of apple being vigorously dislodged from her throat.

Startled and slightly bruised, but otherwise little the worse for wear, Marie Blanche realised she was in a cave with walls of grey stone worn smooth with the passage of water, and sitting on piles of leaves that had been hastily covered with a horse-blanket. She wore her riding clothes, and though someone had tried to clean the blood of her hunts from them, they were still patched with brown stains.

She blinked at the surrounding faces.

There was a tall stranger, anxiously scanning her face. A single shaft of sunlight, piercing the gloom of the cave, gleamed on his bright gold hair.

Another man, who was not quite stocky nor bearded enough to be a dwarf, was watching her with interest.

Hethotain and a number of other dwarves gathered about, looking grave and worried.

"Your Highness, I hope I didn't hurt you," said the blond stranger.

"What happened?"

"You remember eating an apple?"

"Yes. Well, a bite of it."

"It was poisoned."

"*Poisoned?* But Step-Mama gave it to me with her own hands!"

"Yes," said the stranger. Gently, he explained the whole sorry affair.

Step-Mama, it seemed, had ambitions for the babe in her belly, and was even now persuading the King to have Marie Blanche declared dead, and her own son named the heir to the throne.

"But... wait." Marie Blanche shook her head and dragged her fingers through her hair, as though by doing so she could wake up her brain. "How do you know this? And a *son*? Born already? She was nowhere near her time! No, it's impossible!"

"You have been asleep for several months, Your Highness," said Hethotain. "The birds led us to you, the sparrows were gossiping about a dark enchantment and the blackbirds shrieking of murder. We found you and kept you safe, in this cave. We knew it was magic, but not of what kind, nor who had cast it, though... well. We thought it safer to keep you out of sight until we could find out more. Then this young fellow here turns up, and works out how to wake you."

Marie Blanche noticed that Hethotain, normally a dwarf of briskly suspicious nature, looked at the stranger warmly. In fact, everyone seemed to lean towards him, as to a fire on a cold day.

"But... Step-Mama... She was so kind to me..."

"I am so sorry, Your Highness," said the stranger. And he looked as though he really was, solemn and solicitous.

Marie Blanche fell silent. Her hands were cold, her stomach tight.

"You have no reason to trust me," the stranger said. "Especially since you don't even know my name. I am Prince Agradiu on Montaur, and I offer you what service I may in your current, most difficult situation. I know," he said, his handsome face darkening, "what it is to be betrayed by those you trust."

"You are most kind, Your Highness," said Marie Blanche, but she was barely listening to him.

Papa.

Once the child was declared the heir, how long before Papa, too, suffered an unfortunate accident?

She took a deep breath. "We must tell the King," she said. "But how do we get into his presence, without the Queen's knowledge?"

"I think my man Roland and I can manage something," Prince Agradiu said. He took her hand, and bowed over it, smiling at her. "At your eternal service."

Such a warm, sympathetic smile. Despite everything, Marie Blanche found herself smiling back.

THE ROYAL HOUSEHOLD was still at the Chateau, the King having refused, with all the stubbornness left to him, to leave the last place he had seen his daughter. During the ride there, done discreetly and mainly under cover of night, the Prince somehow got Marie Blanche to tell him a great deal more of her life and her thoughts than she had told *anyone*, other than her mother's tomb. He was so good a listener, and when he spoke, he somehow knew exactly what to say.

He talked admiringly of how she had kept the kingdom stable, without ever suggesting she had taken too much on herself. He shot her a look of such sympathy when she spoke of talking to her mother's tomb (and how had he got *that* out of her? She had never told anyone that, not even Hethotain) that she almost wept.

And when she spoke of how she feared for Papa, and whether they would be too late, he tightened his jaw, and urged the horses onward. "Your Highness," he said, "we *will* be there on time, if I have to carry you on my back."

They reached the chateau under cold, brilliant moonlight. With the shutters tight over the windows, it looked strangely blind. Marie Blanche shivered at the sight of it, and wondered if she would ever be comfortable again, in this place she had once loved.

She was certainly uncomfortable as they snuck in by a long-neglected water gate, up through a rough, narrow passage behind the dungeons. The dank cells had never been used in her time, but from the stench and the sobbing, it seemed they were now fully occupied.

The stone scraped at Marie Blanche's hands and her scalp and her back, and her muscles, weakened by long sleep, trembled and burned. But the ache in her unused limbs and the grazes from the rock walls were as nothing to the searing anger and icy worry that grew with every passing minute.

They made it to the centre of the Chateau and the corridor outside the King's rooms, only to see four guards. "Do you know these men?" the Prince whispered.

"No. All our guards were ex-soldiers," Marie Blanche whispered back. "Wait. That one, with the broken nose—he used to be part of a mercenary troop we threw out of the country! Papa would never employ him!"

"That's all right, then," Agradiu said, and so swiftly that Marie Blanche could barely follow his movement he leapt out of hiding, and, neatly as a hunting cat, dispatched two of the guards, severely injured a third (who Roland efficiently finished off), and began a flashy bout with the broken-nosed man—who, it seemed, was a much more accomplished swordsman than his companions. As they ranged back and forth, Roland nipped in and stabbed the mercenary from behind.

"Unsporting," Agradiu said, as the mercenary collapsed, gurgling, to the floor.

"Sorry, Your Highness," Roland said, not sounding it. "But drawing things out might bring us attention we don't need yet."

Marie Blanche found her hands trembling as she opened the doors to her father's rooms.

The King was hunched by the fire, despite the warmth of the day, and seemed not to have noticed the brief ruckus outside his rooms at all. The firelight caught the ridges and hollows of his face. When had he become so gaunt? And when had his beard become so white, and his broad shoulders so hunched? Even after Mama died, he had not shrunk so.

"Papa."

"Marie Blanche!" He sprung to his feet, and almost tripped over his footstool in his eagerness to embrace her. "Is it you? Truly you?"

"Yes, Papa," Marie Blanche said, flinging her arms around him and pressing her face to his chest. Oh, he had grown so thin!

He backed out of the hug and took her hands, staring down at her. "It really is you, and not an illusion. I have so often hoped and longed for you that my mind would conjure you in the shadow of a curtain or the walk of a serving maid.

"I offered half my kingdom," he said, gripping her hands as though afraid she might disappear again. "Half my kingdom only to have you back again."

"Ah, pish, I wouldn't dream of taking half your kingdom!" said the Prince. "I should perhaps mention I have one of my own; or will do, in the fullness of time. One that will need strong alliances. But that discussion is for later." He glanced at Marie Blanche and gave a shy smile, then looked at his own feet. This sudden hesitancy, after such swiftness and resolution, was strangely appealing.

Marie Blanche found herself blushing. The thought of an alliance with such a kind, trustworthy fellow—one who, moreover, had been so gentle and respectful towards her, not to mention saving her life—well, it certainly had its merits.

And he had not minded that she was in breeches, all bloodied from the hunt, either.

"Indeed," she said. "But first, we have less pleasant business."

Roland had carefully gathered up the piece of apple in a cloth, and the court apothecary, discreetly summoned, examined it and declared it, in truth, magically poisoned. "Had Your Highness eaten all of it, or even just swallowed that one bite..." The apothecary shook her head.

The King sighed heavily. "Have the Queen called to me," he said. "But say nothing of my daughter."

Roland coughed into his hand. "May I make a suggestion, Your Majesty?" he said. "A confession makes things easier on everyone. I've an idea." He gave the piece of apple to Marie Blanche.

A few moments later, the Queen swept into the King's chambers, beautiful as ever in crimson silks, with rubies glittering at her ears and the great ruby ring glowing on her hand, as red as blood. She halted on the threshold, staring.

"My dear!" the King said. "See, our beloved Marie Blanche is restored to us!"

The Queen paused only a moment. "Why, how wonderful!" she said. "What can have happened?" And if her voice was a little strained, it could easily be dismissed as surprise.

"Don't you remember, Step-Mama?" Princess Marie Blanche said. "I went to find you some white mushrooms, to help with your sickness. I must have fallen from my horse, and knocked myself out—so careless of me. But this gentleman found me, and has brought me home! And I still have a piece of the apple you gave me, isn't it strange? It must be good luck, to have lasted so long, it hasn't even gone brown! I kept it for you, see? Won't you have a taste? Perhaps *this* will cure your sickness?"

And Princess Marie Blanche held out the chunk of apple.

"Eat," said the King, in a stronger voice than anyone had heard from him in a very long time.

"My King?" said Queen Katherina. "My darling, what have they told you?" She turned to Marie Blanche. "It's only the shock," she said, "of seeing you after so long, that makes him talk so. Where have you *been*? Did you hide for months, just to make us worry? Do you know how much you have hurt us? And then to sneak in, with some—some *stranger*, and tell some wild story... I think perhaps you fell from your horse, indeed, and hit your head. My King, we should get the doctor to her. I know just the man."

"I'm sure you do," said Prince Agradiu.

"If you will not eat," said the King, "perhaps I should feed it to our son, as you fed it to my daughter."

Then the bright colour drained from Queen Katherina's face, and she fell to her knees. "I will eat it, if you wish," she said. "But I beg you spare our son's life."

"Do you really think I would kill him, for *your* crime?" said the King. "Do you think I am like you?" And he made a gesture to the guards, and turned his face away.

*　*　*

THE EXECUTION TOOK place swiftly, with the dignity due to the Queen's station. A wet nurse was found for the baby. The dungeons were emptied of their occupants.

The next few days were a scramble. As Marie Blanche, once again, set her hands to what was in front of them (much of it undoing the Queen's meddling), the Prince seemed to know exactly when she needed him to talk, and when she needed silence. When to challenge her to a horse race to work off her fury, and when to simply sit with her beside the stream, as she stared at the fish in the clear water and envied them their uncomplicated lives.

He took her hand and turned it over, traced a callus with his finger. "This little hand has worked very hard. May I be permitted to lift some of its burdens?"

"Why, what do you mean?" she said, feeling a blush heating her face, and her heart rising within her.

"Come, don't be coy, it doesn't suit you. I'm asking if you'll be my wife. My queen."

"In that case, yes," she said.

His proposal delighted everyone. The preparations for the wedding included a tour of the sections of the palace that Prince Agradiu had not yet seen, such as the treasury, and were just what they all needed to take the taste of betrayal out of their mouths.

Until the next morning, that was.

"Half my kingdom! I promised him *half my kingdom!*" the King raged. "And if it could have been folded up into a sack, he would have taken it! Oh, I am an old fool, and no longer fit to rule, daughter. I shall abdicate, and you must take the throne."

"Nonsense," said Marie Blanche, holding herself very straight, and sharpening her best hunting knife a little more vigorously than needed. "You have a great deal still to teach me that can best be learned by watching you at work, and I am still studying many other things, which will not allow me time to rule a whole kingdom. We must set our hands to what is in front of them." She kissed him on the forehead, and strode off to the stables, and took her best hunter out for a very long ride through the most dangerous parts of the mountains. If, when she returned with the remains of a fine stag across her saddlebow, her eyes were somewhat red, no one was foolish enough to mention it.

And if from that moment she had more time and patience for her dogs, her horses, and her hawks than for people, no one mentioned that, either.

Three Ladies and a Wedding
(The Second Part)

ARIE BLANCHE SAID, "I was humiliated, certainly. But my father was devastated. He thought himself a good judge of character. And he is: our ministers were well chosen, or I could not have managed things so well when he... In any case, it seems neither of us could judge *this* character."

"But he was so *nice*," Lady Bella said. Her eyes brimmed with tears.

"Oh, my dear." Doctor Rapunzel laid a comforting hand on her arm. "They *always* seem nice. How else would such men gain one's confidence?"

"You too?"

"Yes. It is a long and unpleasant story, but I will tell it if you wish."

"I think we need more wine," Princess Marie Blanche said, waving at a footman and waggling her glass.

"My own story begins in the town of Finsterburg," said Doctor Rapunzel, as the hapless servant came hurrying over...

The Orphan Girl and the Sorceress

HE TOWN OF Finsterburg lies in the heart of the great forest called the Trübenholz, its buildings huddling together as though for protection from the louring woods. A huge grey castle frowns down from the hill at the mundane creatures below. The narrow threads of earthen tracks, and a few more solidly paved roads, run out through the dark mass of the Trübenholz. The place smells of pine and moss, of ripening grapes in the summer and wine in the autumn, and always a little of sulphur from its hot springs.

Despite its somewhat isolated and gloomy situation, Finsterburg is prosperous, and possessed of a respected university and many splendid, comfortable buildings.

The building of interest to us, however, is grey, and square, and cold, and ugly, and all its windows are crossed with bars. It is the town orphanage, where the unwanted, the abandoned, and the merely mislaid are hidden away from the sensitive eyes of the more fortunate, until someone can find a use for them.

* * *

"Emilia! Emilia Rapunzel! Stand with the others, straighten your back. All of you, behave!" The overseer shut the door.

Emilia Rapunzel did as she was told. She was lined up with the other orphans, waiting to be picked over like fruit at the market, the stone floor striking cold through her thin shoes.

Her face was still damp from a hasty scrubbing, and she had tidied her straight, coppery hair as best she could, tying it into a rough knot and shoving it under her kerchief. The overseer insisted they kept their hair short, but hers grew very quickly.

The other girls whispered. "This one's fussy. Poor Clara and Twisty have been shut away."

"No one wants the cripple girls."

"*And* she only wants ones who can read."

The orphanage prided itself in providing the girls with a basic education in letters, though this was intended to be used for such things as writing out recipes and reading morally improving texts, not mere entertainment. And even that was considered excessive by some.

"Who do you think it is?"

"I hope it's a baker! So much bread to eat, and a warm kitchen to sleep in..."

"A rich couple with no children of their own..."

"A king looking for his long-lost daughter!"

"A dressmaker..."

"What good's a dressmaker?"

"Pretty clothes. Imagine wearing pretty clothes." The girls were dressed all the same, in brown sack-like dresses provided by the generosity of some local ladyship. This generosity, while much applauded by the townsfolk, did not extend to making the dresses warm, or comfortable, or in any way appealing.

"You'd never get to *wear* them, silly, just fit them on other people."

"No, a dressmaker would be good. Dressmaking's a good trade."

Emilia nodded approval at that. A trade was a realistic possibility. Rich childless couples didn't come to the town orphanage looking for heirs—still less kings.

"So long as it's not the old witch," said another.

"Oh, the old witch is just a tale."

"She is not. She takes girls home and eats them up!"

"Oh, rubbish." Emilia said. "One rich girl disappeared a hundred years ago. If the witch was old then, she's long since dead!"

"So what about you, what do *you* want, Emilia?" demanded the girl who had talked of the witch, a little stung. Life in the orphanage was grey and dull, and tales, even ugly ones, were often all they had of colour or excitement.

"To get out of here," Emilia said.

"I don't know why you didn't already," the other girl said, with a sly look. "You're *good* at getting out of things."

Emilia ignored her, but some of the girls snickered and others looked away.

It was true, Emilia had a knack of avoiding the harshest chores and the worst beatings. Of getting a little extra food. It wasn't much, she just seemed to be able to give things a tiny *nudge;* but in a place like this, where there was little of anything except chores and hunger, it was noticed.

"Hush, hush, they're coming!"

Eager, anxious faces lined up, polished as apples.

The woman who swept in was richly dressed and looked no more than twenty-five. Her dress was of velvet the colour of sherry wine, embroidered in gold; the padded headdress that completely hid her hair was stitched all over with tiny golden sequins that flashed and glittered even in the faint light from the narrow windows.

Her expression, as she looked at the row of girls, was absolutely neutral. "You assure me that these are all strong and healthy? I want no cripples or weaklings. No lung-rot or gut-ache."

The overseer was rubbing his hands as though he were trying to rid them of a particularly stubborn stain, his head tilted towards the woman, his body angled away, in the peculiar posture of someone who wants to be, *has* to be polite, but has no desire to get too close. He had a tight, toothy smile. "Of course! These are our best girls, Doctor. Not a cough or a limp among the lot of them." He started to enumerate the many ways the orphanage produced stronger, cleaner, more hardworking and obedient girls than anywhere else she might look, but the woman cut her hand through the air, silencing him as swiftly as though she had actually cut his voice in half. "I shall see for myself."

"Yes, Doctor."

He's afraid of her, Emilia thought. She looked at the woman again. Rich, obviously, but what else? *Doctor.* Educated, then—even at fourteen, Emilia knew that was enough to frighten some people. There were those who wouldn't take girls from this orphanage just *because* they could read.

The woman began to walk along the row, her heels

*tack-tack*ing on the stone like a clock counting off cold seconds. She looked at each girl in turn, still with that calm, neutral expression. Here and there she paused; "Can you read?" she asked, or "Do you know your numbers?" And whether the answer was yes or no, each time, with a tiny shake of her head, she moved on.

Eventually she stood in front of Emilia, who after one glance at the Doctor's pale face, with its high flat cheekbones and eyes grey as fog, kept her gaze respectfully lowered, tracing the glimmering gold of the leaves and flowers embroidered on the velvet gown. The Doctor's perfume was musky-rich, but underlying it, woven with it, there was another note, austere and metallic.

"Can you read?"

"Yes, ma'am."

"Do you sound out the words as you read them?"

"No, ma'am," Emilia said, raising her chin with a little flicker of pride. She caught that fog-grey stare and lowered her gaze again.

"And do you know your numbers?"

"Yes, ma'am. I can add and subtract and divide." This time she did not look up.

The Doctor moved on. Emilia felt at the same time a lessening of tension and a sense of disappointment. The Doctor was scary. But the Doctor was *interesting*.

Look again, Emilia thought. *Look at me again.*

She never knew whether it would work. Most of the time, it didn't. When it did, she never knew why.

The Doctor carried on, to the end of the row.

That's that, then, Emilia thought.

Then the Doctor turned, and came back, at the same slow pace, *tack-tack,* and stopped in front of Emilia. "This one," she said.

Emilia looked up. The Doctor's mouth was smiling, but her eyes held no expression at all. Emilia felt the cold from the floor creep up into her bones. Perhaps she had made a mistake.

The other girls were completely silent, none of the giggles or commiserations or whispered good luck wishes that usually accompanied one of them being chosen for a place.

The Doctor swept out of the door, the overseer snapped at Emilia to fetch her things and not dawdle.

Emilia went to the room she shared with twenty other girls, and took her things from beneath the thin grey blanket on her bed: a kerchief and a spare shift, both threadbare. She wrapped one in the other then waited outside the overseer's office. She heard the chink of coins, and wondered how many.

The woman came out, crooked a finger for Emilia to follow, and moved away without waiting to see if she did.

Emilia hurried after her—the Doctor moved with a speed that hardly seemed to match her stately walk—and in moments found herself outside the building in which she had spent the last seven years of her life.

There was a coach waiting. A pale hand beckoned her into it.

Holding the reins of the coach was a small fellow with striped stockings and pointed shoes. He had sharp features and keen eyes. He looked Emilia up and down, but his face was no more readable than the Doctor's. He gave something that might have been a shrug, or just a hunching of his shoulders, and turned back to the horses.

Emilia climbed into the carriage and, after a moment's confusion—she had, after all, never been in a carriage before—sat opposite the woman who now, to all intents and purposes, owned her. It was called 'adoption,' but ownership was what it meant.

The woman leaned back against the cushions, scanning Emilia up and down. "My name is Doctor Hilda von Riesentor. I am a doctor in the arcane arts. You have potential," she said. "But try and use the 'fluence on me again—ever—and I will find somewhere far worse than the orphanage for you. Do you understand?"

"Yes, ma'am," said Emilia.

"Mother Hilda."

"Yes, Mother Hilda."

"Did you see the man driving the coach?"

"Yes, Mother Hilda."

"He is not a man, but an imp. He is my familiar, and obeys only me, because I know the thing that has power over him. This is your first lesson: everything has something, a weakness, that will give you power over it. Much of magic is simply finding out what that is, and how to apply it."

"Yes, Mother Hilda."

Mother Hilda smiled, and patted Emilia's knee. "Good girl. I am sure we will deal splendidly together. First, we must buy you some clothes."

THE MORNING WAS spent in a whirl of cloth and measuring and pins. Emilia stood and moved as she was told, relishing the rich colours and luxurious sensations of fine cloth and good shoe-leather, while at the same time feeling a little like a rag doll in the middle of a tug-of-war.

Dressmaking concluded, and Emilia having been thrust into a gown of dark bronze velvet, stockings, and hard shoes that pinched her feet, and having had her hair tidied and simply dressed, they went to dine at the sort of place where, until now, Emilia would have been lucky to get work in the kitchens.

Mother Hilda encouraged her to eat her fill. "You need meat on you," she said, scanning Emilia's frame in a way that made her a little uneasy—she looked almost *hungry*. Though when the food came, she ate sparingly.

Emilia, on the other hand, faced with more and better food than she had ever seen in her life, ate until she could barely move. But she did it carefully, not wanting to stain her new gown, or give Mother Hilda a reason to send her back. She watched every movement Mother Hilda made, from the handling of her knife to the dabbing of her lips with linen, and did her best to do likewise.

As evening fell, they drove out of the town, along a road that wound through the valleys, deep into the forest. Fortunately for Emilia's overstuffed stomach, the carriage ran remarkably smoothly, as though she were riding in a dream, or perhaps as though the wheels turned a little above the surface of the road, instead of upon it.

Emilia stared out of the window as her old life fell away. The tree-covered hills that had always overshadowed the buildings of the town now crowded around her close enough to touch. A huge castle topped one hill, its grey towers looming above the trees like rocky peaks, and Emilia stared. Mother Hilda smiled. "That is the castle where the Prince lives. He thinks a great deal of himself, as you can see. Such display is all very well, but even stone walls tumble, and even princes age, and die."

"Yes, Mother Hilda."

Deeper and deeper into the forest they went, the trees

pressing in around them as though they were curious about the carriage and wanted to see inside. The noise and smells of the city fell far behind, until there was nothing but the sound of the horses' hooves on the road and the creak of the carriage, the song of birds, and the endless secret rustling whisper of the trees.

When the carriage pulled to a halt, the imp opened the door and Emilia stepped out into the great green murmuring forest, to see before her a huge tower, of stone as red as blood. It jabbed at the sky like a raw bone.

"This is the Rotterturm," Mother Hilda said. "Our home."

The walls were glossy smooth, and unbroken by any entrance.

Mother Hilda took a small glass phial with a silver cap from her pocket, and cast its contents on a black stone at the base of the tower. There was a hiss and a smell of frost. "Show, reveal, unlock, unseal," Mother Hilda said, and a great gate appeared in the wall, and swung open.

Within was a courtyard, with lush flower beds full of lilies as big as Emilia's head, pink and orange and cream, striped and spotted and so heavy-scented they made her feel faint. They were quite out of season. Fountains splashed into polished basins of porphyry, and a faint and silvery music was woven with the sound of the water. To one side stood a coach house and stable, plain as bread and quite unmagical, and opposite was a door into the tower's thick wall. The whole space was hollow.

As Emilia stared and marvelled, she realised that the outside of the tower did not match the inside. The space was bigger than it had any right to be, and sunlight somehow fell into the courtyard even though the sun had long passed over the open top of the tower. *Magic.*

The sun falling where it should not, and fragile lilies blooming out of doors and out of season. Emilia was both fascinated and unsettled.

Inside, they climbed a narrow stair to a room that, again, was bigger than the space between inner and outer walls should have allowed. It was richly furnished with chairs upholstered in sherry-coloured velvet, a padded couch, and a table covered with heavy tapestry cloth, on which were many books and gleaming instruments whose names Emilia did not know. That austere, metallic scent—the scent Emilia would come to associate with magic, with knowledge, with fear and power—permeated everything.

"This is where we will begin," said Mother Hilda.

EMILIA HAD LEARNED, early in life, to be cautious. Living with Mother Hilda taught her this lesson anew, and to an entirely new level.

The orphanage had been cold, and plain, and uncomfortable, and sometimes cruel. The Rotterturm was warm, rich, luxurious, and frequently brutal. The redness of the stone somehow soaked into everything, as though even the silk hangings and velvet cushions were all stained with blood. The intense, cloying smell of lilies always hung in the air, mixed with the acrid, metallic tang of Mother Hilda's potions.

And Hilda herself: Mother Hilda could wheel from affection to fury like a weathercock in a March wind. When Mother was happy, she would patiently teach Emilia simple sorceries, or spend hours brushing her hair (always gathering up any loose hair and taking it away), or choosing pretty clothes for her, dressing her up and exclaiming over how well they fitted and how fine she looked. But when Mother Hilda was angry, she would use her sorceries on Emilia, to make her too hot, or too cold, or to make her see nasty things crouched in every corner, waiting to pounce. Sometimes she would forbid Emilia to eat until she gave permission, and then forget to give it—or would tell herself she had forgotten. Then, when Emilia grew faint and trembling with hunger, Mother Hilda would remember, berate Emilia for making herself ill, and tell her to eat her fill.

But she never beat her hard enough to break anything, so Emilia tried, at first, to be grateful.

And she was grateful, for some things at least. She had learned her letters and numbers in the orphanage, but she had always been hungry for more than just food. In the Rotterturm there were *books*. She was not allowed to read them all, but there were far more than she had ever seen in her life. There were herbs of which she must learn the names and uses. There was brewing and distillation and the study of the movement of stars. There were minerals and roots and gems and salts and inks and gleaming instruments of copper and brass, and each of these things had a use and a meaning, and Emilia's brain, long starved, ate up everything it was given.

But in the orphanage, there were other girls. Emilia had not precisely had *friends*, but there were people to compare chores and scoldings and occasional beatings with, to grumble with, sometimes to offer a little cautious mutual comfort. Never quite friends, but company, at least.

Here, there was no one but the familiar. She had known, of course, that witches (or doctors of the arcane) sometimes had familiars, but she had always thought it would be a cat, or a toad, not a frowsty little man—or imp—grumbling about with pails of water and cuts of meat.

Even if they had ever been left alone together, he would not—or could not—speak to her directly. Sometimes he would mutter over his pots, or sing unpleasant little songs under his breath. "Falala," he sang. "See the pretty lamb wag its little tail, come the spring and its blood is in the pail," and suchlike. He scuttled about his chores with his odd, rocking gait, seldom looking at her or at anything but the bucket or mop or bunch of herbs in his hands. Once she caught him looking at Mother Hilda with a look of such utter murderous hate that she blinked and hurried away, hoping he'd not seen her watching, not wanting that look even to brush her. *If that is how a familiar looks at its mistress,* she thought, *I will never have one. Never.*

Mother Hilda often travelled to town, always with the familiar driving her, sometimes with a pack beast roped to the back of the carriage if she was picking up supplies—for no deliveries ever came to the Rotterturm. She always covered her hair, and even when she was only shopping, she always dressed finely.

When Mother went into town to attend parties, she dressed not finely but splendidly, in silks and velvets and brocades, with beautiful matching headdresses. She would stand in front of her mirror for a long time, twisting this way and that, and leaning forward to peer closely into the glass. "Not so bad, not so bad," she would say. "Holding up." Sometimes she'd say, "Well, girl? What do you think, eh?"

"You look beautiful, Mother Hilda. Splendid as a queen."

"I am sure you know a great many queens, my little street sweeping, hmm? You must have met them every day in that orphanage! Well, it is time I left. Do your chores, and if anyone comes, do not look out of the window or go to the door. I shall know if you do."

"Yes, Mother Hilda."

And away she would sweep, in a cloud of perfume.

MOTHER HILDA ALWAYS carried with her three phials: one with a cap of silver, one with a cap of gold, and one with a cap of pale blue chalcedony. The fluid in the silver-capped vial opened the tower, and the fluid in the gold-capped vial, Emilia learned, opened the door to the room where Mother Hilda kept her most precious and powerful things; but the phial capped with chalcedony Emilia never saw used.

The lessons Emilia was taught were all for extremely simple spells and cantrips that relied heavily on memory. "I am sure this seems dull to you," Mother Hilda said, "but some things one wishes to be able to do without thought. The hands, the feet, the tongue should know their moves, without hesitation, as the dancer knows the steps of the dance. Imagine that one must relearn the entire dance, every time one has a new pair of dancing shoes! How tedious would that be?"

Next time the familiar passed her with a basket of logs, Emilia heard him singing, "Falala. The shoe that is new will soon wear thin, when the old dame shoves her smelly foot in." For such a silly song, it still somehow brushed Emilia's spine with cold. "What do you mean?" she hissed. "What are you saying?" But the familiar only turned his back and set to making the fire.

Eager to please, and to learn, Emilia repeated the same few simple spells and the hand gestures and steps that went with each until she was certain she could do them in her sleep. Some were for beguiling and illusion, though none strong enough to work on Mother Hilda, and Emilia would not dare to try. Some were to reveal things, and others were to control the weather—in a small way. "It's so tedious to get wet on the way to a party, or have one's shoes all spoiled with mud," Mother said. "To keep off the rain and calm the wind is much less trouble. Of course, one can also spoil some vain woman's hair with a sudden breeze, which is always amusing."

At first, Mother Hilda sometimes took Emilia with her to town. But as Emilia grew older and more adept, the sorceress went alone more often, always locking away the most powerful instruments and devices (and potions, and herbs) in her treasure room. Emilia was left with a few of the less potent tools and simpler spell books, with lessons to learn and chores to do. Mother Hilda would return, and speak of how much she had danced, and how many compliments she had received, and how this lord and that prince had lost their hearts to her.

Emilia would nod and exclaim, but wonder. For Mother Hilda never seemed to have any interest in these men at all; from her descriptions, Emilia could scarcely tell one man from another. It was their *praise* she liked—especially, it seemed, if they had a wife or a betrothed present at the party. Mother spent far more time describing the faces of the other women than she did the men. "How jealous she looked! Sour as a lemon." "Oh, she pretended it meant nothing, when I danced with him, but I could tell she hated me. All I had to do was snap my fingers, and he'd come running!"

"Why don't you, Mother Hilda?" Emilia asked once. "Snap your fingers, I mean."

"If someone should come along who is worth my time, perhaps."

"Who would that be?"

"Someone with prospects. *Excellent* prospects."

"Aren't you ever lonely, here, with just me?" said Emilia.

"How should that be, when I have my own dear daughter at my side?" Mother Hilda said, smiling. "Come, sit down, and let me brush your hair." Emilia obeyed, and the other woman set to brushing her hair in long, even stokes; but after a few minutes, she stopped. Mother Hilda held up a mirror, bending close so both their faces could be seen. "We look very alike, don't you think? But for the eyes. A little glamour, and we could be mother and daughter in truth!"

"Oh, you don't look old enough to be my mother!" Emilia said, carefully.

"I do my best." Mother Hilda put down the mirror and went back to her brushing.

"What about girls?" Emilia said.

"What about them?"

"Perhaps someone else could come and stay with us? Another girl from the orphanage?" The brushing stopped, with a yank.

"So you'd like a little friend, would you, to gossip with and share my secrets? Don't you think I have enough on my hands, keeping you and dressing you and teaching you?"

"Oh, no!" Emilia said, hastily. "It's only because I've been so lucky, and it seems unfair no one else should have what I do."

"Hah." The brushing began again, harder this time.

"At least you realise how lucky you are. Understand this. Other people will take from you, and take and take again, and never be thankful. Better to take what you want from them first. You understand?"

"Yes."

"'Yes, Mother Hilda.'"

"Yes, Mother Hilda."

The brushing stopped again. "Enough," Mother Hilda said. "I've worn myself out looking after you. Make me a tisane." She went over the brush, carefully picking out every hair, and took the loose hairs away.

Mother Hilda had danced and flirted a great deal at her party, and was, indeed, very tired. When Emilia took her the tisane, she was already asleep, on the chaise, with her shoes kicked off. As Emilia set down the tray, Mother Hilda stirred in her sleep, and muttered, "The first three drops on the hair of the vessel. The next three drops on my own. Oh, so white now, so old-looking. When the vessel is empty, so! Fill it up again. How good to be young and light-footed, and dance all night and ride all day."

Emilia put down the tisane, and went to the window, and looked out at nothing, biting her thumbnail. Sometimes she felt as though the things Mother Hilda made Emilia see when she was angry—the ugly, whispering things crouching in the corners, waiting to spring at her—were not an illusion at all.

But what they were, and how to escape them, she did not know.

EVERY DAY EMILIA looked out over the Trübenholz, the thick, tangled sea of trees. From the blazing beauty of autumn to the cruel winter, the bare branches stark as bones, the firs a dark, unchanging green. She saw the first mist of jade over the branches in spring and the fruit trees shaking out their white blossom like lace, the thick lush growth of high summer turning dusty and then lightening with autumn brilliance. Even the fir trees had their changes, the bright green of new growth against the dark, the bursts of pollen from their cones in summer, as though imps sat in them, smoking tiny pipes. One day, as she leaned out and scented the first frost in the air, Emilia realised she had not left the Rotterturm in a year.

When Mother Hilda next left for the town, Emilia sneaked a pinch of herbs here, a pinch of black salt there, and took out the oldest and most stained of the cauldrons. A spell of illusion, a spell of misdirection.

She hesitated at every step. *Do not look out of the window or go to the door. I shall know if you do.* Would these simple spells of illusion and misdirection be enough to hide the attempt? She would not know, unless she failed.

Trembling, her stomach knotting and coiling, Emilia made for the gate. She had only ever seen it unlocked from the outside; perhaps, from the inside, it would simply open.

But she never even made it as far as the gate. The scent of the lilies seemed to thicken, until her head swam and her feet stumbled and her stomach sickened. Terrified that she would faint, and Mother Hilda would come back and find her in the courtyard, her guilt clear as a bloodstain, Emilia stumbled back up the stairs, and vomited in the nearest basin she could grab. She scoured the basin and the cauldron until her fingers bled, put everything back as though it had never been touched, and crouched in her room, shaking, waiting for the sound of the carriage.

Mother Hilda swept in and called for her. "Emilia! Emilia Rapunzel!"

Emilia took the deepest breath she could—it was hard to get any breath at all—and hurried down the stairs.

"There you are," Mother Hilda said. "I have had a most fatiguing journey. Make me a tisane. Why, whatever is the matter, child? You look quite ill." She thrust her face at Emilia's, that fog-grey gaze running over her like cold water. "You had better not be sickening."

"No, Mother Hilda. I had a little sickness in my stomach, but it's gone now." She had scrubbed and scrubbed, but there might be a lingering trace of vomit; it was a smell that clung.

"Hmm. Bread and water for the next two days, and we'll see how you go on. Are you too ill to make a tisane? Hmm? Are you perhaps needing to lie down, and be fanned, and fussed over, like a little lady?"

"No, Mother Hilda."

"Then get to it."

"Yes, Mother Hilda."

Emilia noticed the familiar sniff the air and look at her. He might have shaken his head, the tiniest fraction, but she was so swamped with relief and exhaustion she could hardly be certain of anything.

But she had learned something. Mother Hilda did not know she had been at the gate. Mother Hilda had lied about the extent of her powers.

EMILIA STOOD BY the window, stretching her aching back. By wary experiment, she had learned that Mother Hilda did not, in fact, know when she had been looking out of the window, though sometimes she would pretend to.

Emilia took the punishments, and said she had not, she would not, she would never disobey. And each time, she felt a tiny little triumph, a crack in Mother's power. On this morning, Mother Hilda and the familiar had gone to buy stores. Emilia had been attempting a new spell with the little equipment that Mother left out for her use. Sometimes out of sheer loneliness she went to the stables, but when the horses were gone there was only an ugly and ill-tempered beast that brayed at her and showed its yellow teeth. The little forest birds avoided the tower; she could not even coax one to her windowsill with breadcrumbs.

Emilia caught a movement from the corner of her eye, and froze. There was a skinny man with a great pack on his back, hung about with pans that clattered and rang. A pedlar. "Hello, the house!" he shouted. "Fine goods for sale! Pots and pans, needles and pins, all manner of useful things!" Emilia waved frantically from her window, flung every spell of revealing and attention-getting she knew, shouted until she was hoarse, but the pedlar only looked about and, finding no doorway, turned around and disappeared again, and never saw Emilia at all. When the clattering of pans had at last faded into the forest, Emilia knelt with her head on the sill of the window and wept for a long time. The red stone drank her tears all away.

Then she washed her face, and went back to her books, and bided her time.

One day, another pedlar came by. This one was short and round instead of tall and skinny, but he carried the same clattering weight of pans, and had the same cheerful demeanour. "Fine goods, fine goods for sale! Needles to mend your hose, kerchiefs to blow your nose! Pots and pans, and spoons to stir 'em! Anyone home? Hello?"

But this time, Mother Hilda was there. She had been in a weathervane mood all month, and pointing due storm for the last three days. Emilia and the familiar were extra quiet, and obedient, and careful, but it took no more than the wrong look to set Mother Hilda off. When she saw the pedlar, she looked at Emilia, and said, "Oh, I see."

"Mother?"

"He's been here before, hasn't he? Did you invite him in, girl? Tell him my secrets? Hmm? What else did you two get up to?"

"I didn't... Mother Hilda..."

"Quiet, unless you want to be a beetle. Worthless girl. Imp! Bring me the copper dish, three leaves of thyme, one dragon scale, and twenty-four grains of black salt."

"Anyone home?" shouted the pedlar, one more time, and sighed, and turned back towards the road.

"Mother, he's going away! He doesn't... please..."

The familiar came ducking and scuttling to Mother Hilda's side with what she had asked for, avoiding Emilia's eye. "Watch," Mother Hilda said. "Don't you dare look away. Watch what happens if you vex me."

She dropped the thyme, the dragon scale, and the black salt into the dish, spoke certain words, and spat into the dish. Silvery-green vapour coiled up.

The pedlar had almost reached the road when Mother Hilda spoke another word.

There was a clatter-jangle of metal, a smell like a forge, a scream as the pedlar's metal pans and the buckles of his pack and the buckle of his belt and the rings on his fingers all became red-hot, and he shrieked and struggled to get free.

The smell of the forge became the smell of a hog roast.

The pedlar's pans dropped to the road in a fused lump. The pedlar writhed and screamed a while longer.

When he stopped screaming, Mother Hilda sighed, and leaned out of the window, and blew, and then there was nothing but ash on the wind, and a tangle of twisted metal by the side of the road.

Emilia clutched the windowsill, her head swimming.

"Such a *mess*," Mother Hilda said. "My head aches. Make me a tisane." And she went to lie on her couch.

So ANOTHER YEAR passed, and another. The lilies in the courtyard bloomed, and did not fade. "Falala," sang the familiar, as he carried coals and she baked bread. "One for the gate and one for the door, and one to trap a pretty bird forever more." She sometimes helped him with his chores, if she had time, and Mother Hilda was not looking, but still he never spoke directly to her.

Emilia watched, and listened, and learned whatever she could, and waited, and tried not to think about the shadowy things in the corners that whispered. If she thought about them too much, she couldn't think at all.

One day, after Mother Hilda brushed Emilia's coppery hair, Emilia pretended to go to sleep. Instead, she crept after Mother Hilda, barefoot and hardly daring to breathe.

She saw Mother Hilda go to the treasure room. Mother Hilda took from her purse the vial with the gold cap, and poured three drops from it onto a purple stone set into the floor. On the first drop, she said, "Unlock." On the second drop, she said, "Unlatch." On the third drop she said nothing at all but put her hand to the door, which swung open.

When the door opened, lamps within the treasure

room sprang to life all of themselves, and lit up shelf upon shelf of black-gleaming mirrors, and instruments of copper and brass. Strange little statues carved of bone and crystal, great twisted bottles whose contents swirled or squirmed or bobbed in cloudy fluids. There were tiny glass vials that seemed to hold pure darkness, and great old books that shifted and whispered.

There was a whole shelf of little bronze caskets, and the light moved strangely on them, as though they had some sort of terrible life of their own—as though they were somehow *breathing*.

There were at least two things that seemed out of place among all this mystery. One was a battered pewter teapot, the other a pair of dusty old boots.

Mother Hilda took down the last bronze casket in the row. The light gleamed on strange figures carved on it, but unlike the others, it was still, and did not have that uncanny false life to it.

Mother Hilda placed the shed hair in the casket, and stroked it with her fingers, and locked the casket with a silver key. Then she put it on the shelf.

Emilia crept away as silently as a cat, and passed the familiar, going the other way with a dead rabbit limp in his hands.

"Falala," sang the familiar, very, very softly. "See the pretty girls, with their pretty hair, dancing, dancing all in rows. One steps out, the other goes there, and who was which, now no one knows." For the briefest of moments, Emilia's eyes met his.

"Familiar, is that you? Stop your nonsense," Mother Hilda snapped. "Bring me black truffles and the heart of a fawn. Now, now, or I'll have you whipped with brambles until you truly sing."

"Yes, ma'am," said the familiar, and scuttled away.

Emilia lay upon her bed, but she could not sleep for the memory of that long row of bronze caskets.

For the first time in a long time, she allowed herself to think of the orphanage, and their chatter and stories, particularly the tale of old witch. The old witch who stole girls, and ate them.

I said she must be long dead. But what if it isn't their bodies *she eats?*

Emilia was growing strong and healthy, with good food and physical labour. Mother Hilda grew no older. Emilia had become adept at learning more than she was allowed, sneaking a glance at an open spell book, listening at doors while Mother Hilda worked at her spells. But still she had learned nothing that would free her from the tower.

She had often been exasperated with the other girls, and thought half of them silly and the rest dull, but now she missed them very much.

"Falala," sang the familiar. "Silver is fine and gold is best, but a simple stone can buy all the rest."

EMILIA STARED AT the people in books and paintings and tried to recall the faces of the other orphan girls, the overseer, anyone at all. The faces she saw in her dreams blurred and melted together.

I will not go mad, she told herself. *I will not turn into her.*

Emilia bided her time. She watched, and she waited, and she wrote down every word she remembered the imp singing, and pored over them, late into the night. She hid her writings in cracks and crevices, and with illusions.

She sneaked threads from the curtains and the tablecloth and whenever she was alone, she wove them into a thin rope, knowing it would not be enough to hold her weight, but hoping against hope that one day another pedlar or a charcoal burner or some other wanderer of the woods might come along, and she might be able to, at least, get their attention. Perhaps they could attach her rope to a stronger rope, and she could climb out of the tower that way.

Mother Hilda looked in her mirror more often, peering closely. She seemed to tire more easily, and sometimes limped a little, as though her hips hurt her.

Emilia slept poorly, and dreamed of copper caskets whose sides moved as though they breathed.

Mother Hilda still went out dancing and flirting, but each time she seemed to come back a little more weary. And each time Emilia felt her eyes on her, hot and greedy, and knew she had to escape before it was too late.

Then, one day, Mother Hilda told her not just that she was going into town, but that there was a very exciting person visiting. "Some prince, I hear. Not only is he handsome, but *very, very* rich, and due to inherit a kingdom that stretches from one sea to another. Think how many thousands of people he rules over! That," she said, leaning and peering in the mirror, and frowning, "is what I call a man with prospects."

"Yes, Mother Hilda."

"He likes to dance all night, they say, and ride out all day, and will no doubt seek someone to match his youth and energy. Ah, well. I must make shift!" She smiled at Emilia, but her eyes were sharp and sparkling, like broken glass.

"Help me dress, girl. Perhaps I will bring you back something pretty, eh? Would you like that?"

"Thank you, Mother Hilda."

Mother Hilda leaned towards her and ran a finger over Emilia's cheek. "Amber," she said. "Some fine amber, to match those eyes. That will be very splendid, don't you think?"

Emilia, trying only to look grateful, and compliant, smiled at Mother Hilda and said, "Oh, yes, that would be wonderful!"

And so she helped Mother Hilda dress in her finest black and silver gown and a matching headdress, and watched the familiar drive her away.

Emilia bit her fingers, and paced, wondering what to do. Mother Hilda had found her man with prospects, and soon he would find Mother Hilda, looking just the same, but refreshed, and young, and able to dance all night and ride all day, perhaps wearing a fine amber necklace, that matched her eyes. (Would he even notice that her eyes were no longer grey? Or would he be too bemused by her beauty and charm and vigour?)

And where would Emilia be? Why, wherever all those girls had gone, whose hair lay entombed in breathing bronze caskets.

Emilia paced, and thought, and made plans, and then she saw movement on the road. Her soul lifted in her body like a bird taking flight.

She spied tall blond man, with a pack on his back and a sword at his side, who even at this distance was handsome as the morning. He was plainly but respectably dressed, and looked to be about twenty-five.

Emilia had been preparing for this as best she could. Sneaking a little copper here, hiding a few herbs from a recipe there, memorising every glimpse of a page when Mother Hilda had one of the more powerful spell books open.

She gathered the herbs and the potions, and made the gestures, and walked the steps, and barely breathed; as the figure on the road drew closer, she managed a little breeze to tug at his hair. He ran his hand through it, frowning.

She managed—oh, it was so hard—to make the breeze whisper, "Look up, at the window. Look up, and see."

He looked up, and *saw her*.

With the last of her will, Emilia forced the window to open, and slumped against the sill with exhaustion. But she was young and strong. She managed to wave.

"Well, good morning," he called.

Out of sheer relief, she laughed. "Good morning!" The air bathed her face with its fresh scent, of pine and clear water, and she felt as though her head was being rinsed clean from the inside.

"I heard there was a tower here, but no one told me it held treasure!" he said.

It took a moment for Emilia to realise what he meant. But there was no time for blushing or simpering. "I am a prisoner here," she said. "Mother Hilda—*Doctor* Hilda von Riesentor—keeps me. She is a very powerful arcanist, and only away for a few hours. The Rotterturm does indeed contain much of great value, and if you help me escape, I will share it with you."

"It would be my pleasure only to free an innocent captive. What is your name, lovely lady?"

"Emilia Rapunzel," she said. "Yours?"

"Liebreizend," he said. "It means 'charming.'" He laughed. "Absurd, I know. Blame my mama, she was somewhat prejudiced in my favour."

Emilia smiled, then bit her lip, staring down at him.

"I can see you are unsure if you can trust me," Liebreizend said. "I understand. Perhaps the last person you trusted locked you in that tower. What can I do?"

"Send me up a lock of your hair," Emilia said. "A sorceress can do much with hair. It might put you in my power. Though, to be honest, it's more likely to put you in hers, but I'd burn it before I let that happen."

"So we must trust each other, then," he said, and smiled, and cut off a lock of his hair with his dagger. Emilia let down the rope she had woven, which was, in truth, more of a string than a rope; and Liebreizend tied the lock to the end of it, and she drew it up and clutched it in her hand.

"Very well," she said. "Mother Hilda is at the celebrations for the foreign Prince. She carries three vials, always. Can you hire a pickpocket to steal one of them, and the silver key she wears about her neck?"

"I can probably ensure that they end up in my possession," he said, grinning.

"Not the one capped with silver—that opens the tower, and if she comes home and can't get in, she'll be furious. And suspicious. And not the one capped with chalcedony. If that's gone too, she'll know. If only the gold one is gone, she might not notice right away, and may believe it was just an ordinary pickpocket, or an accident. Can you get it to me before she comes home?"

"I will do my utmost. Tell me something of her," he said. "The more I know, the easier it will be."

"She is very vain," Emilia said. "She likes compliments, and to break men's hearts. She is looking for a man with great prospects—that's why she is in town, to catch the eye of this foreign Prince. She also has a familiar. He is loyal because he is bound to her, so he has to be. He will do his best to protect her."

"I will be careful."

"You must be *very* careful. That lump of metal, by the side of the road, do you see it?"

"I do," he said, looking puzzled.

She told him what had happened to the pedlar.

He swallowed, blinked, then shrugged and grinned at her. "I am always careful," he said. "You must promise me something in return."

She looked at him warily. "What is it?"

"If I succeed, then let me take you to a party. A lovely, intelligent young woman should not be shut away from society like this, it's a shame and a waste. You must have been so bored!"

Emilia smiled. "If you wish," she said. "But hurry, hurry!"

"As my lady commands." And he smiled, and bowed, and was gone.

Emilia practised her spells and charms, and bit her nails (making sure to swallow any fragments, and not leave them lying about), and waited.

THE HOURS CAME, the hours went. The road stayed empty. The crows called in the high trees, and circled, and settled, and the road stayed empty. The sun set, and the road stayed empty.

In the cool hour before sunrise first one bird dropped a few notes into darkness, then another, then another, until birdsong rose about the tower, thousands and thousands of little throats singing out together until the very air seemed woven from song.

At that moment she saw a figure, and at first it was hard to make out—a grey and creeping thing against the pale stones of the road. But soon it resolved itself into Liebreizend. "Hist!" he called up at the tower.

"'Hist'?" Emilia said, leaning out of the window. "*Hist?*"

He grinned. "I thought it was traditional."

She rolled her eyes, and although she was impatient, and afraid, she felt a smile, still strange and stiff on her face. How long had it been since she had any *fun*? And how was it this stranger managed to make her feel that this was not a deadly endeavour, but an amusing game?

"Do you have the vial, and the key?"

"Yes."

Emilia let down the string, and he tied the gold-capped vial and the key to it, and she drew it up to the window. "Now you must hide until she is home," she said. "Then can you pretend to be an emissary from the foreign Prince? Shower her with compliments, distract her for a while? I just need her to be at the window for a little, and distracted. If you can distract the familiar, too, even better." The familiar might have tried to help Emilia, and she knew he resented his servitude as much, if not more, than she did, but he could not act against Mother Hilda directly, and if he saw her threatened he would have to try and stop it.

Also, she still did not quite trust him. He was an imp, after all.

"That I can do," Liebreizend said.

Emilia, her heart beating high and hard like a live bird trapped in her chest, ran to the treasure room. She poured three drops from the vial with the gold cap on a purple stone set into the floor, and said, "Unlock," on the first drop and "Unlatch," on the second drop, and on the third drop she said nothing at all but put her hand to the door.

It swung open.

Emilia did not pause to look at any of the treasures, but ran straight to the bronze casket that held her hair. She unlocked it with the little silver key. Her hair lay in the box, soft and quiet and gleaming in the firelight. She snatched it up, careful to get every single strand, and flung it all on the fire.

Then she shaved the hair off every part of her with a knife she had sharpened just for this, and flung all of that onto the fire. She even shaved off her eyebrows, just to be safe.

The hair crackled and writhed and stank and burned all away.

She ran back and took the first of the other caskets, shuddering at the way it breathed in her hands. She put the key in the lock, and shut her eyes, and took a breath, then opened her eyes and turned the key.

Hair, curly and black, lay in the box. It did not move, nor breathe, but Emilia could swear that there was a shimmer about it that should not be there.

She thought a wordless something—an apology, a hope—and flung the hair on the fire.

One by one she opened each casket. Twenty-seven caskets, all filled with soft, glossy hair, the lock of each casket a little harder to turn than the last. The very last one simply would not turn at all, and Emilia tried and tried, and in the end beat at it with the fire iron, and did not even know that she was crying until finally the lock broke, and she found her face wet.

She picked up that final bundle of hair—fine and pale

and straight as the walls of the Rotterturm—just as she heard the sound of Mother Hilda's carriage returning.

Emilia cast the hair on the fire and flung her gown back on, lacing it up all askew. She wrapped her head tightly in a scarf, put all the caskets back on their shelf (the one with the broken lock turned to face the wall) and ran to the window just as the imp was hauling on the reins to bring the horses to a halt. He sniffed the air, and Emilia's hands went cold—she had forgotten, in the excitement, what a sense of smell he had. Was it the hair he smelled, or Liebreizend, or both? But the imp only leapt down and lowered the steps for Mother Hilda to leave the carriage.

Mother Hilda got down slowly, as though her knees hurt, but her head was high and she had a cold, glittering smile. She looked up at the window where Emilia waited. "Ah, my dear daughter," she said. "I have a gift for you. Meet me in the red salon."

Mother Hilda climbed the stairs slowly, clutching the banister, with hands that looked a little less smooth and young than they had that morning.

When she reached the red salon, she sniffed the air and frowned. "What is that stink? What have you been doing?"

"Oh, a bird got in the chimney," Emilia said, "and fell into the fire. The poor thing made such a screeching, and was trying to fly out into the room. I was afraid it would get free, and set the curtains alight, so I beat it to death with the poker. But it burned up, feathers and all. It's a terrible smell."

"Well, well," Mother Hilda said. "A pity you could not think of something better. Never mind." And because she did not immediately think of some punishment for Emilia's carelessness, Emilia knew she had been right.

"Hallo!" came a cry.

"Who is that?" Mother Hilda said. "Really, if I wanted visitors I wouldn't live all the way out here! Tell him to go away."

"Oh," Emilia said, looking out of the window, clutching the sill so hard her knuckles were white. "It's a young man. He's *very* handsome."

"Come away from the window," Mother Hilda said, and went to it herself, and looked out. "You!" she said.

Emilia blinked.

"Ah, loveliest of ladies!" Liebreizend called up. "I had to leave, and when I returned to the ball you were gone! Without you it was quite unbearably dull, and so I enquired all about, until I could find where you live. Forgive me. But I had to see you again!"

"And what does His Highness expect, from coming to see me in my tower?"

"Only that I might look on you again, and converse with you—you are by far the most interesting woman I have met in my travels, as well as the most beautiful. If you should consent to, perhaps, ride out with me..."

While this was going on, despite her sudden suspicion and confusion, Emilia conjured a breeze. Just a little one, just enough to tug at Mother Hilda's cap, so she put up a hand to straighten it.

"Perhaps tomorrow," Mother Hilda said. "If I feel inclined."

"Oh, do please feel inclined."

Emilia made the breeze a little stronger, just a very little.

"Such a gusty day!" Mother Hilda said. "Perhaps it will be too stormy to ride tomorrow."

"Should it be so," said the Prince, "I have a little place,

nearby, where we could shelter from the weather. My gardeners grow excellent strawberries."

"So you have property in the town?" Mother Hilda leaned a little further out.

"I have property in lots of places," said Liebreizend.

The breeze and the leaning tilted Mother Hilda's cap a little further, and a single lock of hair crept out from beneath it, thin and grey as sleet. Still conjuring the breeze with one hand, and holding her sharpest sewing scissors with the other, Emilia snipped off the lock, and ran with it, cat-footed, to the treasure room, and put it in the casket where her own hair had been minutes before. She cast the strongest illusion charm she knew, to make it thick and straight and copper-coloured, and ran from the treasure room. She returned to the salon, where Mother Hilda laughed and chattered, and slipped the gold-capped vial into the sorcerer's purse just as she turned back from the window.

"Well," Mother Hilda said. "That was the prince I spoke of. He wants to ride out with me tomorrow. I must make sure I am well rested, he is an energetic young man, and wants someone who can keep up with him! Now since you have been a good girl, and dealt with a scary bird falling in the fire—your face looks scratched; was that the bird, or sparks from the fire? Never mind, never mind. Familiar! Fetch us both a glass of kirsch."

"Both of us?" Emilia said. Mother Hilda never allowed her alcohol.

"Yes, we must celebrate."

The cherry brandy, sweet and dark and red, came, and Mother Hilda took one glass to herself, and made a little gesture over the other as she handed it to Emilia. Emilia did not drink it, but when Mother Hilda was distracted by thoughts of her triumph, poured it into an empty vase that stood on the table.

Emilia yawned and rubbed her eyes. "Oh, I am so sleepy!"

"Come, then, go to bed," Mother Hilda said.

"Yes, Mother Hilda. Oh, what's this?" Emilia pretended to pick something off the floor. "Why, it's a little key!"

"Give me that," Mother Hilda said, and snatched it from her. "Lucky the chain broke here and nowhere else. Go to bed."

Emilia did as she was told, and laid down and closed her eyes, though she had never been farther from sleep in her life.

She heard Mother Hilda go to the treasure room, and held her breath, wondering if she had got all the caskets back in the right place, if Mother Hilda would notice the one with the broken lock, or spot the illusion that disguised the hair. She clenched her hands under the covers. If something went wrong, she would run to the window and scream. If Liebreizend—the Prince (and that was a problem for later, he had said nothing about being a prince)—could do nothing, which was probable, well, she would cast herself from the window and be done with it.

She saw the familiar creep past the door of her room, going towards the treasury, and her heart beat even harder, but there was no screaming, no cursing, no punishment—only silence.

Finally Mother Hilda came to her room. Emilia kept her eyes open a tiny bit. The fire was still burning, and glimmered on the figures on the casket she held in one hand, and gleamed on the chalcedony cap of the vial she held in the other. "Are you asleep, Emilia?"

Emilia closed her eyes all the way, and made no answer. She heard shufflings and mutterings. Could she really hear three drops of fluid fall? Such little sounds, and yet she seemed to hear them, not with her ears but with her *bones*. And another three drops. Though they should have made no sound, falling on the hair growing from Mother Hilda's head, still they echoed in her: one, and two, and three.

She felt the weight of Mother Hilda lying down beside her, and heard the sound of a complex spell in a strange and twisty tongue, and Emilia clutched at the sheets and waited to feel her spirit ripped from her body.

Instead, she felt Mother Hilda grow limp.

Then she heard Mother Hilda's breathing slow, and catch, and change. In, pause, out. In, pause, out.

Emilia dared to open her eyes, and sit up, and look.

What lay next to her was not Mother Hilda. It was an empty thing, that breathed.

Emilia leapt from the bed and ran to the door, not even pausing to look back, and down the stairs. The lilies in the courtyard were wilting in the moonlight, and their scent was fading, and the fountain no longer rang with secret music but dribbled sadly into its basin, and it was quite easy to turn the great handle and open the gate of the Rotterturm.

"Well, now," said Liebreizend. "It seems you managed perfectly without me! Shall I go away?"

"You didn't tell me you were a prince," she said.

"Well, no. Too many people, like Doctor Riesentor, see the Prince for the things he can give them, and don't see the man for the things he is. I would rather you got to know the man than the Prince," said Liebreizend, and smiled at her.

Suddenly it was all too much. Emilia was still less than twenty years old, and had done something that might be terrible, and had been afraid for her life and her sanity, not just tonight but for years. She was unable to hold back a sudden, wrenching glut of tears, all the tears she had not dared cry for fear she would never stop. The Prince patted her shoulder, and soothed her, and guided her back inside, and made her sit down, and gave her his own very fine silk handkerchief.

When she had recovered a little, she showed Prince Liebreizend the treasury, and he said it was far too late, and she must be exhausted, and they could divide things in the morning—if she still wished to do so—but now she should rest. He found the kitchen, and though he did it with noise and clumsiness and having to ask her where everything was, he made her a tisane, and set it beside her. "Oh, mind the vase!" she said. "I put the sleeping draught in it, that she meant to give me. Actually, don't mind the vase, it's as ugly as everything else in this place. Throw it on the fire."

"I don't think it will burn," he said, laughing.

"Then throw it from the window."

He did.

"What should we do with..." He jerked his head towards the room where Mother Hilda lay.

"I'll deal with *that*," said the familiar, appearing suddenly in the doorway.

"You can speak to me now!" Emilia said.

"Yes. Not her familiar anymore." An expression flickered across his face too fast to read, but it left Emilia uncomfortable nonetheless.

"Her hair?" Emilia said.

"I threw it on the fire, like the others," he said.

"Didn't you trust me to do it?" Emilia said.

"I didn't trust *her* not to somehow wriggle her way out of it," the imp said. "Anyway, it's done."

Emilia twisted her fingers together and looked down at them. "Do you know what happens? After?"

"Been fretting, have you? The other girls, they're free of *her*. Beyond that, all I know is people get what they get."

With that, Emilia had to be content.

"After I've dealt with *her*, I'll be on my way." He looked at Liebreizend, who was peering at him with a frown on his face, then sniffed dismissively and disappeared.

Emilia found herself suddenly very sleepy indeed, so sleepy she could no longer keep her eyes open.

THE NEXT MORNING... well, we know how this part of the tale goes by now. The strong room sacked of all its more portable treasures—with the exception of the most powerful of the books, which, like reserved books at a library, did not take kindly to being removed from the Rotterturm. Several of them lay at the entrance, fluttering their pages grumpily. One had some blood on its cover.

Both of the horses and the pack beast were gone. The cup Liebreizend had served her tisane in smelled of sleeping draught.

Emilia searched for the lock of hair he had given her, hoping that she could use it to find him, but of course it was not his, and now she looked at it again, she could see it was quite obviously hair from a horse's tail.

The imp was gone too, presumably returned to whatever Hell had birthed him, and so, somewhat to Emilia's relief, was the empty vessel that had been Mother Hilda.

Emilia did not cry any more. She tightened her lips, and shook her head, and called herself a fool, then she gathered the rest of the books, and the rest of the instruments, and Mother Hilda's notebooks, and set herself to learning what she needed.

She did not plan to do what Mother Hilda had done, but nor did she plan to let anyone take advantage of her—ever again.

Three Ladies and a Wedding
(The Third Part)

HAT'S TERRIBLE," BELLA said. "I'm so sorry. Not just Liebreizend, I mean, everything. And after all that, you became a doctor! I expect your parents would have been very proud, if they'd but known."

Doctor Rapunzel looked faintly startled, as though the thought had never occurred to her—which, to be fair, it hadn't. "Thank you," she said.

"I'm surprised that he managed to fool either you or your... mentor? Is that the word?" Marie Blanche said.

"She was vain, and ambitious. I was desperate. We all have our vulnerabilities. Such a deceiver is good at finding them."

"That's so sad," Bella said. "You see, what happened to me... I don't think... I mean, he really *was* nice, not just pretending. I know people think I was a fool, but Mama and Papa liked him, and they don't take easily to people. I mean, *no one* can pull the wool over Mama's eyes. I'm certain something happened, that we don't know about, because he was just the nicest man. That's why his name was so funny. Charming."

"Wait, who?" The Doctor's grip tightened on her glass.

"Charming. That was his name. I thought I said."

"That is what Liebreizend means," Doctor Rapunzel said. "He joked about it."

Princess Blanche de Neige said, or rather spat, "*Agradiu*. In the dialect of my country, it means 'pleasing.' Agreeable. *Charming*. Either this is a commonly used deception, or..."

"But it was just his name," Bella said. "It can't be..."

"Tell me," Doctor Rapunzel said. "This was the man who turned up to save you from a dreadful situation, who then absconded with valuables? Yes?"

"Well, I was due to wake from the curse anyway, but he was *there,* just as the Good Folk said he would be. 'The very picture of love,' that was what they said, and that was what I *saw*. And yes, at least that's what everyone *thinks*..."

Princess Marie Blanche's eyes were now so dark one could imagine light might never escape them. "Tall? Blond? Strength and grace of a stag? Odd little manservant?"

The three women looked at each other. "His manservant may have been away on an errand," Doctor Rapunzel said, "but apart from that..."

From the next table came a sudden, raucous laugh. A flushed, jovial lady of middle years, who was not so much dressed as *upholstered* in quantities of blue velvet, raised her glass in their direction. "Forgive me eavesdropping, but join the bloody *club*, dears," she said. "Left an absolute *trail* of us, that one. There's probably some rich—formerly rich—woman in Seralia, or the Snow Islands, waking up right now, all ready to run down the aisle, only to find the little bastard's pissed off with half the contents of the strongroom. Should have known better at my age, but I arsing well did not. At least you've all learned your lesson younger than I did! A spinster I shall remain for the rest of my days, and better off for it. Save your tears, he's not worth it."

The three women looked at her, and then at each other. "You..." said Marie Blanche.

"We..." said Bella.

"Who *is* he?" Doctor Rapunzel said. "Do you know?"

"It's said he's the heir to Floriens," the jovial lady said. "Of all the rumours, that's the most consistent."

"But if he's the heir..." said Doctor Rapunzel.

"Got a bit impatient for the throne, didn't he? Put a curse on the King to sicken him, so he could take over, got found out, and bolted just ahead of the Royal Guard. Got a pretty bounty on his head, too. Knowing him, he'll try and find a way to collect it!" She laughed again, shaking her head, and downed the rest of her wine.

"Oh. *Oh*," said Bella. "*Oh*, no, it can't be..."

"The same man," said Doctor Rapunzel. "The very same." A disconcerting glow began to shimmer at the ends of her long, pale fingers.

Princess Blanche de Neige's full mouth was drawn into a tight, white line. She uttered a single, harsh syllable, and suddenly all the birds that had gathered to steal crumbs from the feast exploded up into the air, in a tumult of alarm calls, showering the tables with feathers and droppings and crumbs.

Three Ladies Go A-hunting

ERIA'S GREAT ARENA is largely empty of spectators this morning, which is why Doctor Rapunzel chose it. It is currently being used to train the city's gryphons and their riders, a spectacle few are interested in, since it involves neither the chance to make bets (except, perhaps, on which of the trainees will fall off first) nor, usually, much in the way of bloodshed.

Close to, it smells of sawdust and sweat and the hot smoky-sweet tang of gryphon dung, which persists even as the doctor climbs to the tier where Princess Marie Blanche is already waiting.

Doctor Rapunzel wears a deep blue gown, which, should she wish to ride, would be revealed to have been, in fact, a pair of wide-legged trousers all along. It would also prove to contain a truly astonishing number of pockets, and any thief unwise enough to attempt to pick them would probably regret it, though possibly not for long.

With the gown, Doctor Rapunzel has selected a deep blue headdress. The gown gives her dignity and presence, the headdress both height and protection. She has learned a great deal about the uses of dress, only some of it from Mother Hilda.

Marie Blanche wears a leather jerkin over a green linen shirt, and dark broadcloth breeches, and riding boots. The hawk on her wrist is unhooded, and seems to be watching the proceedings with as much interest as its mistress. At Doctor Rapunzel's approach it opens its beak and raises its wings, but settles when Marie Blanche strokes its head.

"MAGNIFICENT, AREN'T THEY?" Marie Blanche said, nodding at the arena. "Very expensive to keep, of course."

Doctor Rapunzel looked down. A young gryphon, saddled and harnessed and groomed to a gloss, was rearing up, doing its best to unseat the equally young soldier who was clinging to its neck with an expression that even from this distance looked extremely seasick. A small old woman, with an expression of ancient patience and the bowed legs of someone who had learned to ride before they were quite steady on their own feet, flicked the leading rein and clicked her tongue. The gryphon huffed, sneezed, and grumpily dropped to a crouch.

"You keep them at home?" Doctor Rapunzel said.

Marie Blanche shrugged. "I would like to, very much, but the cost of a single breeding pair... we have not yet made up what Charming took from the treasury as it is. We are—or *were*—a moderately prosperous country, but not very rich, and what with Step—with Queen Katherina's extravagances, it is impossible to be so indulgent."

"I should imagine such beasts would be a great advantage in war," Doctor Rapunzel said, leaning her chin on her hand and watching. The gryphon shook its head so violently the young soldier slid half off its back and became wedged at its wing joint, one boot flailing madly at the air. "Or not," the Doctor conceded.

"I would rather avoid a war altogether, especially now."

"Very wise."

"Gryphons are highly strung, extremely temperamental, and vulnerable to the cold at high altitudes," Marie Blanche said. "But fast flyers over short distances—and very loyal, once one wins their trust. I suspect that young man will fail. He is far too concerned with trying to stay on."

"I can hardly blame him," Doctor Rapunzel said, with a slight smile. "Once the beast is in the air, I imagine staying on is paramount. From what I understand, *you* would not have a problem getting the beast to obey you. Or any beast."

Marie Blanche turned her dark, direct gaze on the Doctor. "You have been busy since yesterday."

"I like to know who I've been dining with."

"So. Why did you wish to speak with me?"

"With both of you, in fact," Doctor Rapunzel said, turning in her seat. "Ah, here she is."

Bella, in a rose-coloured gown that, inevitably, suited her to perfection, seemed to float up the steps as though borne on invisible wings, never stumbling despite the steepness of the steps and the fact that she was looking at the gryphon rather than where she was going.

"Good morning," she said. "I hope you both slept well. My room was so charm... pretty. And the people here are very kind. Some young man came chasing after me thinking I had dropped my handkerchief. He was very pink in the face and quite out of breath; he must have run some way to catch up with me. Poor fellow. It was a very nice handkerchief, too—embroidered with forget-me-nots—but it wasn't mine."

Doctor Rapunzel and Marie Blanche exchanged a glance. Doctor Rapunzel looked faintly amused, Marie Blanche rolled her eyes.

"Did it look new?" Doctor Rapunzel said.

"Why, yes, as though it had just been purchased. It wasn't even creased!"

"Probably because it *had* just been purchased, with the sole purpose of giving him an excuse to talk to you," Marie Blanche said.

"Oh. Oh! Oh, dear, and I barely gave him the time of day!" Bella looked positively guilty. "It was a *very* nice handkerchief, too."

Doctor Rapunzel gave a peal of laughter, and Marie Blanche snorted.

"So," Bella said. "The gryphon is interesting—oops, oh, dear, it's treading on him—ouch—oh, good, he's getting up. Poor fellow." She gave an encouraging wave to the young soldier, who, seeing her, promptly tripped over his own feet and landed on his backside again. Bella gave him a sympathetic smile that he could probably barely see through the red haze of his own embarrassment.

"But you didn't ask us here to look at gryphons, did you?" Bella settled herself in a seat in an artlessly appealing flurry of silken skirts. "So why *are* we here?"

"Charming," Doctor Rapunzel said. "Shall we settle on that, for a name? I should like to hear your thoughts."

"Oh." Bella looked down at her hands.

Marie Blanche looked at her hawk, which was watching the gryphon, its head on one side, as though trying to work out what, exactly, it was seeing. "Having been forced to remember him," she said, "I would far rather forget him again."

Doctor Rapunzel raised her brows. "You do not think it would be of benefit to your country to find him, and get restitution?"

"Surely the money is long gone by now?" Marie Blanche said.

"He has taken a great deal," Doctor Rapunzel said, "and not just money. Items of power. Perhaps he only wishes to live a life of luxury. But one day, if he is, indeed, the Prince of Floriens, and if he continues to evade the bounty hunters, which he has been doing with quite *remarkable* success, then he will be *King* of Floriens. I have, indeed, been busy—and among other interesting facts, I found that if the King dies before Charming returns, according to the laws of Floriens, Charming will inherit and all charges against him will disappear, wiped clean by the gloss of kingship—and the inconvenient absence of any other eligible heir. So. Floriens may have, in short order, a king who is very rich, who has magical items in his possession and, apparently, no scruples whatever—dangerous, don't you think?"

Marie Blanche frowned. "A good point," she said. "Yes."

"Not *no* scruples," Bella said. "He could have... I mean, it could have been worse."

"You still have a liking for him," Doctor Rapunzel said.

"I just think, if we *understood*," Bella said. "I'm sure that there's more to it. He was so *nice*."

"He was not *nice*," Marie Blanche snapped. The hawk ruffled its feathers and glared. "Nice men do not deceive and steal. He was very good at *pretending* to be nice."

"If we were to pursue, and capture him," Doctor

Rapunzel said, calmly, "one way or another, an explanation would be forthcoming. Whether we could believe it, without certain... inducements, would be another matter. Personally, while he did indeed help free me from a most unpleasant situation, he also took things from me that cannot be replaced, and I want them back."

Marie Blanche's eyes sharpened. "You think we could?"

"We all have certain skills, do we not?" Doctor Rapunzel said. "And you, Lady Bella, most of all. Let me see: beauty, obviously; dance, or perhaps, *grace*—I heard about your last fencing match. Quite remarkable. The Andirovian champion, wasn't it?"

Bella blushed. "He was very good," she said. "And very courteous about losing."

"Your diplomatic abilities are also, shall we say, notable. That would be the wit, or is *that* the grace... how does that work, exactly?"

Bella turned a slightly deeper shade of rose. "Well, I don't know, really. I like talking to people, and they usually seem to listen."

"Especially when you sing."

"That too."

"Is it true you can mimic anyone?"

Bella said, "'A spinster I shall remain for the rest of my days, and better off for it.'" The blue velvet lady's voice was so perfectly rendered she might have been sitting there, grinning at them all.

"And of course," Doctor Rapunzel said, "the Good Folk recognise you. Something of a two-edged sword, that, but it might come in useful."

"It seems to me," Marie Blanche said, "that the Lady Bella could bring this fox to ground herself, quite without any help from us. But she does not wish to."

"Well, if that's true," Doctor Rapunzel said, watching Bella closely, "there's nothing to be done. Is it true?"

Bella fidgeted with a fold of her skirts, then shook her head. "I don't know."

"He hurt you very badly, didn't he, my dear?" Doctor Rapunzel said.

"I was so *happy*," Bella said, and her voice caught. "And I thought he meant it all. But Papa said he just laughed and went on his way."

"You are used to being loved," Doctor Rapunzel said. "It probably hits harder, that way."

Marie Blanche shot Doctor Rapunzel a glance, but the Doctor was smiling at Bella. "If we find him," Rapunzel continued, "you will know for sure. Perhaps there really is a reasonable explanation."

Marie Blanche made a face, but only to the hawk.

"You think there is?" Bella said.

"I think that I will pursue him in any case," Doctor Rapunzel said. "If either of you wishes to join me, the chance of success certainly increases."

"And what will you do if you catch him?" said Marie Blanche.

"Get back what he took from me," Doctor Rapunzel said.

"If I can regain some, at least, of our treasury, and bring him to justice," Marie Blanche said, "my father may regain some dignity in his last years."

"The justice of your country is quite *sharp*," Doctor Rapunzel said. "If I remember rightly."

"A blade is generally an effective cure for treachery," Marie Blanche said.

Bella looked from one to the other. "I'll come," she said. "Just... If we catch him, let me talk to him first. I truly believe there is more to it."

Marie Blanche made a noise somewhere between a snort and a hiss, but said nothing.

"We are agreed, then? We will pursue him, and if we catch him, he gets a chance to explain himself? Excellent," Doctor Rapunzel said. "Now. First, we need to get him within reach. Your Highness, you are the huntress; what is the best way to trap a wary beast?"

"Bait," Marie Blanche said. "Nice plump bait. But this beast is *very* wary, and not alone."

"True," Doctor Rapunzel said. "And his ability to escape capture is notorious. That is partly because he possesses a pair of exceptional boots. We need to get the boots, or he will escape us, too. And there is his manservant."

"Oh, yes, Roland," Bella said. "Such a strange little man."

"Roland, is it?" Doctor Rapunzel's mouth quirked. "A *useful* little man, to judge by your story."

"A creature of very misplaced loyalties," Marie Blanche said.

"Oh, indeed," said Doctor Rapunzel. "Without him, I suspect Charming would be less cunning, and more vulnerable."

"You're not to hurt Roland," Bella said. "I won't have it."

"Why are you so concerned for the manservant?" Marie Blanche said.

"He's a *servant*. What choice does he have?" Bella said. "He has to do what Charming tells him."

"True enough," said Doctor Rapunzel. "Very well, we shan't punish him for what he can't help, hmm? Now, the plan."

"You have a plan already?" Bella said, her eyes wide.

Marie Blanche smiled, a little darkly. "That was only to be expected, it seems," she said.

The Princess and the Mountain Men

HESE ARE THE mountains of Ödlakullar, famous for their stark beauty. The high peaks, snowy even at this season, rise brilliant against the sky like white shoulders discarding their green gowns. A hawk wheels, hovers, pinned to the blue air, then swoops in a heart-catching dive. But whatever it pursues sees it coming, dives down some barely visible crevice in the rocks. Thwarted, the hawk sweeps away, with a harsh cry.

Princess Marie Blanche knows that that dramatic shriek is actually a scathing condemnation of useless, lazy rodents who don't appreciate the honour of being eaten. She takes a deep breath of the clean, cold air, gulping it like wine. A slope of grass so brilliantly green it is almost painful to look at, speckled with tiny bright flowers, sweeps away below her.

Marie Blanche is wrapped against the chill in a coat of dark blue wool beautifully embroidered with those same tiny bright mountain flowers. She keeps a careful eye on the small herd of plump lowland cattle making good use of the grass while they can. They are weary from the long climb; older cattle, past breeding and tenderness—cheaper that way. But still sufficiently tempting, Marie Blanche hopes, to anything that might be foraging up here. Despite their age, she has had no trouble persuading them up the mountain. She very seldom has trouble persuading an animal to trust her. And how, precisely, has Doctor Rapunzel found *that* out? Not to mention everything else she seems to know. Of course, at weddings, everyone gossips like sparrows, but still, it gives Marie Blanche pause.

For the porters that accompany the herd, Marie Blanche has relied on money. Not to mention generous quantities of the local spirit, which is a gentle yellow and smells of summer meadows. It doesn't have quite the eye-watering potency of the Oakapple Clan's stone brandy, but it still punches like her father's blacksmith.

She is travelling alone, under a pseudonym—which in itself gives her a quiet, and slightly bitter, amusement. She is calling herself Lady Winter.

MARIE BLANCHE HAD not, of course, told Papa what she was up to.

She had talked instead of the possibility of a marriage, a useful—potentially *very* useful—alliance with the heir of a powerful kingdom. "But, Papa, I plan to spend some time at his court, first. And not as myself. After our recent experiences, I wish to see how a man behaves when he is not putting on a show. So I will travel alone, as minor nobility, and see what sort of person he is."

She hated to deceive Papa so, but otherwise, he would never allow her to go. Certainly not without the sort of entourage that would instantly alert the quarry that it was being hunted.

Papa had taken her hands in his—still too thin, still with that faint tremor—and she had almost weakened.

"Well, if you think it best, my dear..." He grimaced. "Though I wish you did not have to go away."

"It would hardly work if I invited him here," Marie Blanche said.

"But how will I manage without you?"

"You will do very well, Papa. You ran the kingdom perfectly without me for many years before I was even born."

"And how would you know that?" he said, with a flicker of his old humour. "Ah, I was young then, and I thought I knew everything."

"Nothing has happened that cannot be undone, Papa," she said, though looking at him, she wondered.

As for herself, she felt like Mama's stone flowers: pretty enough to look at, but only warmed by the sunshine, not by any life within.

"You will be careful, won't you?" the King said. "I could not bear it, should anything happen to you."

"I will be extremely careful, Papa." She began to say that she was, at least, no longer in danger of falling for a pretty face, but closed her mouth on it.

And once again, after she had made every arrangement she could think of to keep things running in her absence, and adjured the chamber groom for at least the tenth time to keep an eye on Papa and make sure he ate, she found herself uncomfortably glad to be leaving the Chateau behind her. This time, she hoped, she would come back with a far better prize than the last.

In the meantime, she was enjoying the freedom, the lack

of fuss, the anonymity, and the chance to spend entire days out of doors, on horseback or on foot, in the company of people who could talk sensibly about livestock.

Given a sufficiency of the sweet-smelling spirit, they could also be persuaded to talk about certain colourful local stories and old legends. "All respect, ladyship, but what you're looking for, they're not found around here," said one of the younger men, who was going through that stage of growth where he was all gangle and freckles and attempted beard. "Just a story, good for making the girls squeal, *yah?* Well"—he blushed—"not *you*, ladyship. You don't seem the squealing... type..." His voice trailed off on the last words, and he blushed even redder and buried his face in his glass.

"No, I seldom squeal," Marie Blanche said.

"Ah, you youngsters," the head of the team said, breaking the sudden howling silence that had descended on the table. He was an older man, whose bald patch was surrounded by a foam of white curls like a smooth rock in a rough sea. "So quick to say everything's a story. My grandfather told me *his* father saw one once, when he was out looking for a sheep that got itself stuck.

"*Sheep*," he went on. "Stupidest creatures alive, walk out onto a ledge they can't get off for the sake of a patch of grass that's just like every other patch of grass. Can't stand 'em. Never could, even as a boy, except on a plate. That's why I took up this." He gestured to the team. "People aren't so stupid. Mostly." He eyed the blushing youth, with a look that said, *Later we will be discussing why you tried to suggest to this nice,* generous *lady that she didn't need to hire us.* "Anyway, he saw one, right enough. Took it for part of the mountain, until it moved."

"You understand the risks?" Marie Blanche said.

"Well, no," the team leader said, "never having, you might say, dealt with one myself."

"Well, I do." She hoped she did, at any rate. "So, apart from helping me get where I need to go, please follow my lead in all things."

"Yes, ma'am," the leader said. "You're paying, you're in charge."

They were high above the little lodging house; it looked like a dollhouse abandoned on the mountainside. In the quiet, Marie Blanche could hear the tear and crunch of the cattle feeding as they mowed their way across the slope, as clear as the occasional *clonk* of a cowbell. The bearers talked quietly among themselves.

A ptarmigan gave its rattling cry, and Marie Blanche raised her hand. The bearers fell silent.

Ptarmigans were, like sparrows, gossipy creatures, fussy and easily scandalised, but they watched *everything*.

...her nest was quite destroyed, one rattled, *her own fault, she* would *build on that slope...* my *nest is much better, strong and safe...*

Well I was going to build over on the side where the sun hits in the morning, just above that stand where the best catkins grow in the spring. But there's something there, bigger than an eagle...

Nothing's bigger than an eagle.

Yes, it was—much, much bigger! Big enough to shadow half the mountain!

That, Marie Blanche hoped, was an exaggeration. But it would be worth a look.

The ptarmigans flew off, still arguing.

"Around to the east, first thing tomorrow," she said.

"Yes, ma'am. Settle in, you lot, rest your feet." The

bearers made themselves comfortable with sighs of relief and the ease of long experience.

Marie Blanche herself, despite the long climb, still felt as though she could run up one side of the peak and skip back down again.

Some of it was the air, no doubt; but some of it was simply that she was at last—at last!—putting her hands to the business of Charming.

Once it became clear that he was beyond reach, she had bitten into clearing up the messes that he and Queen Katherina had left, and hung on to life, grimly, filling her days from edge to edge. But it had been a joyless effort. Finally taking some action felt like a worthy hunt on a fine morning. Which, she supposed, it was. She didn't— except very occasionally, in her more bitter moments— wish to see Charming limp and bleeding across her saddlebow. But she did want some sort of justice, some more satisfactory ending to this sordid little tale.

And yet she was not entirely easy.

Who *was* Doctor Rapunzel, really? A woman of intelligence, obviously. But though her story had been harrowing, it was the story of one girl, not a country. One life in jeopardy, not thousands. And she had, it seemed, continued to live a life of bookish isolation— though one could hardly blame her for that. *If* she was telling the truth.

And if she *was*... she was someone whose knowledge of the world came mainly from books. Not a leader. Not someone whose hands were used to taking the reins.

Yet she had come up with the plan. Marie Blanche would reserve judgement—for now.

As for Bella... the very thought of the Lady dei' Sogni made Marie Blanche roll her eyes. Open as a book—a children's book, in bright, simple colours. A sweet, spoiled, wide-eyed innocent. Her first experience of the real world seemed to have rolled off her like rain off a shiny red apple.

Don't be unfair, Marie Blanche. The poor child was heartbroken.

Yes, and still determined to be forgiving. A liability, but probably not actually dangerous.

Unlike this part of the plan, which was what she should be concentrating on, and which might, indeed, be dangerous.

For all her skills, she was uncertain. A dog, a horse, a stag she could get to trust her—even an injured wild hawk, ready to stab at anything in reach. This, though; this might be something of a challenge.

But she was the only one of the three of them who could do it, so do it she must. She would set her hands to what was in front of them.

She laid out her bedroll, hoping the spot was flat enough that she wouldn't find herself back at the bottom of the slope by morning, and watched the stars and wondered how Papa was, and if he had taken more than a mouthful of supper, as the cattle crunched and the bearers snored and the wind sang faint, sweet songs in the mountain grasses.

Five Ladies and a Prince

HE ANCIENT CITY of Allegra is known for its extraordinarily talented and frequently temperamental artists, its equally talented and even more temperamental musicians, and its great public buildings, as airy and fantastical as its glorious cakes.

At the heart of the most fashionable area of the city, there is a room full of people who either *have* exquisite taste, would like others to *think* they have exquisite taste, or want everyone to know that they can afford to *buy* exquisite taste, even if they, personally, wouldn't know it if it sat on them. The most fashionable and expensive perfumes battle it out in the air, drawn out by the heat of so many bodies crowded together.

The room swirls with excited chatter. In the centre stands a veiled statue, with a handsome young man hovering nearby, chewing on his fingernails and quivering like a plucked harp string.

* * *

"AH, LADY BELLA!" A tall man, his silvering beard trimmed to a point, bowed over her hand.

"Francesco, I hope you'll forgive the intrusion," Bella said.

"Intrusion? *Assurdita*, I couldn't be happier." Conte Francesco Morosini patted Bella's hand and tucked it into his arm. "And Gia will be utterly delighted. He's been *so* nervous, but your taste is already legendary. Still, I needn't ask you to be kind, I know."

"As if I'd need to be. Papa was *delighted* with his statue of Mama. So was she, though she claims it flatters her terribly."

They moved towards the front of the crowd. Conte Morosini murmured, "May I just say how happy I am to see you out of seclusion again, at long last?"

"Oh, I'm not the only woman ever to be unlucky in love," Bella said with a sad little smile. "One can't mope forever."

"Society would be bereft, had you decided to do so. And, indeed, you're not the only one." He gestured to a stunning young woman in green damask, who was standing by the window, laughing at some remark made by one of the half-dozen men surrounding her. "Madame la Marquise de la Tour, there, though she seems to have recovered remarkably well from the experience."

"Oh, yes! I have been wanting to speak to the Marquise. I wonder, after the unveiling, would you be so kind as to introduce me?"

The Conte shook his head at her. "You, her... Really, these fellows, what are they about? To abandon such treasures, for the sake of mere *gold!*" He smiled at her. "Were my tastes not otherwise, I'd offer for either of you in an instant. *And* mean it."

"Were your tastes not otherwise, I would be delighted to accept," Lady Bella said. "Who else could teach me so much about art, and the nature of beauty?"

"You teach more than I ever can about the nature of beauty, by your mere existence," said the Conte.

Lady Bella laughed, and tapped him with her fan. "Flatterer."

He turned to her, his lively face suddenly solemn, and took her hands. "My dear, I understand your wish to speak to the Marquise. But don't spend your youth chasing a ghost. It seldom ends well, and I should hate to see your heart broken twice over."

"I am an old lady now, my youth was spent in sleep," said Lady Bella. "Besides, can a heart be broken more than once?"

"Oh, Giacomo's heart is broken whenever some wretched critic takes a pen to his work, poor darling. But he starts anew, and people are kind, and so, it is mended."

"I don't think it is quite the same," Lady Bella murmured. "Now, hush, poor Giacomo is waiting."

The statue (*Young athlete, sleeping*) was unveiled to gasps of delight. Giacomo was lauded, patted, and handed a large drink.

"Madame?" Conte Morosini bowed to the Marquise. "May I introduce Lady Bella dei' Sogni?"

The two women smiled and curtseyed. "Dei' Sogni," the Marquise mused. "Now where have I... Oh. Oh!" Her eyes sharpened.

"I understand you had a... similar experience to mine," Bella said. "And I wondered, could you bear to tell me what happened?"

The Marquise turned to Conte Morosini. "*Mon cher.*

A salon. Small, private, and with wine and a servant of the most intimidating mien, to stand at the door and keep out the curious? S'il vous plait?" She beamed at the Conte. "I *know* you are well supplied with all those things."

The Conte rolled his eyes, laughed, and made the arrangements. "Now," he said, as he ushered the two women into the cosy blue-and-gold salon and placed one of his most broad-shouldered footmen outside the door. "No weeping. If you come out with red eyes, Giacomo will think you hate his work."

"Giacomo is far too busy being inondé with congratulations, commissions and prosecco to care about any such thing," the Marquise scoffed.

The Conte rolled his eyes again, more vigorously. "You have *met* Giacomo, have you? Well, at least try not to make each other miserable."

"Impossible. In such company, how could anyone be miserable?" The Marquise tucked Bella's hand into her arm and swept her into the room, closing the door meaningfully in the Conte's face.

"Now," she said, as soon as they were both seated, with wine in their glasses. "Tell me everything. Or ask me anything. Both! And if you should happen to cry, I have a dozen handkerchiefs about me. I have the habit, nowadays."

Something about the Marquise made it easy for Bella to get through her miserable story. She did cry, but perhaps a little less than she might have expected.

"Well," the Marquise said, passing her another handkerchief. "Ma pauvre, if it is of any comfort, that all sounds *disturbingly* familiar. He was so very attentive, so very kind! One knows, now, of course, that it was merely..." She looked at Bella's expression and cut herself off, waving a hand. "Tant pis. In my case, I had been rendered invisible. So inconvenient, cherie, you cannot imagine. One is always stubbing one's toes, and terrifying servants quite unintentionally! *So* much broken crockery.

"I had irritated a witch by refusing to marry her son. She should perhaps have taught him to wash, and make interesting conversation, or at the very least take his meat *cooked*, but I digress. So, he comes, the Prince... I wonder if that too was a lie, but certainly he seemed like nobility, and he was so very..." The Marquise fluttered her fan.

"Well. So it happened that he broke the spell, and trapped the witch and her son in their cave. Naturally I was grateful, and he declared himself, and I... Well. After the witch's son, he was even more appealing, no? And I was perhaps not quite myself, and a little too ready to fling myself into a pair of arms that were muscular but not smelly and bloodstained. If I had had a little more time to consider... But they were *very* good arms." She sighed. "In any case, three days later, where is he? Why, nowhere to be found! Nor was half the gold in the treasury, not to mention my grand-mére's magic bird, which upset me more than all the rest."

IN A HIGH, many-windowed room overlooking the snowy mountain slopes of Trollmansted (a country even smaller than Ödlakullar, but considerably richer), the last notes of Lady Bella's performance of the song 'Chrysophrie's Lament' fell on the ear as crystalline as the mountain air.

Her Highness the Sovereign Princess of Trollmansted

applauded with tears glittering on her cheeks. "My dear Lady Bella," she said, dabbing at her eyes, "it's as though you *knew*. That last verse is enough to break the heart, is it not? If one's heart were not already broken, of course."

"Who would dare to break Your Highness's heart?" Bella said, looking prettily aghast.

The Princess had been reserved even before The Incident, and had gained a reputation for being more guarded than the royal treasury since. Somehow in the aftermath of the song and the sudden, unexpected release of the tears she had not previously permitted herself to cry, she found herself seated in a quiet corner with Lady Bella and confiding every humiliating detail.

"I was weary of my place in the world," she said, "and made a foolish remark that my crown weighed heavy and I wished I could fly away. Perhaps the Trickster was listening. In any case, it followed that I was turned into a raven, by day. That is a fine joke, since the raven is a bird of wisdom. By night I was myself, but imprisoned in a room of glass, up in the mountains, wearing a crown of diamond. You see that peak, where the setting sun hits? That was the place.

"I do not know how the Prince discovered how to free me, though now I suspect it was not even he who discovered it, but his manservant. He seemed to know a great deal, for a manservant. But I did not think of it then, only that the young man looked so very handsome, and the snow all around him pink and white with the sunset, like apple blossom, almost as though he had timed it. And I had been so very lonely, by day and by night. But it was not me he wanted at all, it was the crown of diamond.

"I should have known, because two ravens appeared and quarrelled, just as he got down on one knee. Here, that is an omen of a bad marriage to come. But I suppose I should be grateful that there was no marriage at all, and that the wretch escorted me down the mountain, instead of leaving me there to freeze to death." She dried her tears and forced a smile. "They do say, though not in my hearing, that my heart was frozen up there on the mountain, and that it will take a true hero to melt it, but I think I am done with such things."

"Oh, don't say so," Lady Bella said. "You wept at my song. What were those tears but the meltwater of a thawing heart?"

Her Highness actually laughed. "You are as charming as he was," she said. "But unlike him, you *have* a heart. A very tender one."

Lady Bella's heart felt, still, not so much tender as tenderised. She was adept at making herself pleasant, at keeping the smile on her face, at being kind and appropriate and drawing people out of themselves. That, of course, was why *she* was the one going from palace to salon to ball to military parade, and talking to people. But once she was alone, she let the smile drop, feeling the muscles of her face ache with relief. She no longer wept into her pillow, at least—or not very often. But she did wonder where Charming was, and what he was doing, and if he ever thought of her at all.

THE BALLROOM OF Welland Castle looked like some fantastical dream: herons and eagles, cats and bears, wolves and foxes, all dressed in silk brocades or velvets and delicate shoes, bowed and spun and fluttered their fans and laughed. Along one wall stood a table crowded with every form of refreshment the dancers could desire, filling the air with the smell of roast meat and sweet puddings.

A woman in a snarling tiger mask seated herself next to Bella in one of the fragile-looking gold-leaf chairs that lined the ballroom of Welland Castle. Despite the mask, the brilliant red hair elaborately piled above it marked her as Lady Buckforth-Welland herself.

"Not dancing, Lady Bella?" she said. "I admit, you do rather put the rest of us to shame, you know. I wish you could teach me to glide the way you do, as though you were floating."

Bella smiled and set aside the white egret mask she wore. "Your ladyship dances very gracefully, and I didn't notice *any* shortage of partners. That last young man looked dreadfully disappointed when you turned him down. Even with the mask on."

"That's Lord Telforth. A frivol, and far too handsome without his mask. I no longer trust handsome men."

"Oh?" Lady Bella said. "Why might that be?"

"You didn't hear? The story is much told!" She leaned forward. "I was being held captive by a bear. Not an ordinary bear, a talking bear. I got rescued by a remarkably handsome young man. Looking back, I think I rather preferred the bear. At least he was honest about his intentions."

"I don't suppose you could introduce me to the bear, could you?" said Lady Bella, rather to her own surprise.

Lady Buckforth-Welland threw back her head and laughed aloud.

Bella only managed a smile. "Oh, how absurd life is," she said.

"However would we stand it otherwise?" said Lady Buckforth-Welland.

LADY BELLA ACCOMPANIED the Landgravine of Uswald-Brenate as she walked among the vine rows, occasionally pausing to tuck a piece of cloth more tightly around one of the gnarled branches. Throughout the vineyard other figures could be seen bending, inspecting, adjusting. The smells of lamp oil and frost hung in the air.

"Deepest apologies, Lady Bella, for not taking time out of my day to speak with you, but my weinbauer is sick. At this time of year, one has to be so careful that a late frost does not the crop ruin. Since what happened, we rely even more on our wine trade. How much do you know?"

"I had heard something," Bella said, "but not the details."

"A sorcerer turned my sister into a *chicken,* to begin with. Because she would not dance with him. And they say *women* do not like to be scorned! My poor Sophia, she still is not herself." The Landgravine straightened, putting her hands into the small of her back and stretching.

"Of course she's not herself, she's only *been* herself again for a few months!" Bella said. "You must have been so worried for her."

"I was, greatly. The worst of it, she says, is that it is so very, very dull. Chickens become overwrought at the sight of grain because it is the most exciting thing that happens to them all day. And that is another thing!" The Landgravine bent to yank furiously at a weed. "What did he hope to gain? Was he planning to turn Sophia back, in the hope that she would be so pleased to be human again that she would immediately forgive him and offer him her hand in marriage? Or did he think other women would be so afraid of being turned into poultry that they would flock—I did not mean that—*run*, into his arms, instead of as far away as they could?" She shook the weed free of earth as though shaking the sorcerer by the neck. "*Men.*"

Bella discreetly brushed earth from her coat. "And... the Prince?"

"Ah, yes, the Prince. He arrives, as I am at my wits' end. He is so very concerned, so earnest." She shook her head. "Since our dear parents passed, we have dealt with assassins, spies, cheating traders and overambitious relatives. I thought I knew a rogue, but no."

"But he did free her?"

"Oh, yes. It appears he managed to eavesdrop on the sorcerer gloating about his spell—of course, he was a boasting fool—and how no one would work out the way to break it, since it involved knowing his mother's maiden name. I hope his mother never learned what sort of man he had become."

"What happened to him?" Lady Bella asked idly.

"The servant... Ronald? Reynaud? No, Roland. Roland managed to turn one of his own spells against him, and turned *him* into a chicken. A roast one. Which he ate."

"Oh," Lady Bella said. "Um..."

"*Not* in front of my sister, fortunately. We no longer eat chicken in the palace. Then His Highness The Crown Prince of Untrustworthiness offered her his hand. I *did* suggest she wait, after what she'd been through—but she said being married would make her feel more human again. Of course, the morning of the wedding..."

"What did he take?"

"My opa's ruby ring, a phoenix egg, and a good third of our gold reserve. As to how he carried it all, perhaps a magic pouch or some such thing, and if *that* was not stolen I would be shocked."

"What can he possibly *want* with all that treasure?" Bella said.

"My sister wondered if he was secretly a dragon, and building his hoard. Somehow that thought helps her feel a little better. Myself, I think he was simply a thief, and a greedy one." The Landgravine slapped dirt from her gloves. "Sophia swears now that she will never marry. For myself, I have informed my fiancé that I wish for a quiet, *inexpensive* wedding. Fortunately, he is a sensible man."

"Is he kind?" Bella said. "I do hope he's kind."

The Landgravine smiled. "Yes," she said. "I think that is the most important quality in a husband, do not you? And honesty, of course."

Lady Bella smiled, a little sadly, and said nothing.

IN THE OAK-FLOORED gymnasium of the Epigny Palace, the stroke of steel meeting steel rang from the walls. "Oh, very nice!" The Baroness d'Epigne put up her sword. "I concede! An excellent bout, Milady. Quite in the old style."

Bella, since she was wearing breeches, bowed. "I am a little behind in my techniques," she said, "but I am learning."

"Well, you defeated me soundly, without any modern trickery." The Baroness took off her mask, revealing a laughing face and eyes a startling shade of amber. "The last time I had such a bout I lost a great deal more than the match."

"Oh?" Lady Bella said. "How did that come about?"

"My parents were pushing me to marry, and I vowed I would only wed the man who could complete a number of tasks—stealing a dragon's egg, getting a hair from the head of the sea witch, and defeating me at fencing. I was overconfident."

"But he succeeded?"

"In a manner of speaking. The dragon's egg was a painted rock, the sea-witch's hair was nothing more than a strip of seaweed, both ruses enhanced with magical illusions, and the promises as false as either. But he did beat me at fencing honestly. The only honest thing about him. The next morning he was gone, along with several of the more interesting items from the treasury and Papa's personal collection." The Baroness stretched, and winked at Bella. "I should be grateful. At least after that Mama and Papa *finally* stopped trying to get me to marry. Champagne?"

"You know, I think I will," said Bella. Meeting someone whose pride might have been dented but whose heart was entirely unbruised by the wandering prince felt like a cause for at least a small celebration.

But even as Bella sipped, and smiled, she was going over every story, every reminiscence, looking for something that would explain it all in a way that would soothe her own sore heart. Something that meant they were not all the same man, though that was increasingly hard to believe. Something that proved the Prince's actions were the result of an evil spell, or a geas, or anything other than mere greed and lack of feeling.

There was *something*, she was sure of it.

There *had* to be.

The Doctor and the Demon

ERE IN THE heart of the Trübenholz, near enough to town to be convenient and several miles from where the blood-red tower, the Rotterturm, slowly crumbles in upon its own empty heart, is a small house of white plaster and dark timber beams, with a delightful garden. There are many herbs, some of them extremely rare, and all flourishing. There is fennel and rosemary, madder and saffron. There are roses and pinks and violets and wallflowers. The scents mingle and wind around the house, always harmonious, never overwhelming.

There are no lilies. Not a one.

DOCTOR RAPUNZEL TUCKED herself into her lushly padded chair like a cat. A fire in the grate, hot tea to hand, a heated brick at the feet. Having grown up without luxuries, she was a believer in allowing herself a few, especially if they were comfortable ones. Besides, one could work a great deal harder—and longer—if one were comfortable.

On the table in front of her stood a scrying mirror, gleaming obsidian in an oval black frame. Unlike the chair, it was plain to the point of austerity. No scrollwork, no frame of writhing demonic figures—or, worse, smirking cherubs; all that nonsense was nothing but a distraction.

Distractions, when scrying, were not only inefficient, they could be lethal.

The Doctor lit two candles in heavy black onyx holders and placed them to either side and slightly to the rear of the mirror. Her own reflection appeared, dim and watery; she tilted the mirror so her face was no longer visible, only the black, gleaming surface.

She placed her hands in her lap, and focussed.

Deep in the blackness lurked a flicker of fire. Smoke curled about the frame.

Abruptly, a gaping maw of jagged teeth and writhing, dripping tongues lunged at the mirror.

Doctor Rapunzel did not flinch.

"*Peeking, seeking, sneaking,*" said a voice. It was a thoroughly unpleasant voice, somehow *viscous,* thick with suggestions of ooze and rot.

"Greetings, Elathiel," said Doctor Rapunzel.

"*Oh, it's you.*" The maw disappeared. In its place was a small, pot-bellied, red-eyed creature which resembled the results of a mutually-regretted liaison between a bat and a toad. Though a lot less threatening in this form, it still had rather too many teeth and tongues, and its voice still dripped.

"How are things in the Infernal?" Doctor Rapunzel asked.

Elathiel shrugged. "*Political. I stay out of it.*"

"Very wise."

"*What do you want, O wise and noble doctor?*" Elathiel somehow managed to make the flattering words and well-earned title sound like the grossest of insults.

Doctor Rapunzel had prepared carefully for this. As with the Good Folk, the choice of words when dealing with the Infernal was of the greatest importance. A misused tense or unclear term could get you into the kind of trouble even lawyers could only admire from a safe distance.

"I want you to find me the imp who was bound to Doctor Hilda von Riesentor in the Rotterturm until the time my captivity ended. I have questions to put to it, as to certain things that were stolen after I fell asleep that day."

"*You wish me to find* one *demon, who could be anywhere in Hell?*"

"No," said Rapunzel firmly. "If it has entered another magician's service, you'll simply say it is not in Hell and your service is completed. Find the imp in whatever world it is in."

Elathiel scratched itself, snorted, and grimaced. "*And what do I get?*"

"The usual."

"*For that? Oh, no. To search* all *worlds I need to talk to The Thousand-Eyed. You want me to deal with them, it'll take a* lot *more than that, thank you very much.*"

"Half again. One live and one egg."

Elathiel sighed and studied its extremely dirty fingernails. "*Try harder, or go away. I have stuff to do.*"

"Twice the usual price. No more."

Elathiel huffed. "*I could end up splattered across six*

worlds, if I catch The Thousand-Eyed in a bad mood, you know. At least six."

"If you're not interested I shall ask your littermate."

"*Pathifel? You'd trust Pathifel?*" Elathiel sank back on its haunches and mused. "*I'd almost let you, just to see what The Thousand-Eyed would do to them. I mean, that could be fun.*"

"Very well, then." Rapunzel said. "I will ask Pathifel." She shifted the mirror slightly, so that the cage with the two pure white doves was visible to Elathiel.

Elathiel groaned. "*You didn't tell me they were white doves.*"

"A dove is a dove," Rapunzel said, knowing full well that in the peculiar currencies of the Infernal white doves were particularly rare and valued. "But these are pure white, yes."

Elathiel gazed at the doves and wrung its hands together. "*Oh, all right. I get both of them, alive, right?*"

"Yes. But I need the information in no more than three days from now, by my world's time. I shall call you again at midnight on the third day. If you do not have what I ask for by then, the agreement is void."

Elathiel writhed, and twisted, and grumbled, and eventually, with a last, longing look at the doves, agreed, and disappeared in an explosion of particularly foul-smelling, snot-coloured smoke.

Doctor Rapunzel covered the mirror and opened the windows; cleaned the cage and fed and watered the doves. She did not allow herself to become fond of them, but while they were in her care, she would look after them. What exactly the denizens of the Infernal *did* with the doves, and why they placed such value on white ones, she had not yet been able to discover, though when she had once suggested to Elathiel that they ate them, it had been so shocked and offended it had tried to throw a curse through the mirror. It had almost got through, too. And the room had reeked of sulphur and rotten fish for *weeks*.

Doctor Rapunzel knew she had made a misstep there, but she remained determined to find out, one day. Knowledge, after all, was power—*I know the thing that has power over it,* a voice murmured in the depths of her mind—and some knowledge, she thought as she shut the doves' cage, was best kept to oneself. Would the doves be better off for knowing their fate? Surely not.

The Prince and the Thieves

HE MOTTLED CROW tavern huddles in the rain like a large, sulky cat, its firelit windows gleaming like narrowed eyes under its dripping eaves. Inside, it is low beamed and tolerably well lit; the long tables stand in fairly clean straw, the chairs are sturdy if not particularly comfortable. It smells of smoke, cooking, damp clothes, wet dogs and beer. The clientele are mainly weary farm labourers, a couple of shepherds (with crooks to hand and dogs asleep at their feet), and a few of what look, from their clothes, to be moderately prosperous travelling merchants.

Two of the clientele do not belong to any of these groups. They sit slightly removed from them, tucked in a corner.

"Now *THAT*," ROLAND said, "was what I call a meal. Sometimes all you want is a proper fry-up."

Charming pushed his own plate away with a grimace.

"I think there was more grease in that than in an entire roomful of lawyers."

"Says His Royal Highness of the Moral High Ground."

"Hush with the Highness, would you?"

"Oh, come on, no one's listening. And who's going to believe a prince is dining in a common tavern, anyway? Although that bacon wasn't at all common. That was exceptional bacon. Fit for a prince, in fact," Roland said, leaning back and loosening his belt.

"Please," Charming said, "keep your clothes on."

"Scared I'll get all the ladies?" Roland smirked.

"What ladies?" Charming looked around. "*Ladies* don't go to taverns."

"Poor ladies! How dull for them," Roland said.

The tavern door opened and a new group blew in with a gust of rainy wind that set the lanterns flickering.

They had a look about them that was somehow both swaggering and wary. They made for the counter in a bustle of colourful but slightly tattered finery, one or two of them casting sharp looks about the room, as though checking the exits.

Charming and Roland exchanged a glance. Charming tugged the hood of his cloak over his hair, and they both slumped a little, let their faces drop into dullness, and generally became as inconspicuous as it was possible for such a pair to be.

The newcomers dragged a couple of tables together and settled in. One of them, a lanky, sharp-bearded fellow with a flashing grin, raised a tankard and took a long draught, wiped foam out of his curled moustache, and said, "Well, that was a good day, my lovelies."

"Nice to have enough for a decent meal for a change," said the handsome woman beside him, rolling her sleeves up to show notably muscular forearms, before attacking a leg of mutton with enthusiasm and a disturbingly large knife.

"Leave some for the rest of us, Gilda," complained a tiny woman with a mop of pale hair. She wore a collection of knives which, while most of them were smaller than Gilda's great blade, verged on the excessive. She turned to Moustache. "Tell her, Dance."

"Leave Gilda alone, Mouse," said Dance. "She worked hard today."

"We all work hard," Mouse grumbled.

"Gilda worked hardest. That guard..." Dance lowered his voice, though not so low Roland and Charming couldn't hear him. "Right over the wagon and into the lake. Squawk, splash. Spectacular."

"He was stubborn," Gilda said. "I told him, just let us take it, no one wants a fight, right?"

"Liar," said another man, stocky and curly-haired. "You *always* want a fight."

"I do not. That wasn't a *fight,* anyway. I just got him out the way."

"So where next, Dance?" said the curly-haired one.

"Well I *was* thinking about Eingeten."

"Ooh, Eingeten," said Curly. "Eingeten's rich as cream. Nice."

"Yeah. Though not now."

"Why?" Gilda said, around a mouthful of mutton. "What's happening in Eingeten?"

"Oh, come on, you must have heard," Mouse said. "They were talking about it in that place we stayed two nights ago."

"All I remember about that place is bad fish and worse privies."

"They've got a dragon," Dance said.

"A *dragon*? When'd that happen?"

"About a month ago? Maybe? Anyway." Dance leaned forward. "The Grand Duke's been at his wit's end, trying to work out how to get rid of the thing. Burning up cattle and crops like it's taken a personal dislike to the place, apparently."

"Shame," Gilda said. "No point going there, then."

"He even," Dance said, "thought about offering it the Eingeten Necklace."

"No!" Gilda paused with a forkful of potato partway to her mouth. "Really?"

"The Eingeten Necklace," Mouse said dreamily. "What I'd give just to wear it. Once."

"Wouldn't suit you," Curly said. "Rubies aren't your colour."

"Eff off, anything worth that much is my colour."

"*Anyway*," Dance said. "He consulted his court astrologer first, which is just as well because it'd be a crying shame if someone burned up the Eingeten Necklace..."

"Do rubies burn?" Curly said. "I mean, I suppose they might get discoloured and the setting'd melt, but..."

"A dragon wouldn't *burn* it," said Mouse. "It'd *keep* it. On its hoard."

"If I was a dragon and I had the Eingeten necklace I'd get rid of the rest of the hoard and buy a decent bed," Curly said. "I mean, it's supposed to be worth more gold than a man can measure, isn't it? Why sleep on a load of coins and stuff if you can have a nice bed *and* a really fancy necklace? Mind you, I don't suppose it'd fit, would it? Not on a dragon."

"Shut up, Curly," Gilda said. "What'd the astrologer say, Dance?"

"*Thank* you, Gilda," Dance said. "Honestly how I ever get you lot to listen long enough to take instructions... The astrologer said the Grand Duke has to offer up his daughter, Ysoude, to the dragon. Tie her to a rock, dragon comes, sees the girl, devours her, bish-bash-bosh, no more dragon."

"Ysoude the Virtuous? Fed to a *dragon*? Ouch," Gilda said. "That's going to be popular."

"You'd be surprised how quickly people are all right with some lass getting chomped once they're staring down a starving winter," Curly said, gloomily.

"But they *love* her," Mouse said. "She feeds the poor and everything. They cheer her every time she shows her face out of doors."

"It *is* a very pretty face, from what I hear," said Gilda. "Shame."

"Be a shame even if she *wasn't* pretty," Mouse snapped.

"All right, all right, don't get up in one, I'm just *saying*," Gilda said. "The Grand Duke must be in a state. Didn't he lose his wife last winter?"

"He did that," Dance said. "No other children, either. *Dotes* on Ysoude. Done nothing but mourn and wail since the astrologer told him, apparently. But what else can he do? It's his daughter or his whole city, unless someone can find another way to sort the dragon out."

"Well that's all a bit shit, then, isn't it?" Gilda said. "I'm depressed now. Let's get some wine."

Charming looked at Roland and raised an eyebrow. Roland shrugged and nodded. Quietly, they paid their bill and left the tavern, slipping out into the wet night.

The Lady, the Dragon
and the Ruby Necklace

HE TOWN OF Dornslatz, seat of the Grand Dukes of Eingeten, is tiny, steep and almost absurdly pretty. Cobbled streets wind uphill between picturesquely crooked but sturdily built houses of silvery stone. The town is overlooked by the Grand Ducal Residence, a small castle so spiky with slim, flag-topped towers that it looks like a hedgehog has run through some bunting. All around are lush forests, fruit-dotted orchards and fields like a patchwork quilt made by a loving grandmother. The only uncomfortable note is provided by the brutal jab of mountain that looms above it all, stark as a bone.

"NICE PLACE," CHARMING said. "Be a shame if it got burned."

Roland sniffed. "'Sall right, if you like that sort of thing."

"You have no taste, you know that?" Charming said.

"I have taste. Just not the same as your taste," Roland pointed out. He sniffed again and turned around, like a short, ugly weathercock, then pointed. "Look, over there."

In the distance was a blackened field and a rising column of smoke.

"Ah. The dragon, you think?"

"Looks like it."

"So what do you know about this place?"

"Bugger all," Roland said, cheerfully.

"Seriously?"

"The whole place is about the size of a giant's hanky. Not one of the *big* giants, neither. What d'you expect me to have heard about it? No important wars, no notable plagues, no raging tyrants. Dull as a plain pudding until the dragon turned up. But now they're suddenly living in interesting times. The Duke was already in mourning, now he's scared for his people, he's scared for his daughter, all his choices are bad ones. Talk fast, be reassuring, do that noble but caring thing you're so good at, he *should* be an easy mark."

"Don't say that. I hate it when you say that."

"What, calling someone a 'mark'? What d'you want me to call 'im? The target? The victim?"

"You just make it sound so... *nasty.*"

"It is nasty. Suddenly you've a problem with nasty?"

Charming pouted and kicked at a cobblestone. "It's not like I don't have a *reason*."

"Said every thief ever," Roland said. "Always got a reason. Are we doing this or not?"

"Yes, we're doing it."

"Good. Let's go take advantage of the grieving widower."

"Oh, I see what you're doing," Charming said,

straightening up. "You're trying to provoke me so I'll get rid of you. Not happening, *Roland*."

Roland grinned, nastily. "Worth a try."

"I still feel really uncomfortable, you know," Charming said.

"Don't worry," Roland said. "You'll talk yourself out of it soon enough. Come on, beast."

The Mostly Donkey complained its way up the hill towards the castle, farting extravagantly and leaving several piles of droppings so extremely sulphurous that even the town's dogs and dung collectors avoided them.

The guards snapped to attention, their spears crossed before the gate. Their uniforms were an eye-watering combination of purple and yellow, their hats befeathered, and their boots extremely shiny. Under all of this frivolity, however, could be seen a rather impressive collection of muscles and scars. "Good morning," Charming said, beaming. "We're here for an audience with His Royal Highness the Grand Duke."

"Are you indeed?" the older guard said, looking them up and down. "All three of you?"

"Just me and my man here," Charming said. "Border wars?"

"'Scuse me?"

"I know veterans when I see them. A place this size, surrounded by bigger neighbours, keeping the borders must be hard work."

"Seen a bit of action," the guard said. "His Imperial Highness rewards good service."

"Nice to hear it," Charming said. "Not everyone remembers those who've risked their lives in their service."

"You got that right. But I'm sorry, sir, the Duke isn't seeing visitors. I'd let you in, but it's not up to me."

"Oh, I don't expect you to go against orders, but would you be so kind as to take a message for me?"

"That I can do," the guard said, and whistled sharply between his teeth.

A small boy, also adorned in purple and yellow (and looking extremely proud of the fact), popped out of the guardhouse. "Message for His Imperial Highness," the guard said.

"Yessir." The boy drew himself up to his full height, which came to about the guard's elbow, and put on the face of one determined to listen with every ear he had.

Charming smiled at the boy, who attempted to stand even straighter.

"Please to tell His Imperial Highness that Prince Lothrik of Brode-Bassen is here, having heard of the terrible curse under which his noble house currently labours, and hopes to free him of this burden. Can you repeat that back to me?"

The boy did, in a slow but accurate monotone.

"Very good. And here"—Charming prepared to draw the large ring from his finger and give it to the boy—"my seal, in case the Duke requires proof I am who I say I am." The sun caught the seal ring and the design carved in its face flashed in the light.

Roland coughed loudly. "'Scuse me, Your Highness," he said, grabbing Charming's hand.

"What in Goose's name?" Charming said.

"Terribly sorry, it's filthy, that ring, can't send it to the Duke in that condition, what would he think?" Roland babbled, yanking it from Charming's finger and rubbing it frantically on his jacket, a procedure not likely to clean anything at all.

Both guards raised their eyebrows. Charming's

expression was that of a man whose patience with his foolish servant was reaching its limit, when Roland thrust the ring at him. "There, that's better," he said. "Don't want to give a bad *impression*, do we?"

Charming glanced down at the ring, and anyone watching very closely might have seen a moment of realisation flicker across his face. "No, indeed," he said, "quite right." He handed the ring to the boy. "Off you go now."

Charming exchanged war stories with the guard until the boy reappeared, accompanied by a man in scarlet and rose pink livery, embellished with so much thick gold braid and so many vast gold buttons that it must have weighed nearly as much as a suit of chain mail. The man wearing it was very tall, very wide, and so extremely dignified he almost managed to make the ridiculous livery look like a deliberate personal choice.

"I am His Imperial Highness's Steward of the Inner Household," this vision declared, and bowed, with a slight creaking noise. "Please accompany me and I will take you to His Imperial Highness, and someone will take your... that, to the stables."

"I thought he was a duke," muttered Roland, under cover of the Beast's sudden loud braying. "What's this 'Imperial Highness' business? Thought that was just princes."

"Some dukes are Highnesses," murmured Charming under his breath. "Some are Imperial Highnesses. All depends who they're descended from."

"Huh. Well, Prince Lothrik of Brode-Bassen is descended from King Lothrik III, and is *not* the Marquis of Carabas, whose ring you had on, and who is still wanted for thievery and deception not nearly far enough from here."

"All right, all right, you caught it, didn't you?"

"Just as well I did. Getting careless, Your Highness. Or Your Marquisness, depending."

"Oh, pooh, as though they'd have heard about it, *and* recognised the seal, especially with a dragon on their hands. Hush, now."

The Mostly Donkey was led off to the stables. "Careful," Roland called out to the stable hand. "She bites. And kicks. And is just generally a lot more trouble than she's worth."

The Mostly Donkey blared in response, and Roland grinned.

CHARMING AND ROLAND were ushered through a series of increasingly elaborately carved doors, and with each section of the palace they entered found themselves the subject of more and more whispered conversation and wistful stares. The guard's uniform stood out against the occupants of the palace like a fairground lollipop in an empty fire grate. Everyone was dressed in black or grey. The delightful frivolities of the palace's interior—barley-sugar twisted banisters, ornately gilded and painted furniture, extravagantly elaborate clocks—were alike draped in gloomy swags of cloth. Even the statuary was in mourning—a marble nymph's smile was rendered chilly and slightly sinister by grey veiling, and a group of dancing marble children appeared to be caught in a terminal struggle with reams of black velvet, only a single small white hand waving from the folds, as though appealing for help.

The syrup scented smoke of powerful incense permeated the halls, lying on the air in hazy swirls. Roland sneezed and scowled.

Charming drew back his shoulders, lifted his chin and projected an air of solemn, reassuring strength. Roland looked sideways at the crowd, sniffed the air, and sneezed some more.

Before they could quite reach the last and most extravagant set of doors, these were flung open. "Is it true?" the figure that appeared demanded in quavering tones. "Can you help us? Can you save my darling girl and my poor, beleaguered people from this awful beast?" Then he fell into a coughing fit, waving a hand in front of his face. "Sorry about the incense, it's supposed to bring luck."

The Grand Duke of Eingeten, Sovereign Prince of Lisfar-Bendril, Count of Rithlevish, Defender of the Borders, and Holder of the Most Noble Office of the Ruby Star, appeared to have been compressed by the sheer weight of his titles. He was barely taller than Roland, and as skinny as his steward was broad. His elaborate robes (black) and fur-trimmed crown (also black) looked as though they had expected someone rather more impressive, and remained attached to him only by sheer force of protocol. White locks escaped the confines of his crown and his grey eyes swam with tears as he reached his trembling hands out towards Charming.

Charming knelt, bringing his head roughly level with the Grand Duke's narrow chest. "I have heard so much of your benevolent rule, of your beautiful country, and of your beloved and virtuous daughter. Hearing then of your great trouble, how could I not offer whatever help I may?"

"O kind and noble stranger," the Grand Duke said, his voice choking with emotion. "Only free us of this curse and we will give you whatever you ask." He blew his nose loudly on a silk handkerchief (black) and cried out, "Our salvation is come!"

Cheers echoed through the corridors, with such vigour that the marble nymph's veil fell off. Charming kept his gaze modestly lowered.

The cheering grew suddenly louder and Charming looked up to see a young woman standing behind the Grand Duke. Unlike her father she was tall, and dressed in a simple grey gown that matched her eyes. Her hair, plainly dressed, was a pale, silvery blonde. She rested her hand on the Grand Duke's shoulder and he clasped it with one of his. "Ysoude, my dear," the Grand Duke said, sniffling, "this is the man who will save us all."

"He is most welcome," she said. Her voice was soft but very clear. She looked at Charming with a frank, open gaze as he got to his feet and bowed. A faint frown creased her brows. "Alone?" she said. "Against a dragon?"

"Not *quite* alone," Charming said, gesturing at Roland, who responded with a grimace that could perhaps be called a smile, if one were in a generous and forgiving mood. "I have fought dragons before, Your Imperial Highness," Charming said. "And here I stand, alive and unsinged. And even if I had not, had I never fought anything bigger than a sparrow? For you, Milady, I would find the courage."

Ysoude gave a tremulous smile. "Find courage not for me, but for our poor people," she said, tucking her father's stray locks back under his crown. "My father puts great faith in his astrologer, but should she prove wrong, then the dragon will consume me, and continue to ravage their farms and their homes. And I will be gone and unable to provide what little help or comfort I can."

Charming blinked. "From what I have heard," he said, "you would be a greater loss to your people than any number of farms."

"Whoever thought so did me too much credit. I cannot feed them on virtue, or shelter them with fine words. But come! You have not been properly welcomed. We cannot offer you a feast, I fear, but we can make shift to feed you, at least."

The Grand Duke patted his daughter's arm. "She emptied the palace pantries to feed the families who lost everything to the dragon," he said. "Cook was furious."

"Oh, now, you know Cook has a generous heart," Ysoude said. "He simply hides it well."

"A crust, in such company, would be reward enough," Charming said, and suddenly winced, as though someone had kicked him in the ankle.

AFTER THE SPARSE, if excellently cooked, supper, the Captain of the Guard came to show Charming where they must go the following morning. He was a broad-shouldered, greying man with a broken nose; the yellow and purple tabard over his armour did nothing to make him look less tough. He eyed Charming and Roland in the manner of someone used to keeping his counsel, and led them to the beginning of the mountain path mostly in silence.

"Up there," he said. "The path's suitable for horses for most of the way, but where the trees end, you'll have to go on foot. And you see that rock platform? That's where..." He broke off and turned away. His great shoulders shuddered, once.

Charming and Roland glanced at each other. Charming said, "Be of good cheer, captain. We will not let any harm come to Milady."

The captain coughed and said, "Right." Then, "I'd

like to hang that astrologer from the gatehouse, and damn my pension."

"Well, you can trust His Highness to get the job done," Roland said. "As to astrologers..." He spat, extravagantly. "Wouldn't trust 'em an inch. All moonshine and verbiage, them. Ever get a straight answer off one? No. No one has."

"Are you quite finished, Roland?" Charming said.

Roland glowered, and continued to mutter about astrologers as they rode back to the palace.

"Thank you for the vote of confidence, by the way," Charming said to him, when the captain was out of earshot. "My cockles are positively glowing with warmth."

"Didn't say he could trust you to save Ysoude, did I?"

"You do know how to undermine a compliment, don't you?"

"That's why I don't give 'em, as a rule."

Charming sighed and looked at the captain's back. "They *really* seem to care for her a great deal, don't they?"

"Yeah. They actually do."

"You sound surprised."

"Oh, come on. You of all people know that all the fawning on royalty is usually as genuine as a lead penny. Soon as you were out of favour, what happened to all those dear friends and loyal servants of yours?"

"You're dreadfully tiresome," Charming said, and urged his horse on to catch up with the Captain.

Roland smirked to himself.

THE ROOMS PROVIDED for the hero and his man were, at least, not draped in mourning. Although for anyone *not*

177

delighted by baby blue walls, rose pink ceilings, a great deal of gilding and an excess of dimply cherubs carved into every available surface, a bit of black drapery might have been a relief.

Charming took in the décor, groaned, and flopped down on a loveseat upholstered in bright pink satin. "My eyes are never going to recover from this."

"Your eyes? What about my nose?"

"What *about* your nose?" Charming looked at that impressive organ.

"The incense is bad enough. You haven't noticed the perfume? People reek of it. Even some of the guards."

"I suppose you'd prefer everyone to smell of cabbage."

"Cabbage? Well, you can't beat a nice bit of steamed cabbage, touch of nutmeg, maybe..."

"Do you ever think of anything but your stomach?"

"Hard not to when you keep turning it. I mean...! 'A crust, in such company, would be enough'?" Roland quoted in a voice that sounded like syrup poured through gravel. "That much honey'd gag a bee."

"Ladies *like* that sort of thing. Not that you'd know."

"Just 'cause she's virtuous doesn't mean she's thick."

"Of course she's not—appalling word—*thick*. She struck me as a most intelligent woman." Charming leaned towards the nearest mirror, frowned, and shoved a lock of hair behind his ear. "Is that grey? Roland?"

"You've got away with this for so long you think you're smarter than everyone. Going to get you in trouble one day, Your Highness. Speaking of which... Worked out how we're going to deal with this dragon, have you? Or is that up to me... again?"

Charming was twisting his neck in front of the mirror in what appeared to be an attempt to see the top of his own head. "What? Roland, look, be honest with me, is that *grey?*"

"It's *mud,* you plonker."

Charming gave a gasp of relief and clasped a hand to his chest. "Thank the Goose for that. Wait, no, I sat at dinner with *mud* in my hair and you didn't tell me? That's awful. Do you think Lady Ysoude noticed?"

"I think she probably had slightly more pressing matters on her mind. Like her impending fiery death? Like we're facing? Tomorrow?"

Charming sat down and began pulling off his boots. "Oh, you're such a worrywart, Roland." He smiled and patted his boots fondly. "We'll be fine. I've got these, and the arrows, and the cloak, haven't I?"

"*You've* got the cloak. What about me? I en't got no cloak."

"I'm sure a little fire won't bother you, Roland, all things considered."

"Dragon flame is not just a *little fire.*"

"You've known worse." Charming held the boots up to the light and scowled. "I do wish these were smarter. I don't suppose we can do something about that? An illusion, or something?"

"You *are* joking. You don't just bung extra spells on top of a powerful item. They *interact,* spells do."

"How?"

"No telling beforehand. But an illusion, on top of those? How about you have an illusion that the dragon's gone while you're actually about to be toasted like a crumpet? What if the illusion stops the boots working? There you are, not moving an inch, and boom—or rather, whoosh, scream, crackle, crackle, crumble to ash."

"All right, all right, you've made your point. No illusion on the boots."

"So do you have a plan?"

Charming grinned. "Of course I have a plan. Avoid the flame, kill the dragon, grateful populace goes huzzah, ride off with the necklace." His grin wavered a little on that last item.

"So the detail's up to me, again."

"I did actually succeed in a plan or two before you came along, Roland."

"If by 'succeed' you mean 'got away with by the skin of your teeth,'" Roland said.

AT THAT MOMENT, there came a knock on the door. Charming and Roland glanced at each other, and Charming yanked his boots back on.

Roland opened the door. "Milady!" he said. "Er... come in?"

"Thank you, but this is not a social visit," Ysoude said. "I would like to show you something."

"Of course, anything," Charming said.

"So long as it's not the dungeons," Roland muttered, as they left the room.

They walked through the palace, amid the black and grey draperies. Occasionally one of the palace's other occupants would appear, and bow to Charming, or press a luck-charm into his hands, and mutter incoherent, tearful words of encouragement.

Charming's usual irrepressible cheer began to wither at the edges. Ysoude glanced at him and said, "Forgive them. After the first excitement, now..." She shrugged. "I am sure you will defeat the dragon"—and her voice *almost* hid the lie—"but they are very frightened."

"Of course, of course," Charming said. "I do understand. The trust of strangers is hard won."

"Here." Ysoude gestured at a massively barred door guarded by a pair of heavily armed and even more heavily muscled guards. "If you please, Francisco."

The guard thus addressed bowed, clanking slightly, took a massive iron key from a ring at his belt and unlocked the door.

Ysoude led the way into a small, candlelit chamber.

There was nothing in it but a pedestal holding a white marble bust of a woman with high-piled curls and a glare no less intimidating for being carved in stone.

Around her neck, its glittering, blood-red glory perfected by candlelight, was the Eingeten Necklace. A thick choker of deep red stones, from which depended gold chains attached to looped swags of more red stones lying across the bust's—well, bust.

"Now that," Roland said, "is *nice*. Nice work."

Charming was, for once, rendered entirely speechless. Ysoude stared at the necklace, her expression hard to read in the candlelight.

"We *offered* it to the dragon, you know," she said. "It was hard—the people consider it a symbol of the city, and they like to see me wear it on special occasions, as my mother did, and her mother before her. That statue is my great-grandmother, for whom it was made.

"One of the councillors even suggested we take a copy, but our astrologer said a dragon would know the difference between real and paste immediately, and be angered.

"The captain volunteered to take it up to the rock, and the dragon actually turned up, and looked at it, and flew away, flaming a field as it went! At least it left the poor captain alive. That's what matters, after all." She sighed. "But we realised the astrologer must be right, and I was the only sacrifice it would accept."

Charming retrieved his voice. "I see," he said. "Well, beautiful as the necklace is, the dragon obviously has more refined tastes."

Ysoude managed a slight laugh. "I am beginning to understand how you got your name," she said.

"Oh, it's the greatest embarrassment to me, but my mother, you know... May I ask why you wished me to see the necklace?"

"Only so you might understand a little more about the dragon. I didn't know if it would help, but I thought..." She shrugged and shook her head.

Charming smiled. "I understand, and appreciate it more than you can know." He took her hand and bowed over it. "Milady is as wise as she is beautiful. Far more so than any necklace." He straightened up and spoke over his shoulder: "Roland, I'm becoming concerned about these coughing fits of yours. Perhaps you should see the palace physician; I'm sure they've some dose of boiled snails, or something of the sort, that could help."

BACK IN THE cherub-infested chambers, Roland said: "So what if your much-boasted skill with a bow fails?"

"What do you mean?"

"Well, it's Ysoude the dragon's after. If you miss, or just wound it, it's still going to come for her. And if you're still alive, the people aren't going to be happy that you let their beloved Lady get toasted, or eaten—do we even know which? Or is it one, then the other?"

"I am not going to allow either of those to happen to Ysoude!"

Roland paused for a moment, eyeing the Prince. "Well, then," he said slowly, "how are you going to prevent it?"

"By providing a decoy, of course."

"If the dragon won't be fooled by a paste necklace, it's not going to be fooled by a paste Lady, either."

"Roland. There only needs to be a decoy long enough to attract the dragon's *attention*. Remember what she said? It came and looked at the necklace. If it comes close enough to look at what it *thinks* is the lady, I can shoot it."

"Ah, I see. Then we keep Lady Ysoude and her men out of sight, so if you merely wound it, if I'm waiting with the Mostly Donkey, we can have it away on our toes, without anyone being the wiser. Well, *you* can, anyway. Me and the Donkey will have to make our own arrangements. As usual. So when do we grab the necklace?"

"*After* the fight. I am not intending to miss."

"No, I can see that," said Roland.

THE NEXT MORNING dawned cool and drizzling. Roland pulled aside the curtains and glared at the spot where smoke had risen the day before. "Wakey wakey, Your Royal Sunshine."

"I'm awake," Charming yawned. "Oh, no, is it *still* raining? This is a very wet country."

"You'd better get a move on. The family's been up for hours, getting Milady ready to be chained to a rock. Wish we'd had a chance to talk to that astrologer."

"What good's an astrologer?" Charming fluffed his hair. "They're always so vague, what they say could mean anything."

"That's the thing, innit? This one wasn't. Remarkably precise, in fact. But she's off somewhere, just as things are likely to get proper nasty. Suspicious, I call it."

"Maybe she's off feeding her crystals, or whatever it is they do. We know what we need to know, don't we?" Charming got out of bed, stretched, and began to splash his face vigorously from the ewer on the nightstand.

"S'pose," Roland said, frowning at the rain.

Charming checked his arrows. Three of them had pale, translucent heads, with an odd oily shimmer. "These had better work, they cost enough."

"They'll work if your aim's good enough. Even dragonstooth arrows won't get through dragonhide if you never actually *hit* the dragon."

"My aim is excellent, thank *you*."

"Then you've nothing to worry about."

"Don't forget the cloak, will you?"

"I won't forget the cloak."

THE PALACE WAS filled with grey light, subdued murmurs and the whisper of rain. The Grand Duke pushed his porridge about without eating it, his eyes fixed on Charming like a stray dog hoping for a biscuit. Ysoude, pale and shadowed about the eyes, seemed more concerned with getting her father to eat than doing so herself.

"Milady should try to eat something," Charming said, gesturing at her untouched plate. "A ride up the mountain, then a walk, and then"—he smiled reassuringly—"back down again! You'll need your strength."

Ysoude tried to smile back, and nibbled at a slice of apple.

Soon after, Charming and Roland were riding out on (in Charming's case) a fine horse, provided by the ducal stables, and (in Roland's) the Mostly Donkey. Ahead rode the Lady Ysoude, accompanied by the Captain of the Guard and two of her father's most valued knights.

Despite the drizzle, a small crowd had gathered. "Don't wave," Roland snapped at Charming under his breath. "This isn't a parade. They think their beloved Lady might be about to be served up brulée, with us as amuse bouche."

"Are you hungry or something?"

"Plain porridge is not a breakfast."

"It's very good for you."

"Not so much as a *sausage*," Roland grumbled, as the gates swung open. "I could really have gone a sausage."

Charming drew his horse closer to Ysoude, who raised her chin and smiled determinedly. "The captain showed you where?"

"Yes."

"The astrologer chose the site;" she said. "She has some knowledge of dragons, and they like to... to feed... from bare rock ledges. The attempt with the necklace proved her right."

"Did she have any other useful knowledge to impart?" Charming said.

Ysoude shook her head.

"How very unhelpful of her. Well, though you are no doubt a most tempting meal, Milady, please have no doubt that I will send the beast hungry to its grave. Now, let us talk of something more pleasant. I couldn't help but notice the guard's uniforms. Most... eye-catching. A long-standing tradition?"

Ysoude's smile was, this time, rather more genuine.

"A recent one. And entirely my fault, I fear. They used to dress all in brown, and as a child, I found it terribly dull. I asked, for my seventh birthday, that I be allowed to design new uniforms for them. My parents, being dear, indulgent creatures, allowed it. And Mama, bless her heart, was utterly delighted with them. She laughed so much... they still made her smile, even when she was very sick. Papa has refused to change them ever since."

"Well now *I* am utterly charmed, and intend to ask your palace tailor for a copy of the designs, so that I can dress my own guards the same. It will create a permanent link between our countries."

The lady actually laughed. "Oh, no, please don't force your poor guards into such a show!"

"Your guards seem to bear no grudges."

"Yes, well." Ysoude blushed. "They're good people."

"I believe they would do a great deal to please you. Don't you think, if I tell my guards the story, they will wear such uniforms with pride?" Charming glanced over his shoulder. "Roland, wouldn't *you* be delighted to wear something with such an adorable history? It would certainly be an improvement on your current ensemble. In fact I think you would look absolutely *spiffing*."

Roland's face was a picture, although perhaps one painted by someone in great mental distress. "If Your Highness insists," he managed to grind out.

"Don't tease the poor man," Ysoude said.

"I always tease him. He wouldn't recognise me if I didn't."

At that moment Roland yelped, and brushed furiously at the top of his head.

"Are you all right?" the lady asked.

"Fine," Roland muttered. "Bloody rowan berry."

"A… rowan berry?"

"He's allergic," Charming said. "Or something."

"How… inconvenient," said Ysoude. "Perhaps a hat?"

As they drew around the side of the mountain, the path ahead emerged from the cover of the trees, and the bare ledge became visible. The party fell silent. Charming surveyed the landscape with what appeared to be a knowing eye. Roland did likewise. Charming gave him a glance, and he nodded. Charming held up his hand to halt the party. "We should dismount here. Milady, I have a plan."

Roland rummaged in his pack and drew out a length of glimmering brocade.

"We intend to make a decoy," Charming explained. "The visit to the necklace last night inspired me. It only needs to be enough to draw the dragon close."

"And—forgive me—should you fail," Ysoude said, "then I can step forward and take the decoy's place."

"Should it come to it," said Charming. "But believe me, Lady, I do not intend to fail you. In the meantime, it is safest if you remain here, in the trees, out of sight. All of you," he said, looking at the guards. "You are the last line of defence."

The guards nodded.

Ysoude took Charming's hands. "Brave and noble prince," she said. "Good fortune go with you."

He raised one of her hands to his lips and kissed it.

"I ask no better fortune than your favour," he said, and smiled, and walked away up the path. Roland scuttled behind him, rolling his eyes so hard it was amazing they didn't fall right out of his head.

* * *

THE ROCKY LEDGE was wider than it appeared from below, with plenty of room for even a large dragon to land. Jutting from the base of the cliff was a spear of rock, that might almost have been designed for chaining people to.

Roland rummaged about, picking up two fallen branches and pulling from his copious pack a turnip, some wool, and the brocade he had earlier shown Lady Ysoude. He set these up against the spur of rock, made a couple of passes, and in remarkably short order, there appeared the figure of a woman, chained to the rock, her long hair and brocade gown blowing in the mountain breeze.

"Better hope that dragon turns up soon," he said. "She won't last long. And she don't smell right. If they hunt by scent it's, 'Goodnight ladies, enjoy being charcoal.'"

Charming pulled a cloak out of Roland's bag. Even in the grey, rainy light, it shimmered; blue-green from one angle, purple from another. "I can't believe you know so little about dragons."

"I don't know *everything,* Your Highness, I just know more'n you. Speaking of dragons..." Roland said, peering into the drizzle. "I think we've got company."

There, indeed, flying towards them with majestic speed, was the unmistakable shape of a dragon. It glimmered copper-bronze, its great wings flexing and beating the air.

Roland whistled. "Ooh, that's bigger than I remember. Look at them claws!"

As the dragon neared, the clouds broke, and a shaft of clear, glassy light caught Charming in its glow. He paused, and—possibly aware that from this angle anyone watching from the tree line could see him—struck a defiant pose, bow in hand.

"Stop messing about and get on, or those arrows'll go to waste!" Roland shouted.

Charming nocked an arrow. Its head shimmered in the weak light.

The dragon's head swung about, and it roared. The sound echoed off the mountainside, sending deer fleeing through the forest and birds clattering into the air.

"Think it's seen the poppet," Roland said.

Charming let fly.

The dragon swooped aside, the draft of its passage blowing Charming's hair back from his head. It was impossible to tell whether it had seen the arrow and dodged it or had simply never noticed its existence. Charming cursed and nocked another arrow.

"Watch it," Roland shouted. "It'll be close enough in a—"

With a hissing roar, a gout of flame scorched a line across the rock. Charming leapt backwards.

The air filled with the powdery acrid scent of hot shale. Charming stared for a second at the scorch mark marring the rock, bow and arrow forgotten in his hands. "Ow?" he said.

"You're fine," Roland said. "It wasn't even close; woulda missed you by miles. Let's move before it gets its eye in."

"Well, at least the cloak works," Charming said. "Didn't even feel the heat."

They ran around the corner, where the shelf narrowed and the terrain dropped steeply away. The smoke caught the dawn light and draped the valley in golden mist, which swirled and spun away in wreaths and vapours as the dragon made another turn.

Charming nocked the arrow again as the dragon swooped below the shelf and reappeared to the left. He took aim, the dragon twisted in mid-air, the arrow spun off into nowhere. The dragon directed another gout of flame along the stony ledge, where the few plants that had managed to cling there withered instantly to ash.

"Thought you said you could aim?" Roland shouted, as the dragon circled for another approach.

"Just getting my eye in!" Charming yelled over the rush and boom of the dragon's wings, and the roar of its indrawn breath.

"Well hurry up! It's already got *its* eye in!"

"Stop panicking!"

"Thought you were supposed to be"—Roland leapt backwards as another gout of flame seared unpleasantly close to his face—"good with a bow! Won competitions, you said! Beat some foreign whatsit called Lark or Thrush or something over the Manche, you said he was famous for it and you beat him, you said!"

"Trying to concentrate, here," Charming said through gritted teeth, narrowing his eyes and nocking his third and final dragonstooth arrow. "Just got to hit the weak spot."

"Can I remind you that *I'm your* weak spot?" Roland yelped. "Ow! I *felt* that!"

"Quiet." Charming drew, and aimed, and loosed.

It struck the dragon's side. The dragon jolted in mid-wingbeat and shrieked, its cry reverberating among the rocks and sending shale tumbling down the mountainside. Roland clapped his hands over his ears. The dragon spun in mid-air, as though seeking what had hurt it, convulsed, yawped, then tried to flame.

The dragon opened its mouth, but there was no flame, only a sad drift of pale smoke.

It gave them an incredulous look. Its wings beat once, twice, a third time, and went limp.

Agonisingly slowly, the dragon tilted head downwards. Wings fluttering helplessly in the updraught, it plunged, faster and faster, spiralling and trailing smoke, down into the fog.

"Gotcha!" Charming yelled. "Told you! Hah! Am I or am I not the best? Roland?"

"Your hair's on fire."

"*What?*" Charming shrieked, and clapped his hands to his head. "Nono*no*, not the hair, Roland, help me!"

"Oh, stop fussing, it was only smouldering. It's out now."

"But it *stinks*," Charming wailed, "and it'll be all *charred*, I shall have to wear a hat. How long does hair take to grow? Can you do a charm or something?

"Anyone would think you'd been horribly injured. It's *hair*. It'll grow back."

"Yours didn't."

"Where I come from, baldness is a sign of virility." Roland grinned and made a thrusting movement as disconcerting as it was suggestive.

"I really did not want to know that," Charming said.

Roland peered over the edge of the cliff. "Are you sure it's dead?"

"Got it right in the guts. You saw, didn't you?"

"It made a proper meal of it, all right. Probably a young one, never seen such bad aim. Not from a dragon, anyway."

"Was that a *remark*, Roland? Are you making *remarks*?"

"Who, me? Wouldn't dream of it, Your Highness." Roland leaned further over the cliff. "Can't see a thing, except a couple of broken trees. By the way, if you're thinking of applying that boot to my backside, can I remind you that you still need me?"

Charming sighed. "As if I didn't know. And do you *really* think I'd kick you off a cliff?"

"You're happy enough to kick an entire city off the cliff, metaphorically speaking. Why should I be any different?"

"What *are* you talking about?"

"If that dragon isn't dead..."

"So you distrust my aim, I *get* it, Roland, but I assure you it's dead. And even if it isn't, it's badly injured enough that it won't be coming back."

"At least for a while, by which time we'll be happily on the road and far away, right? Leaving the people with an even more pissed off dragon to deal with. Oh, well, maybe it'll calm down if it actually gets to eat the lady next time."

"Shut up. It's dead."

"Hey, no skin off my nose." Roland thought for a moment. "Skin off hers, though. And the rest of her. Shame."

"If you don't shut up I really *will* kick you off that cliff."

Roland, smirking, moved away from the edge. "Shall we head for the palace, and the cheers, and the acclaim, and the offer of marriage, then, O My Hero?"

Charming, ramming the lid on his quiver, shot him a look almost as smouldering as the surrounding landscape, and strode off.

LADY YSOUDE RAN towards them. "You're alive! Did you...? Is it...? I heard the most awful noises, I..."

"The dragon is slain, Milady."

Ysoude bit her lip, hard, and pressed her hands to her

eyes. "Thank you," she said, in the strained voice of someone determined not to cry. "Thank you."

At that moment Charming suddenly found himself enveloped in an armoured embrace, as the older of the two knights crushed him in the manliest of hugs. The knight recollected himself, flushed, and backed away. "Forgive me. I'm just so thankful..."

"Oh, really, no..." Charming said, shifting his shoulders to check that all his ribs were still intact.

The younger knight was entirely speechless, but clasped Charming's hand and shook it so vigorously his chainmail rattled.

The captain merely nodded, and blew his nose on a large linen kerchief.

Charming smiled, and made deprecating noises.

One of the knights slapped Roland on the shoulder, making him buckle slightly. "Splendid!" he said. "And so quick, too, after all these months!"

"Oh, he's a fast worker," Roland said. "Known for it, he is."

By the time they reached the ducal residence, they could barely move for the cheering, weeping crowd. Flowers, ribbons and kisses flew through the air. The ducal musicians played a triumphal air, with a great deal of oompah, enthusiastically if somewhat randomly accompanied by various tin whistles, fiddles and cowbells in the crowd. The smell of food from the kind of vendors who seem to appear via spontaneous generation whenever there's a crowd made Roland whimper and crane his neck.

The horses, trained for battle, remained remarkably stolid, even when a flower landed on one's head, or a ribbon draped another's neck, or a beaming if slightly confused child was held up to pat one's nose. Charming responded to all this with a look of modesty, mouthing, *Oh, no, really—no, I—please—* and patting the head of the occasional child with the enthusiasm of someone who associates children with stickiness.

Even Roland came in for some of the adulation. Much to his disconcertion a small, curly-haired child decided that he was the best thing she had ever seen, and flung herself at him from her father's arms with such enthusiasm he was forced to grab her before she fell into the street. He held her out at arms' length, looking bemused, as she giggled and beamed at him, until her father managed to catch up and take her back.

"You have a fan, Roland," Charming said.

"Leave it out," Roland growled. "I don't *do* children."

When Charming wasn't looking, however, Roland might possibly have looked over his shoulder and waggled his fingers at the child, who waved both chubby hands in the air yelling "Gah!"

"'Least someone appreciates me," he muttered.

Inside the palace the celebrations were even more intense. "Hip, Hip!" and variations on "For they are jolly good fellows!" rang through the ducal corridors. The mourning drapes had been whisked from the statues. The Duke emerged, beaming and weeping, his black garments replaced with robes of rich blue embroidered with gold. He seized Charming's hand in both of his. "Ah, my daughter—my friend—oh, how wonderful it all is! We've no food to feast you with, yet, but I've sent for some, the best that can be got!"

"Your Imperial Highness, I'm only too happy to have been of service," Charming said, gently removing his hand from the Grand Duke's surprisingly powerful grip. The Duke had not grown any larger, but it seemed as though the tremulous, agèd man had fallen away, revealing a bouncily enthusiastic and hearty fellow of middle years.

"Come in, come in, don't stand in the rain! Couldn't bear it if you got a cold! After all that! You're sure you're not hurt? Either of you?"

"Slightly scorched," Charming said with a smile. "It's nothing."

"But my physician shall attend you immediately!"

"No, no, Roland can do whatever's needed. Although a bath... I'm sure I smell like a damp fireplace!"

"Of course, of course. Prepare a bath for His Highness! And His Highness's... fellow here! And provide them with whatever they require! But you will feast with us, of course? Only in a straitened manner, you understand—it will take a while for the city to recover..."

"Of course," Charming said. His smile, to the observant, was beginning to appear slightly strained. This was perhaps not surprising in one who had fought a deadly beast. Most of the surrounding crowd simply did not notice.

"You look exhausted," Ysoude said quietly. "Please, Papa, let the Prince have a little time to himself."

Charming shot her a look of absolute gratitude. "Most kind," he said, and allowed himself to be ushered away, into a flurry of steaming jugs, and towels, and scented oils.

He was sunk in hot water up to his chin when Roland bounced unceremoniously into the room. "Wotcha."

"Give a chap a little privacy, can't you?" Charming said, but without his usual zest.

"Someone's got the megrims right and proper." Roland

frowned. "What *is* a megrim, anyway? Sounds like some sort of small burrowing insect to me. The sort that lays eggs under your skin and it goes all squidgy and manky and there's green stuff."

Charming merely sighed, resulting in a small cloud of scented foam taking off, to land on Roland's bald head. Roland grimaced and wiped it away. "You're going to smell like a very expensive brothel," he said. "Not that Her Imperial Virtuousness would know. Probably."

"Did you bother to take advantage of the bath that these nice people took the trouble to pour for *you*? Or are you going to remain as disgusting as usual?"

Roland shot him a shrewd look. "Oh, I washed," he said. "Just 'cause I don't want to smell like a Weekend Special at Madame Belinda's—'Extravagant Tastes Our Speciality'—doesn't mean I didn't *wash*."

"You amaze me."

"So," Roland said, sitting on the edge of the bath, "are we doing the usual?"

Charming sat up, sloshing. "No."

"No?"

"No. This place... I want to get out of here. No proposal, no hanging around smiling at everyone and being"—he waved at himself—"*Charming*. We'll get the necklace and head out the second we can."

"All right," Roland said, in a carefully casual tone. "So. Before or after the 'feast,' such as it'll be?"

"During," Charming said. "Everyone will be otherwise occupied. About three quarters of the way through, so they're all drunk. Well, probably not her, she doesn't seem the type. But everyone else."

"And what about the treasury?"

"To Goose egg with the treasury. The necklace is worth

more than everything else in there put together, by the sound of it."

"What if she's wearing it?"

"At the feast?"

"It's a celebration, why wouldn't she be wearing it?"

"Can you get it?" Charming said. "I *know* you can."

"Come on, you've seen the thing, it's the size of a piglet, it's bright red, and it's *sparkly*. I mean, I can *try,* but I'm a bit worn out after making that poppet. Can't guarantee no one'll notice."

"Why are you making this difficult?" Charming sank back down into the water and blew a despondent bubble.

"I'm not," Roland said. "But I'm finding it pretty interesting that *you* are. What's got under your skin, eh? A megrim?"

Charming invited him to perform an act upon himself that is as a rule impossible for most, though not all, beings.

"What, right now? You can't be *that* bored."

"Go *aw*—" Charming caught Roland's expression and stopped abruptly. "Go get me a towel."

Roland scowled. "As Your Highness commands," he said.

THE FEAST WAS less sparse than might have been expected. Delighted that their Lady was no longer at risk of being turned to charcoal—not to mention their crops, cattle, and selves—the townspeople had dug deep into their cellars. The result, while not as extravagant as some feasts that Charming had experienced on his adventures, was definitely celebratory.

Roland, in his post below the salt, dug in with a will.

Charming, on the other hand, ate sparingly—though he drank slightly more than was his habit. Ysoude also ate sparingly, but drank only water. She seemed to know the name of every servant, and asked after their families; she watched her father with tender concern, encouraging him to eat, and subtly added a little water to his wine when he was distracted. She checked frequently to make sure not a single guest, above or below the salt, was being neglected.

"I hardly like to," said Charming, as a third helping of roast lamb was placed in front of him. "Surely the townspeople..."

The serving maid gasped. "No, no, Your Highness, we'd gladly... After what you did? Anything. Anything for you." She blushed, curtseyed, apologised, and hurried away.

The Duke waved his goblet, spilling a bit of wine down his robe. "Now the dragon's gone, before it destroyed too much of the harvest, they're feeling a little extravagant. And grateful. They were riding up to the palace with stuff on carts, bless 'em. How would you feel about doing a little walkabout, tomorrow? Shake hands, pat children's heads, that sort of thing? They think you're the absolute knees of the bee, you know. Well, so do I." The Duke wiped his eyes, and patted Charming's wrist with a hand that was once again trembling with emotion. "Can't tell you enough. So grateful."

"Oh, now, really," Charming demurred, pushing his plate away. "No, my pleasure."

"Daughter's very taken with you," the Duke said, in what was probably supposed to be a whisper, but was audible all the way to where Roland sat. "Thought perhaps we could come to some arrangement."

Charming could not help glancing at the Lady Ysoude,

who gave him a look of helpless embarrassment and mouthed *Sorry*.

Before Charming could come up with a response, there was a flurry at one of the doors, and a figure in deep blue robes swept into the room.

They threw back their hood in a jangle of bracelets to reveal a mane of white hair, framing a gaunt face and large eyes rendered larger by the dramatic, if not perhaps very accurate, application of kohl. She fixed her gaze on Charming. "Ah, the man himself, the saviour of the hour! Look how everything has fallen out as I foresaw!"

"Our astrologer," the Duke said.

"I'd never have guessed," said Charming.

The astrologer simpered, holding out one thin, white hand. Charming bowed over it. The astrologer stared intently at the top of Charming's head, then drew her hand back to fling it in the air. "Lo!"

Charming blinked. Everyone paused, expectantly.

"More visions came upon me as I was contemplating the Infinite," the astrologer declared.

Those seated closest to Roland may have heard mutterings about, "Infinite my hairy backside, contemplating the smoke from one of those whiffy pipes more like."

"Visions all coloured in scarlet and crimson!" the astrologer went on.

This caused some disturbed looks and anxious whispering. Charming shot a glance at Roland, who was glowering at the astrologer and didn't notice.

"Not more bloodshed!" cried the Grand Duke. "Have we not suffered enough?"

"Oh, no, no." The astrologer smiled a smile with a definite condescending air about it. "Colours of *love*.

Of *passion*. Of most blessed matrimony! It is foreseen!"
She beamed at Lady Ysoude, who was biting her lip and
blushing furiously.

Charming gathered all his considerable aplomb and
smiled. "Ah, how wonderful to have such visions! And
how fortunate is this dukedom to have such talent at
its call! And should a man be so fortunate as to dare to
aspire to be the one to fulfil not one, but *two* prophecies,
why, he could only hold himself the luckiest man alive.
But the final decision, as always, must rest with the lady
in the case. Only the noblest of men could possibly be
worthy of such a match, and who but a popinjay would
dream of considering himself the noblest of men?" He
bowed to the astrologer again, and managed, on the
way back up, a glance at Lady Ysoude filled with such
puppyish hopefulness that she smothered a laugh in her
napkin. Her eyes, brimming with amusement, sparked
in Charming perhaps the first genuine smile of the
evening.

It quickly dropped away. As the astrologer went into
further raptures, drawing attention back to herself,
Charming gestured to Roland with a jerk of the head,
excused himself from the table and, meeting Roland in
the corridor, pulled him into a small empty room. "That
astrologer..." he hissed.

"Oh, *her*. Never heard such a load of malarkey in all
my puff." Roland's usual attempt at a whisper grated off
the walls.

"But all that stuff about scarlet and crimson... what if
she was talking about the necklace? What if she *knows*?
I think we should just leave."

"Oh, please," Roland said. "Even if she did get a
vision—I admit, it's possible, sometimes you find a

grain of corn in a pile of bullshit, but it usually didn't get there on purpose, if you follow me—she thinks it's about marriage." He tilted his head to one side, and rubbed his nose. "Personally, I don't think this is about the astrologer. I mean. We had that captain of the guard in Afalta who *told* the Queen, straight up, that you were far too interested in the treasury. In *front* of us. And you *still* smarmed your way through the proposal, danced all night and off we popped the next morning with our pockets stuffed. Something's—Oh!" Roland's eyes widened. "Oh-*ho!*"

"What do you mean Oh-*ho?*"

"You *like* her."

"What, the astrologer? Are you quite well?"

"The *lady.*"

"Ysoude? Of course I like her," Charming said. "She's a nice person, not that you'd recognise anything of the sort. But if you mean I *like* her—like, writing bad poetry and going all unnecessary at the sight of a rose 'like' her—then no. I've just got a bad feeling."

"Hmm."

"Stop it."

"What? I was clearing my throat."

"No, you weren't," Charming snapped. "When you clear your throat I can hear *chunks*. That just now was, albeit less revolting, nonetheless *intended* to annoy me, and I'll thank you to stop doing it."

Roland rolled his eyes. "So we're just going to go, then? Fine by me; unloading that necklace would take more than the usual amount of finesse. I mean, anyone who knows anything is going to recognise a piece of heritage flash like that in an eyeblink. Just because it's worth more than anything else we've picked up, no reason to take the risk. Yeah, we got rid of that diamond crown okay, but still. Since you've got a *feeling...*"

"Stop saying it like that. Fine. Fine. We'll take the wretched necklace, right now. And then we're straight out of here."

"You sure? Don't want to think about it some more while everyone wonders where the guest of honour has disappeared to, maybe starts sending people to look for you? The poor Lady, feeling all abandoned at the victory feast...?"

"Be quiet and come on."

The guards were not the same as the ones from the morning. In place of the two mountainous veterans stood an older, scrawny man with a snow-white but surprisingly stylish beard, and a bulky, round-faced lad who had some impressive muscles but whose beard was more ambition than substance. The older was sitting on a chair against the wall with his helmet tilted over his eyes, and the younger was sitting on the floor, frowning over a figure—either a short-legged horse or a lanky dog—he was whittling out of a piece of wood.

"Like Afalta?" Roland muttered.

"Like Afalta." Charming swayed out of the corridor, beaming. "I say... I say there! I seem to be a bit lost."

The younger guard jumped to his feet, and yanked the older one up by his arm. The older one coughed, shoved his helmet back, peered and blinked. "You one of the new servants? I dunno, in *my* day..."

"Shut up, Uncle!" The younger one elbowed his elder in the side. "It's *him*. Your Highness!" The young guard bowed, then—obviously feeling that was insufficient—bowed again. He seemed to find it difficult to stop.

Charming, eventually, waved his hands. "I say, no need

for that. Stop. Please, I'm getting dizzy. You fellows all on your own?"

"Everyone's at the feast," said the young guard. "'Cept the gate guards. We lost the draw. Hah. Joke's on them. *We* got to actually talk to *you*. Didn't we, Uncle? *Uncle!* Oh, dear, he's fallen asleep again. Sorry about that. He's too old for this, really," the young guard said in a whisper almost as loud as Roland's. "But he won't be told."

"Don't worry, don't worry. Tell you what." Charming pulled a gold coin out of his pouch. "If you can guide me back to the dining hall, I'm sure he won't wake up until you get back. Then he can tell you some story about how back in *his* day, guests knew their way about!" He grinned.

The young guard beamed. "Of course. Follow me, Your Highness." He shuffled and coughed into his fist. "Your Highness? What was it like? Fighting the dragon, I mean? Have you done it loads?"

"Oh, a few times. That's how I got the dragonskin cloak," Charming lied. In fact, Roland had acquired the cloak for him; the wizard it originally belonged to had an unfortunate taste for cards, and Roland's luck was, one might say, uncanny. But that was not what the guard wanted to hear.

As they strolled away, with occasional swishes and swoops as Charming demonstrated his more impressive moves (insofar as the confines of the corridor allowed), Roland made sure the sleeping potion he'd used on the other guard was still in effect, and let himself into the strongroom.

The candlelight woke tiny fires in each of the necklace's deep red stones, making it glimmer and flash like something adorning the neck of a demon queen.

"Lovely," Roland muttered. "Really lovely bit of kit, aren't you?" He took a moment more to admire it, then lifted it carefully from the statue of the old Duchess. "Sorry, ma'am, but you'll have to do without. Go for sapphires next time, they're more you. Trust me."

He laid the necklace on a piece of velvet, gently wrapped it, tucked it into his ever-present backpack, and left the room, locking it carefully behind him.

Roland glanced down at the sleeping guard and sniffed. A brief frown crossed his face. Then he shrugged and slipped away, down a succession of side passages and out into the night.

Charming was waiting for him at the back of the stables where the Mostly Donkey was tethered, biting his nails and pacing. "Have you got it?" he hissed.

"'Course I've got it. You could have got the beast."

"She always makes a fuss and tries to bite me. I didn't want her raising the alarm. Come on, let's get out of here."

"All right, all right, Mr Twitchy, give us a minute." Roland went into the stable. No one here needed a potion—all the staff were in the palace, celebrating.

The Mostly Donkey was in a stall by itself. Roland leaned on the stall door. The Mostly Donkey laid back its ears and drew in a breath to bray.

"Quiet," Roland said, pointing at it.

The Mostly Donkey's lips froze over its teeth. Its chest heaved. Then it shut its mouth, glared, and kicked at the rear of the stall.

"None of that, either," Roland said. "Come on."

He put its bridle on and led it out of the stall.

An Interlude

N A BARN tucked into the trees near the foot of the mountain where the fight had taken place, lamplight slid over the heaving sides of a great gleaming copper-bronze shape.

One woman knelt at its side, solicitously. Two more stood nearby.

The dragon hissed, turning its head to look reproachfully at Marie Blanche.

"I know, I know," the Princess soothed. "There, look, all finished."

The dragon inspected the small scratch—now covered with a strong-smelling mulch of herbs, salt water, and mud—and jetted smoke from its nostrils.

Marie Blanche waved smoke away from her face, coughing. "Now, that *is* rude," she said. "I have done my best. You know we did not intend you should actually be injured."

The dragon huffed and turned its head away in a pointed fashion.

Marie Blanche sighed and got to her feet. "Try to keep still," she said. "And do not fly until morning, at least."

The dragon made a deep grumbling noise that went on for some time.

"Yes, I understand," Marie Blanche said. "We will make arrangements. Come on," she said to the other two. "Leave her be, she wants to sleep." She ushered the other women out of the barn.

"What arrangements?" Doctor Rapunzel said.

"She has demanded an increase in the fee. Not unreasonable, under the circumstances. I agreed."

Doctor Rapunzel raised her brows. "You took that on yourself, I see."

"Well, who else is to do it?" Marie Blanche pointed out. "You do not speak her tongue."

"And?"

"Thirty more head of sheep, and thirty of pigs." Marie Blanche said. "And a shepherd and swineherd, their wages paid for five years. She wants the herds for breeding, and they know we are better at keeping them in good health."

"That is double the stock she asked for! Can she not pay for it out of her hoard?"

"It is the males who establish hoards, to attract the queens. She does not yet have a mate. And she did not expect dragonstooth arrows!"

"Perhaps *you* should have expected them?" Doctor Rapunzel said. "You *are* the expert huntress."

"Do you have any idea how rare they are? I had no way of knowing he would have such a thing. We were fortunate they were poorly made, and his aim imperfect, or the result could have been a great deal worse."

"Yes, it could!" Bella snapped. She had been uncharacteristically silent since the fight. "He could have been *killed*. You promised she'd be careful! His *hair* was on fire!"

"I told you," Marie Blanche said. "Dragons use fire for territorial display and mating dances. They do not target their prey, or each other. When I saw that wretched cloak of his, though, I was worried. If that skin had been from one of her clan, no bargain we could make would have saved him."

"She still set fire to his hair!"

"That was his own carelessness," Marie Blanche said. "Either he forgot to put up the hood of the cloak, or failed to secure it. And whether or not he succeeded, he *intended* to *kill* her."

"Well, he did believe her to have attacked the country, and that *she* intended to kill Lady Ysoude," Doctor Rapunzel pointed out. "I think that everyone's intentions, clear or otherwise, are irrelevant to the issue. Between us, we can afford to make the required payment, yes?"

"I will have to send to home," Marie Blanche said, "but yes."

"Is that all you care about?" Bella said.

"We are *all* the poorer for our interactions with the Prince," said Doctor Rapunzel. "And as I, at least, do not have a country and its coffers at my back, I must make my own way. So yes, I care that he has robbed me, and continues to cost me money, of which I do not have an endless supply."

"Neither do I," said Marie Blanche. "Thanks not only to Charming, but to my stepmother and at least one other thief, my country's coffers are not precisely overflowing."

"And you think what he stole from me means nothing?" Bella said.

"I understood he stole a great deal from you," said Doctor Rapunzel. "Why would you believe we think it means nothing?"

"Because he didn't steal either of your hearts!" Bella burst out. "I don't believe either of you loved him, not really, or you wouldn't... wouldn't..." The rest dissolved in tears.

Marie Blanche's eyes blazed. "You think *money* is all he stole from me?"

Doctor Rapunzel cast Marie Blanche a warning glance and put an arm around Bella's shoulders. "It has been a long day, and we are all overwrought. I don't think you have eaten today, have you? These kind people have supper ready for us. Food will make you feel better. Go wash your face and make yourself even more beautiful, and then come down and eat, hmm?"

Bella blew her nose and straightened her shoulders. "I'm sorry," she said. She turned to Marie Blanche. "I *am* sorry."

"It is of no matter," Marie Blanche said, staring past her into the dark wood.

Bella sighed, and slipped away to a side door of the main house.

"You indulge her too much," Marie Blanche said. "She is a child."

"Yes, she is," Doctor Rapunzel said. "She is a tender plant still with a deal of growing to do. She is also a child who has at least in the past been of great interest to the Good Folk. I would prefer not to risk their anger. Or even their attention, if I can avoid it."

"Gah." Marie Blanche slapped her gloves against her thigh in irritation. "Better they turn their anger on the Prince."

"I rather hope they will not. If he is turned into a frog, or a tree, or some such thing, we may never recover what he has stolen."

"So we must listen to her simperings and handle her like a day-old foal. And if she decides, in the crunch, that her loyalties lie with him?"

"She is young and overindulged, not stupid. I hope that sufficient evidence against him will change her mind," Doctor Rapunzel said.

"Evidence is not always enough, in the face of infatuation," Marie Blanche said. "Why are you so defensive of her? I find it hard to believe her charms have blinded you to the danger she represents."

Rapunzel sighed. "Perhaps I am jealous."

"You? Why? Not the gifts, surely?"

The doctor laughed softly. "No, not the gifts. What I have, I have earned, and I take pride in that. I envy her belief that there is good, even in someone like Charming. I lost that early, and am unlikely to regain it."

"I thought *I* was the cynic," Marie Blanche said.

"Well, and so you are. Perhaps we need someone like her, to balance us out, hmm?"

Marie Blanche shrugged. "I think I prefer to remain cynical," she said. "It's safer."

They walked on to the large farmhouse, an L-shaped building, three stories high, with a red-tiled roof, white painted walls and a dozen small windows aglow with light.

SEATED AT THE large table in the farmhouse kitchen were the Grand Duke and the Lady Ysoude. The latter looked considerably less harrowed than before, though still with a dark streak under one eye that on close inspection appeared to be makeup, so that one side of her face looked rather more weary than the other.

There was also a sharp-bearded gentleman, a small woman with white hair, a much larger woman with notably muscular forearms, and a curly-headed gentleman. All parties present had been regaled with a hearty meal and a generous supply of ale, wine, port, and some of the local pear cider (yet another local brew noted for its exquisite fragrance, rumoured health-giving properties, and ability to send the unwary into a coma unless treated with extreme respect). The usual formalities had been flung out of the window, at least temporarily.

Doctor Rapunzel and Marie Blanche seated themselves. The house cat, a normally standoffish creature, immediately installed itself on Marie Blanche's lap, and the Grand Duke's spaniel leaned against her knee. The cat glared at this insolence, but decided it was too comfortable to move.

A moment later, Lady Bella appeared—and as always, all eyes turned to her (except those of the cat, who had gone to sleep, and the dog, who was still gazing adoringly up at Marie Blanche).

The Grand Duke beamed at everyone. "What a day! I do hope the poor creature isn't too badly hurt. Magnificent display, I must say. Watched from the roof of the palace. Better than the fireworks we had for your birthday, m'dear."

"A *little* more alarming than the fireworks, when one was that close," Lady Ysoude said.

"You got far *too* close," her father scolded. "You were supposed to stay in the trees."

"Well, I couldn't resist," Ysoude said, grinning. "I must admit I was hoping he would get at least a *little* scorched, after what he did to poor Melinda Buckforth-Welland. She *did* seem well, yes?" Ysoude asked Bella, who had taken a minute slice of pie and was doing very little about eating it.

"Oh, yes, very well," Bella said.

"I always thought Melinda was the sort to see through a man like that," Ysoude went on "Though of course, in the circumstances, she can hardly be blamed for falling for his act. I mean, if I hadn't known what he was like, I might have done the same. Hollow as a walnut shell! He did have an amazing capacity to jump, though. I swear he leapt *over* the flame at least once!"

"Quite the athlete," said Dance. "Tempted to ask him to join the troupe, one way and another. And you, your Imperial Highness, Milady. That was a fine show you put on."

The Grand Duke giggled and stroked his beard. "Well, I did do a bit of acting in my younger days, you know. School, and so on. Such fun to do it again!"

"You were quite shameless," Lady Ysoude informed him fondly. "All that wailing and weeping and black drapery, I almost began to believe I was doomed myself! And you two"—she pointed at Dance and Gilda—"were *terrible* guards."

"I dread to think what your captain thought of us," said Dance.

"You made a simply marvellous astrologer, though," said the Grand Duke to Mouse.

"Oh, she was fun." Mouse scratched her head. "But that wig itches something fierce, even after you take it off. I need a better one."

"I was wondering," the Grand Duke said. "Would you be interested in a permanent posting? Official acting troupe of Eingeten? You could buy all the wigs you want, then. What do you say?"

The troupe looked at each other. "It's incredibly generous of your Imperial Highness," Dance said, carefully. "And we wouldn't wish to insult you..."

"Oh, please." The Grand Duke waved his glass and added another stain to his robe. "Please be honest. You'd rather keep to the road? A new town every few days, new vistas on the horizon?"

"Well," Dance said, "Yes. For a few more years, at least."

"Quite understand," the Grand Duke said. "Liked to travel myself, as a younger man." He sounded wistful.

"Perhaps a compromise could be reached," Lady Bella said. "A return visit, once a year? And then the Duke could hear all your stories, and you'd be assured of at least one regular engagement, yes? I should imagine that could be quite useful in your line of work."

"Maybe not *all* our stories," Gilda murmured. Mouse nudged her in the ribs.

"Sounds like an excellent idea," said the Duke.

"It does indeed." Dance bowed. "We should be honoured. And in the meantime, if you ladies need us again, a message to the Running Hare at Calmwater will always find us."

That decided, more alcohol was obviously required to toast the arrangement.

"So the Prince has got away with the necklace," said Mouse, blinking. "Um... maybe it's the cider, but I still don't understand: if he's robbed all of you, why let him get away? Not that it's any business of mine, your royalnesses," she added, hastily. "And doctor."

Marie Blanche looked at Doctor Rapunzel. "*Some* of us thought that using an enchanted necklace to track him was a better idea than simply capturing him," she said.

"Oh, that necklace!" Ysoude said. "Great-Grandmamma adored it, and insisted it be worn for all state occasions. I've never been able to stand the thing. Makes one look as though one's throat's been cut."

"Is it really valuable?" Mouse said.

"Well, not quite as valuable as the Prince believes," said the Grand Duke, "but not paste, either."

"We couldn't risk that," Doctor Rapunzel said.

"And you let him run off with it?" Mouse asked.

"Happy to sacrifice it to a good cause," the Grand Duke said. "Besides," he gave a small shudder, "reminded me far too much of my grandmother. Terrifying woman."

Doctor Rapunzel said, "With luck, Charming will take it to some hideout, with the other loot. He cannot possibly have got rid of everything he's stolen, and much may still be restored to its former owners."

"Well I hope we don't live to regret letting him slip," Marie Blanche said.

Lady Bella said nothing at all.

Another Interlude

HERE ARE PLENTY of places in a landscape like this where, if someone chooses, they might pose dramatically against the skyline. A cloak may be helpful, depending on the desired effect. But here, for once, there is no cloak, no noble stance. Instead, a hunched figure regards the spectacular sprawl of a brilliant sunset, the reds and golds of the sky echoed in the ember-like glow of the turning leaves below. A murmuration of starlings twists and swirls across the sky like a silk scarf waving in the breeze, before pouring into the forest and disappearing.

The figure has its hands in its pockets, and might, if it were an artwork, be titled *Man Having a Thorough Brood*.

"YOU WANT SUPPER or what?" said Roland. "'Cause we need to get a move on if we're going to get anywhere before dark."

"Am I a bastard, Roland?"

"'Scuse me?"

Charming, still staring out over the valley, said, "I'm asking, am I a bad person? Not just, you know, a rogue, a devil-may-care troubadour of hearts, a man to leave the ladies sighing but smiling... all right, all right, there's no need to make retching noises, Roland. I don't know why I bothered asking you a serious question."

"Nor do I. Not that one, at any rate. You've met me."

"So? Doesn't mean you can't have a moral perspective, does it?"

"Well, I can *have* one. Whether it's one that's exactly what you're looking for... I mean, why are you asking? Seriously? Why'd you care, all of a sudden?"

"No reason," Charming said, with studied casualness, flicking a bit of leaf from his sleeve. "A man can have a philosophical moment, can't he?"

"So it wouldn't be anything at all to do with a certain lady, then?"

"Pfff," Charming said.

"Or the way she seemed like someone who actually gave a toss about her people, and doted on her dad. Mind you, the one with the apple was like that, too."

"Nothing to do with that."

"Universally adored... but then so was whasserface, the sleeping one. Smart... but there've been quite a few smart ones, as I recall, specially that lass in the tower. Still *something's* given you a poke in the place people usually have a conscience."

"She was *nice*, all right?" Charming snapped. "I *liked* her."

"Well, she liked you too. They all do. And now she knows she's been done over, she probably doesn't like you any more. Never bothered you before."

"I wish you wouldn't put it like that. We're not common thieves. At least, *I'm* not." Charming kicked a stone over the edge of the cliff.

"Well, that's true enough," Roland said, backing away from kicking range, just in case. "*You* rob entire kingdoms, and you don't even use an army to do it. That's pretty uncommon."

"I don't know why I should care. I mean, so she won't like me anymore. She's just judging me on one thing, it's not like she actually *knows* me."

"Of course, if the dragon *does* prove not to be dead, she'll have another reason to dislike you. Assuming she survives, that is. If she gets toasted, well, at least you'll know she's not out there, *disliking* you."

"Oh, shut up." Charming said. "Why are we still hanging around here, anyway? I thought you wanted supper?"

Roland opened his mouth, thought better of it, shook his head, and went to fetch the Mostly Donkey.

The Perils of Fairy Circles

ND HERE, A hunting lodge, with gabled windows, overlooking a lawn now striated with long tree shadows by the setting sun. Rabbits crop the grass. Every few seconds one of them sits up, ears twitching, wary. They are all over the lawn, except within the ring of darker grass, still just visible in the fading light.

At a mere fifteen rooms, its owner considers the lodge little more than a cottage, but it is snug and well appointed. He has happily leant it out for what he believes to be a romantic assignation. It smells of woodsmoke and roasting meat, and slightly of damp.

Fortunately its current occupants do not require staff for the night. It is hard to keep staff, here. They complain of odd lights and whisperings, start to behave strangely, abandon their posts without warning, packing their few possessions in a cloth and fleeing for the nearest village. Occasionally, forgetful creatures that they are, they don't even take their things, and never seem to find their way to the village, either.

*   *   *

IN WHAT WAS normally the dining room, a long table was strewn with paper and quills, a small astrolabe that gleamed and swayed in the lamplight, various other intricate devices and a cage in which two white doves shuffled and cooed.

"He is taking a very *wandering* route." Doctor Rapunzel frowned at the map in front of her. Glimmering red light shifted over it, concentrating in a single spot that left behind a faint trail, like a tiny comet.

"He probably suspects he is being hunted," said Marie Blanche.

"He *is* being hunted," Rapunzel said. "And has been since he left his father's kingdom, if our information is correct. We are not the only ones seeking him out. A hunted animal is, rightly, cautious."

Bella, who had been making kissing noises at the doves, spun around. "Stop it! Stop talking about him as though he's a... a..."

"Rat?" said Marie Blanche mildly. "Weasel? Rabid dog? Oh, no, you prefer to see him as a stag: nobly at bay, fighting for his life against the ravening hounds..."

"If all you two can do is snipe at each other like children, please do it elsewhere," the good doctor said. "This requires concentration."

"All you care about is catching him," Bella said.

"Well, yes." Doctor Rapunzel raised her eyebrows at Bella, then returned to the map.

"And then?" said Bella.

"And then justice," said Marie Blanche.

"Vengeance, you mean." Bella said.

"No," Marie Blanche said. "I wish to see him in chains, yes. I wish to see him pay for his crimes, yes. Do I wish done to him what he did to me, to my father? No. *That* would be vengeance."

"I do not think it would be possible, in any case," said Doctor Rapunzel. "To suffer as his victims have, he would have to be capable of feelings for other people than himself."

"He *does!*" said Bella. "I know he does! There's a reason for all this!"

"My dear"—Doctor Rapunzel shifted her shoulders, sat back and sighed—"I know he convinced you. He convinced all of us. And I, at least, should have known better than to trust the appearance of kindness. His is no less a performance than we had from those players."

"Please don't call me 'my dear,' when you despise me," Bella said.

Doctor Rapunzel pressed her fingers to the bridge of her nose. "I do not despise you. I think your life has been, in general, a gentle one. Reality for most of us is somewhat sharper."

"I was *cursed*, in case you've forgotten."

"To sleep," Rapunzel said. "Protected by everything around you. And you woke in safety, wealth, and love."

"You despise me because I was *loved?*"

"Despise? No. Envy, perhaps, yes. One must admit one's faults before one can correct them. Now will you *please* let me concentrate?"

Bella's eyes glimmered with tears, like caught starlight, and she left the room without another word.

MARIE BLANCHE STARED into the fire. "I am beginning to think perhaps this was a mistake."

"The necklace?"

"Her. She is still under his spell."

"Yes, she is." Rapunzel sighed. "But I should not have spoken so to her."

"I recovered from my obsession with the man. So did you."

"And your father?"

Marie Blanche felt a jab at the thought of her father. "What has he to do with this?"

"When your father succumbed to *his* obsession, you bore the brunt of it."

"I do not see how that is relevant!"

"Don't you?"

"Tell me, doctor, what do *you* want?"

"I want the return of my property."

"And?"

"There must be an *and*? Or is it simply that you do not trust me, either?"

"That's not—"

"Studying the arcane arts does not make me your stepmother. *Or* mine. Or make it any easier to concentrate when surrounded by people who insist on *talking* at me." The sorceress rolled the map up, thrust it into its case, snapped the catch shut, and left the room.

Marie Blanche muttered the worst words she knew, in three human languages and one known only to eagles. She stretched out a hand to where it would normally have found the top of a dog's head and, that comfort missing, snatched up a poker and attacked the fire until the sparks flew.

She spent the next hour going over her understanding of the dragon tongue—the dragon had been amused by some of her mistakes, and they could have proved expensive had the beast been less eager to come to an arrangement.

Then she went to the stables, only to find that the horses had everything they needed. She was reduced to polishing some perfectly clean tack and re-organising what little equipment had been left by the owner, knowing full well that his staff would probably rearrange it all the moment they returned.

She wondered how the stables at home were being managed, and if her favourite hunter was being properly exercised, and if Papa had been out hunting at all. And at the back of her mind, the doctor's words itched and stung, like an insect bite that could not be reached to scratch it.

BELLA STOOD ON the steps of the lodge, wrapping her arms about herself. Though it was autumn, the night was unseasonably mild, almost like midsummer. All around were soft shiftings and rustlings. Stars scattered across the sky, jewels cast by a hand careless in its generosity.

Bella was not afraid of the night. She had never had reason to be.

She kicked off her shoes and walked barefoot onto the cool grass. Her insides churned. She hated arguments, and unkindness. She hated *being* unkind, and argumentative. And for all their determination to hunt the poor Prince down like a—yes, a stag—she liked and admired these women, they seemed so knowledgeable, so... well, so *grown up*. Especially the doctor, whose life had begun so hard, and had nearly been taken so early, and which she had *made* into something through her own efforts.

And though Marie Blanche was sharp and bitter, she had been so cruelly betrayed by her stepmother, and had had to run a kingdom by herself when she was hardly more than a child. Younger than Bella had been when the curse fell on her.

Bella, on the other hand, had never had to organise so much as a party by herself. Even when she had travelled about, speaking to the other women who had encountered Charming, everything had been made easy for her. Could she have done it unaided? Could she have made her way from country to country, inveigled her way into each of those noble houses, with nothing but her own resources, without the gifts of the Good Folk and the power of her family at her back?

What, like Charming did? And would you, too, have lied, and stolen, and run away?

But she would not listen to that voice. *He had a reason!* Her heart cried out.

They all thought that...

She began to cry in earnest, head bent, tears dropping onto the grass, and did not notice when she crossed the circle of darker grass, and her tears fell within the ring: one drop, then two, then three...

"Why, my darling child, what do you do so far from home and weeping as though your heart would break?"

Bella looked up with a gasp.

The voice was softly musical and full of gentle laughter; the figure it came from was tall, and had skin as pale as ivory. Though there was no moon that night, the silver hair that fell like a cloak to the woman's thighs glowed as though bathed in moonlight. Her eyes glimmered the pale, frosty lilac of dawn.

"My Lady!" Bella started to curtsey, then—remembering she was wearing breeches—bowed instead.

The figure's laugh rang like a glass bell. "Oh, now, such formality! Bella, do you not know me?"

"I'm sorry, my Lady…"

"I am Ione. I was at your christening, little one. Not so little anymore, but grown into quite the beauty. Beauty should never weep. Especially when you were saved from my sister's curse, by my hand."

"I'm sorry," Bella said again.

"Tell me what has made you so sorrowful, my sweet. The sorrows of mortals—ah, how cruel they are! Have you lost someone?"

If Bella had not been still tearful, and startled, and not sure where to look (since the Lady wore nothing but her own silver hair), she might have seen an expression that did not match the beauty of the face that wore it. Something like curiosity, and something more like greed, and certainly very little of kindness.

But when Bella looked up, there was nothing in that lovely face but gentle concern.

"The Prince," Bella said. "The one who was there when I woke. He… he left."

"He *left*? The Prince who was foretold? The very picture of love?"

"Yes."

"That was not what was supposed to be," the Lady said, a presentiment of frost creeping into her voice. "That is not the story. Why did he leave? Was he tempted away? Some creeping charm or sneaking spell, pulling a thread and spoiling the weave?"

"Do you think it might have been?" Bella said. "Because they say he robbed the treasury, and that he's done it to other people too, but I'm sure that he wouldn't have done so without good reason! If he was under a spell, that would explain everything!"

"I'm sure it would," the Lady said.

"Unless it…" Bella looked at her feet. "Unless it was me."

"What do you mean?"

"I have been given everything," Bella said. "Sometimes I think, without the gifts, would I be anything at all? Maybe that's what he saw. Underneath, there's just… me. Maybe that's why he left."

This time the Lady's voice was hard and cold as eternal winter. "Do you *reject* the gifts? Were they not fine enough?"

"Oh, no, not at all!" Bella said hastily. "How could I be so ungrateful? No, it's just that I wonder who I'd be without them, that's all."

"Foolish child," the Lady said. "What does it matter? You are what you are, with all your gifts, and they must not be wasted! Now, what is to be done?"

"The others… They want to hunt Prince Charming down," Bella said. "And I don't think they're going to listen to him. They won't listen to *me*."

"Others?"

"Doctor Rapunzel, and Princess Marie Blanche. It seems he robbed them, too. They don't believe he's good at heart. I mean, I know he's done bad things, I'm not completely—"

The Lady waved her hand again. "It is of no matter. What matters is that he is the one that was foretold. That is how it is supposed to be."

"Well…" Bella pushed her toes through the soft grass. How simple, how nice, to be grass—or better still, a rabbit, with nothing to worry about but *eating* grass—though it seemed, when she looked around, that all the rabbits had disappeared.

"Ah, my little one, you seem confused, and sad. How can it be otherwise? You and the Prince are supposed—

destined, *fated*—to be together, is it not so?"

"I thought so, yes." Bella said.

"And you are quite right."

"Truly?"

"Truly."

"Then what should I do, Lady?"

"Find your Prince and be with him. Declare your love, and he will declare his, and how perfect it will be!"

"But what if he *doesn't* love me?" Bella said, her voice smaller than a blade of grass.

"Do you want my help or not?" The Lady's eyes narrowed, and despite the warmth of the night, Bella felt a little cold.

"Yes, Lady."

"Then do as I tell you, and all will fall out as it should."

The Lady gave a whistling cry. The lake at the end of the lawn rippled, and shivered, and heaved, and out of it rose a black horse of uncanny beauty, its coat as glossy as a beetle's wing, its mane a cloud of silky threads, and its eyes as silver as moonlight.

"He will bear you towards your Prince, as swiftly as a dream; and as swiftly as a dream your Prince will come to you," the Lady said. "But he will carry you only until the dawn, and then he will return to me. So go now!"

Hardly knowing how she got there, Bella found herself on the horse's back, without saddle or bridle, clinging to its mane.

"But..." she said, looking back at the house, and the single lit window where no doubt Doctor Rapunzel was still working.

"Ride," the Lady said, and slapped the horse's rump, so that it shot forward, bearing Bella away, into the night, without a cloak to her back or shoes on her feet.

*   *   *

ROLAND WOKE TO see Charming standing by the window of the small, scruffy inn. He was staring at the night.

"What's going on?"

"I've been a fool," Charming said. "She was The One, Roland."

"What? Who?"

"The Lady Bella dei' Sogni. I had a dream... I have to go."

Charming turned away from the window and made for the door.

"Wait a minute! What?" Roland hauled his breeches on over his sagging underwear and shoved his feet into his shoes. "Oi!"

But Charming had already left the room. Roland scurried after him, and caught up with him in the inn yard.

"I need a horse," Charming said. "A fast one." His eyes were open, but they were focussed on something far away.

"Hey, Yer Highness," Roland said. "Wake up!"

"I am awake. Awake for the first time. Oh, my love, wait for me, let me fly to your arms..."

"I smell magic," Roland said. "Well, I don't—life'd be a lot easier if I *could*—but if ever I saw someone under the influence..."

"Yes, it's magic," Charming said, wandering towards the stables. "Pure magic. Wonderful. I've never felt this way, Roland, it's like floating..." He splashed through a suspiciously noisome puddle, and took no notice, despite being in his stocking feet.

"Oh, Bloody Norah," Roland said. "Look, you haven't even got yer boots on!"

"What do I care for boots, when my love is waiting?" Charming said. "Which of these horses do you think is fastest?"

Roland attempted to get between Charming and a lean chestnut gelding who was shifting uncomfortably and side-eyeing the Prince.

"You're going to get yer head kicked in," Roland shouted. "That horse can sense it too. You're under a spell!"

"Poor Roland," Charming smiled down at him. "You've never known true love, have you?"

"No more have you!" Roland snapped.

"Maybe one day you'll find... someone... some*thing*..." Charming frowned, his floaty bliss briefly derailed.

Roland ignored this, digging frantically in his pockets. "Conker... no... yarrow root... no... dammit... can you at least wait until I get my pack?"

"Love waits for no man!" Charming declared and swung a saddle onto the horse, which bucked. Charming clucked at it. "Or horse."

Roland ran for the other end of the stables and whipped a bridle and saddlecloth onto the Mostly Donkey, leapt on, and just made it in time to see Charming, atop the kicking, balking, sidestepping horse, exit the inn yard.

Swearing with inventive vigour, Roland followed.

DOCTOR RAPUNZEL WAS not sure what woke her, but she was immediately bolt upright in the dark. She reached for the lamp, then hesitated.

Some things fear the light. Other things are better not illuminated.

Instead, she listened. A soft night breeze stirring the branches, the faint crunch of a deer eating grass. Doctor

Rapunzel lowered her feet to the floor and moved quietly towards the window.

Sweet air, a little warm for the season, swirled through the open casement. The moon spilled a wash of light across the lawn.

There were smudges in the dew-laden grass, perhaps footprints.

Doctor Rapunzel scooped her jacket from the chair and pulled it on over her nightgown. She scanned the table, picked up a vial and a small pouch, and trod softly to the door. She stood for a moment, listening, then inched the door open, catching her breath as the hinges groaned.

Nothing stirred in the corridor.

Cat-quiet, she moved to Marie Blanche's room and edged open the door.

Quiet breathing, the rustle of linen as the Princess stirred in her sleep.

Doctor Rapunzel closed the door and went to Bella's room.

When she got there, she paused, resting her hand on the doorframe. *Please, you silly girl, please be asleep in your bed*.

But when she pushed open the door, the moonlight fell stark and undeniable across rumpled, empty sheets.

Doctor Rapunzel bit her lip, and glanced over her shoulder at Marie Blanche's room.

Not yet.

She crept down the stairs, placing her feet at the edges so the boards would not creak. She was suddenly, desperately hungry. In just this way had she snuck down the stairs of the Rotterturm to steal a bite of cheese from the kitchen after three days without food.

You are not in the Rotterturm now. She turned away from the tempting smells of the kitchen, where a dried ham hung in the pantry and a fat wheel of cheese sat smugly in its wrappings.

The door of the lodge was open.

Doctor Rapunzel turned slowly in the hallway, wary as a deer, the vial in one hand and the pouch in the other, stretching her senses for the tang of magic, or the slightest sound or shift of air that would suggest an intruder in the house.

Nothing.

She slipped out of the door and down the steps, watching, listening.

The faint smudges in the dew seemed spaced rightly for footprints. Her imagination painted Bella, barefoot, walking across the lawn, and then...

The footprints ended.

Focussed as she was on the prints, Rapunzel almost stepped into the fairy ring herself before she realised it was there. She stepped back hastily and slipped on the dewy grass, barely avoiding a fall, feeling her heart clatter in her chest.

Was there the faintest sound of laughter, as she stumbled?

She raised her chin and walked back to the house, holding herself rigid, shut the door behind her, and leaned against it for a moment with her eyes shut.

Then she ran up the stairs to the room where Marie Blanche slept.

"We have trouble."

Marie Blanche blinked and squinted at the lamplight, then scanned the doctor's face. "What has she done?"

"I think it is more what has been done to her. You are the huntress, come tell me what you see."

Marie Blanche stood and looked at the lawn, hooding the lamp with her hand. "These clearer prints, these are yours?"

"Yes."

Marie Blanche followed the footprints, bent and touched the grass, careful not to enter the fairy ring, and sniffed the air. Then she stood for a while frowning at the woods.

"She walked to the ring, and then her footprints simply end. She did not leave—at least, not on foot. She stood for a while, here." Marie Blanche pointed to a set of prints that seemed no different to Doctor Rapunzel's eyes than all the rest. "And this... see that patch, there? And that?" The doctor peered, but could see nothing. "The grass is bruised, as though someone else stood upon it, but they barely bent the stems."

"Ah. Well, it is a fairy ring," Rapunzel said. "And the laws of weight and pressure do not always apply to the Good Folk."

"And here, just at the edge of the ring: a hoofprint, I think. Again, it barely bent the stems, so..."

"A fairy horse."

The two women looked at each other, and as one, turned away and walked back to the lodge, and closed the door.

There is something comforting about kitchens. They are places where the everyday work that keeps everything else running is done: where stomachs are filled and wounds are dressed, where tears are dried and comforted with apples—or biscuits. Here, Doctor Rapunzel lit the fire and pulled the kettle over it, and they sat on the hard plain chairs.

"So one of the Good Folk came and took her up upon their horse, and rode away with her." Marie Blanche said. "It seems she called on them for assistance, and they gave it."

"I am not so sure," Rapunzel said. "You think she went willingly?"

"They have showered her with gifts," Marie Blanche said. "Why would she not go willingly?"

"One of them also cursed her," the sorceress pointed out. "But then again, being Bella..."

"Being Bella, whether or not she summoned them, she undoubtedly believed a member of the Good Folk who appeared to her in the middle of the night is kind, and generous, and without any sort of ulterior motive whatever... How that girl survived travelling the courts of the continent without being robbed, married or buried is entirely beyond my comprehension," Marie Blanche said.

"In any case, she is gone. We must find her."

Marie Blanche chewed her lip. "Even if I had my dogs, tracking a fey horse is beyond them—or me. And..."

"And?"

"Dragons, I can negotiate with," Marie Blanche said. "Wild boar, giant bears, enchanted stags, all these I can manage. Sea serpents, probably. But I have no idea how to deal with the Good Folk!"

"Carefully," Doctor Rapunzel said. "And we cannot simply abandon Bella to her fate."

"I do not say we should. I am merely pointing out that we have few resources against a powerful fey, especially since we do not know which one took her, or why."

"*I* have a few resources," Doctor Rapunzel said, "But you are right." She drummed her fingers on the table. "Let's see... There were seven of the Folk at Bella's christening, but there are, I think, two main possibilities. Either it was Ione, who turned aside Carabosse's curse, or it was Carabosse herself. If it was any other, then I do not even know where to begin. If Ione took her, then I suspect what she desires is to have the marriage to Charming take place. Charming, after all, turned up in the right place at the right time to fulfil the tale, and Ione wants her version of the tale to take place. If it was Carabosse..."

"She wanted to kill the girl." Marie Blanche's voice shook a little. "Do you think...?"

"I think she would not simply kill her out of hand. That is no story. They each want to tell a story, a different one. Carabosse's is a tragedy, and Ione's is a romance, and the puppets must play their part."

"You think the entire business with the curse and the gifts is simply about rival *stories*?"

"My dealings with the Good Folk have been as few as I can make them, but they do have a liking for making mortals pawns in their various games," the doctor said. "The rivalry between Carabosse and the Lilac Fairy is a long-standing one."

"And how are we to tell which story is being told?"

Doctor Rapunzel stared at the instruments piled on the table. "I don't know," she said. "And even if we find out, I don't know what to *do*."

MORE TIME PASSED, while the doctor muttered over her maps and implements, and Marie Blanche paced and glanced out of the window.

"I have it!" Doctor Rapunzel said. She smiled, though there were shadows like bruises below her eyes. "I am a fool. I should have thought of it before."

"What is it?"

"The necklace. Consider the likelihood that whoever took her wants to facilitate a meeting with Charming. That being the case, if we find Charming, we find Bella. It will eliminate one possibility, at least."

"Surely it will be better to simply let the King's men know where he is and let *them* deal with it."

"Let them be turned into toads, more likely. And we lose any chance of finding the loot. And what chance will they have of saving Bella?"

"I really wish that girl would learn to save herself, instead of making everyone else do it!" Marie Blanche growled.

"She has not yet had much opportunity," Rapunzel pointed out. "You and I, we had to save ourselves. My parents were nowhere to be seen, and yours... well. Your mother, for her part, could not help dying, of course."

"What do you mean by that?"

"Merely that in some ways your father abandoned you as much as my parents did me."

Marie Blanche froze. "He did nothing of the sort!"

"As you will. But I am not ready to give up. And there is another card that has yet to come into play."

"What card? What are you talking about?" Marie Blanche fixed her gaze on the Doctor.

"I made certain... arrangements." Doctor Rapunzel fidgeted with a compass, tucked a non-existent stray hair back under her cap. "Perhaps I should have told you, but..."

"You kept something from me." Marie Blanche's voice could have frozen a deep lake and all that lived in it, right down to the crawlers in the mud.

"I thought it safer for you," Rapunzel said. "The Prince is so very good at getting things out of people."

"You think, if we met, he could have *charmed* me into giving away our plans? That I am as much of a fool as Bella?"

"No, not at all! It was only that it seemed..." Doctor Rapunzel looked at Marie Blanche's expression, and made a helpless gesture. "I am in the habit of working alone," she said.

"Then you will no doubt be much happier when I have left." Marie Blanche stood up, pushing her chair backwards with excessive care. "I have wasted enough time. I shall return to my duties. If you wish to continue with this wild-goose chase, then that is up to you, but I will no longer take part in this foolishness."

"I didn't mean... I had no intention..."

"You deceived me," Marie Blanche said, and left the room, shutting the door behind her in the pointedly controlled manner of someone who very much wants to slam it so hard the frame breaks from the wall.

Rapunzel flung her hands up, then clapped them to her head and groaned.

After a moment she pushed herself to her feet and hurried after Marie Blanche, but by the time she reached the stable, there were only her own mount and Bella's, staring with mild interest at the empty stall between them.

BACK AT THE kitchen table, the doctor stared at the two untouched and now cold tisanes, slumped back in her chair and rubbed her eyes. She should go and look at the map, and work out where that wretched man was. She should send a message—probably several messages. Or write them, at least. They could not be sent until she could reach the village.

And then what?

Then, she supposed, she must follow where the map led, and hope it led to Bella, and try to extract her from whatever ghastly entanglement she was now in, while fending off a powerful fae *and* keeping track of the Prince. And she had no idea if she was even right. It could be someone else who had taken Bella—perhaps even Charming himself, with magical assistance. Who knew?

Suddenly, she was dreadfully tired. Everything felt, at once, too much. The idea of working with Charming's other victims had seemed so right, at first, so perfect— had they not complementary skills, and resources? Bella, particularly! But now it had all fallen to pieces. Was it her own fault? Perhaps it was. Yes, certainly it was. She had been too sure of herself, too certain that she knew best.

Better, perhaps, to give up. To go home. To wrap herself in the tatters of her dignity and sneak away before the dawn.

It was not quite Doctor Rapunzel's own voice that told her these things. It was at least partly a voice she had once heard every day, demanding tisanes and obedience, and making sure she knew that she was only as important, or as clever, as Mother Hilda allowed her to be.

But Mother Hilda wasn't here, and Doctor Rapunzel was. She straightened up, put the tips of her fingers together, and stared into the dark glass of the window.

THE SWEET PRE-DAWN air, the first sleepy notes of the waking birds, no matter how trivial their conversation, the feel of a good horse beneath her—all these would normally have lifted Marie Blanche's mood.

Somehow, this time, they failed. With every pace she drew further from the lodge, she felt an uneasy churning growing in her. Her hands tightened on the reins and she forced herself to ease back, not wanting to pull on the horse's mouth. The beast, after all, had done nothing wrong.

But who did?

Bella. Silly, *silly* girl. A pity the Good Folk had not added a little sense to their gifts. And the doctor, of course. She had lied, or at the very least concealed a truth. That was not forgivable, not when Marie Blanche had trusted her enough to abandon her duties and leave Papa alone.

It is not the truth she concealed that is biting at you, Marie Blanche, but the truth she spoke.

What truth? Nonsense.

But how was she to face Papa? It was for him she had really come. For him she had wanted justice.

So you decided to behave just like him. Abandoning your responsibilities, while you obsessed over a lost cause.

The thought pulled her up so abruptly that the horse, feeling her shift, snorted and shook its head.

And there, suddenly, alone but for a stranger's horse and a crowd of gossiping birds to whom she meant less than a pebble, Marie Blanche felt the full force of her resentment.

Had she really left for him? Or had she left because she was tired of it all, because she wanted *him* to wait, and to worry, and to realise how it was without her? Did she want, really, to pay him back, just a little, for his absence, for his selfishness, for falling in love with the wrong person?

Bella had fallen in love with the wrong person, too.

Marie Blanche rode on, so slowly the horse eventually halted to crop grass at the path's edge, and Marie Blanche simply sat, the reins loose in her hands, as the sunlight strengthened and the birds quieted and the great contemplative silence of the woods rose around her.

THE NIGHT REACHED out to Bella as she rode. Branches combed her hair, the wind rouged her cheeks and brightened her eyes, giving her a wild, nocturnal beauty even greater than that she already possessed.

Not that Bella knew. She was used to beauty, and thought little enough of it. Instead, even as the horse bore her on, she thought of the women she had left behind. Doctor Rapunzel, reaching out a hand to her, at that dreadful wedding dinner. Marie Blanche, so tenderly anointing the dragon's wound, reassuring the great and lethal beast in her no-nonsense fashion.

And then, suddenly, the woman she had left even farther behind: her mother.

What would Mama make of this wild ride? She had, with some difficulty, persuaded Papa to let Bella go on this—mission? expedition? this *quest*, then—though she had given her daughter one of her shrewd glances, and said, "If you are chasing justice, well enough, child. But I hope you are not chasing a mirage. Those who do so in deserts thirst and die." That was very similar to what Conte Morosini had said, too. *Don't spend your youth chasing a ghost.*

But Bella had given her sunniest smile and promised that she was chasing no mirage. Because, perhaps thanks to the gifts of the Good Folk, she could sometimes fool even Mama, and very few people could do that.

"I am sure your marriage to Papa was much better organised," she said, laughing—and what a lie that laugh was! "And it actually took place, of course."

"My choice was marriage or the nunnery, child. And, having seen my mother's life, the nunnery had a great deal to recommend it! But your father was..." She smiled and, to Bella's eternal astonishment, actually *blushed*, something Bella would not have thought possible. "Let us say there was that about him that made me reconsider the contemplative life. But passion is a glue that dissolves with age. Liking, respect, a shared interest in the welfare of our country... these things have lasted."

Liking, yes; certainly she *liked* Charming, how could she not? But... everyone liked Charming. And he appeared to like everyone. As to respect... he had handled the meeting with the Serenissima with great diplomacy, he had deferred to her and to her parents as appropriate, she could respect him for that... but had it only been a façade? And how much respect had he shown to her, to leave so, and laugh as he left?

Perhaps it was for the sake of his country he had done it—but surely if he cared for the welfare of his country, a match with Caraggia could hardly be bettered.

Perhaps he knows something I don't. It wouldn't be hard.

Bella shook her head furiously, as though she could dislodge the doubts that swarmed her brain like flies.

He will come to you, the Lady had said.

She would meet him, and look into his eyes, and then she would know. Surely, then, she would know for sure.

She gripped the horse's mane and blinked at the flying night, and tried not to think about how far she was from the lodge, and the doctor, and Marie Blanche, and Mama, and home, and everything she knew.

The Bird and the Fox

HEN SHE HEARD the footsteps, Rapunzel blinked at the chart she was studying, rubbed her eyes, took up a pinch of some unpleasantly soft grey powder and a small but efficient dagger, and faced the door.

"Oh," she said, at the sight of Marie Blanche. Then she made a quick, barely perceptible cast with the powder, which drifted wider and faster than should have been entirely possible.

Marie Blanche sneezed. "I hope that was not poison," she said, eyeing the dagger. "I understand you are annoyed, but that would be excessive."

"Revelation powder. I had to be sure you were... you."

"And am I?"

"Yes. Why are you here?"

"I am here. I intend to go on with this folly. Does the *why* matter?"

"I think, yes, if we are to trust each other at all," the doctor said.

"If we are to trust each other at all, then perhaps you would put away your dagger?"

"Oh, that." Rapunzel thrust it into its sheath. "It would probably be little use against someone of your skill, in any case."

"I am merely competent, with anything other than a skinning knife. Bella is the artist with blades."

"So?"

"So," Marie Blanche said, "I am here because you were right. I *am* a fool."

"I never said so," the doctor pointed out.

"You did not need to. What you did say simply made me realise that I was behaving like one." Marie Blanche spread her hands and gave a slightly twisted smile. "This journey is a revelation in itself, no?"

Doctor Rapunzel snorted. "Indeed. Now, the other card I mentioned. If we can drag Bella out of this current imbroglio, then that will come into play. It—"

Marie Blanche held up her hand. "No. If we are to trust, let us begin with that. Tell me when it becomes better for me to know." She looked at the desk, covered in maps, and papers, and quill pens, a covered mirror and little clicking devices, and at the Doctor, whose eyes were sunk in shadows. "You have been working all this time?" She shook her head. "Of course you have. I am sorry," she said, abruptly.

"For what?"

"Everything. And I have left too much to you."

"You negotiated with a *dragon*. That alone is a fair exchange."

"Have you had any success?"

"I have some information, but I am not sure what it means."

"Tell me."

"Charming. He is coming *towards* us." Doctor Rapunzel pointed to the glimmer on the map, which moved, like a slow, dim firefly, through painted forests.

"What?"

"He has turned back on his original route and is heading in this direction, at a canter at least. And there is something else going on." She glared at the map. "The scrying is diffuse, unclear. Something is interfering with it."

Marie Blanche frowned, tugging off her riding gloves. "*Towards* us. Why?"

"I have no idea! Unless he realised, somehow, that someone was on his trail and has changed direction to confuse any followers—but why come back in this direction, where he would meet anyone who had been hunting him?"

"A hunted animal may turn to evade pursuers," Marie Blanche said, "but not generally *towards* its pursuer, unless it is at bay. And then it turns because it has nowhere to run."

"*Could* someone else be pursuing him? His father's men, perhaps, or some bounty hunter?"

Marie Blanche stepped up beside her and the two heads, one under short bronze curls, one in an embroidered cap that covered every hair, bent over the table. "But, again," Marie Blanche said, "why would he retrace his steps, when he might go in any other direction?"

"It could seem the best route, if he has no idea we are after him. Perhaps he is leading someone away from the loot?"

"I think," Marie Blanche said, slowly, one finger hovering over the glimmer on the map, "either something chases him that he fears, or something draws him that he desires. Another victim?"

"Of course," Doctor Rapunzel said, in weary tones. "Oh, no. Not *another* victim; the same one. *Bella*."

"You think he has changed his mind? That he wants to marry her after all?"

"I think someone, or something, has persuaded him that that is what he wants. That interference I spoke of; I think it is magic surrounding him. A glamour."

The sorceress stared at the map, as though that faint red glimmer were a deadly beast, sneaking towards them through the trees. "You know that Bella was cursed by Carabosse, yes? And that the curse was turned aside by her sister, Ione of the Lilac?"

"I knew the first, but not the second."

"Bella is a game piece. Charming is a game piece. Ione is making a move, to get the result she wants; she is willing and able not only to move Bella into place, but Charming too. She is probably willing and able, then, to ensure the marriage takes place."

"This we already suspected, no?"

"Suppose she succeeds? Bella is married to Charming. The glamour that was put on Charming wears off, but Charming is still Bella's husband, with all the privileges that implies... full of resentment at being trapped into marriage... not to mention the political implications—he is being sought for the attempted murder of his father! There could be a war!"

"Let us not buy trouble before we reach the market. You don't think Bella will notice beforehand that he is under a glamour?"

"When we see something we want very much, it is easy to ignore all the signs that it will be bad for us."

Marie Blanche thought of a bright, red, poisoned apple, and a woman in a bright red dress, with a great ruby on her finger. "Yes. But what of Bella herself? Is she, too, under a glamour?"

"No. She seems to be immune—one of her Gifts. What she feels for Charming, poor child, is all her own doing. And his, of course. Ione gets what she wants," Rapunzel went on. "Charming is trapped. Bella is trapped. We are robbed of both justice and restitution. And then, if we are all even more unfortunate, Carabosse realises that she has been outsmarted, and makes a countermove..."

"And if we attempt to help Bella out of this situation, perhaps we too become pawns in the Good Folk's game," Marie Blanche said. "Frankly, I would rather negotiate with a dozen dragons. Hungry, pregnant, *irritated* dragons."

"But if we don't, then we abandon both Bella and our hopes."

"Can we reach Bella before she reaches Charming?"

"She left hours ago, on a fey horse," the doctor said. "What do *you* think?"

Marie Blanche began to pace again, slapping her riding gloves into her palm. "I should have ridden after her immediately."

"We did not know where she was going. We still don't, apart from the general direction."

"If we know Bella's direction, and Charming's direction, we can make at least a guess," Marie Blanche said. "Where those lines intersect on a map... Can your devices interfere with the glamour on Charming?"

"Hmm. Possibly, but... well, I can try."

"If she sees him run away the minute he is free... You said sufficient evidence would bring her to her senses."

"I hoped so. Now..." Doctor Rapunzel shrugged.

"Do your best, and I will do my best to find us a means to follow Bella. That horse did not fly, it ran. Can you make a beast run more swiftly than is its nature?"

"I can make a potion that will do it, though only for a short time if I am not to kill it."

"I will be back shortly."

"Best you don't come back in the house until I call," Doctor Rapunzel said. "I must do something which might be dangerous."

"Very well."

"NOBLE BIRD, IN *time of need I stand, I summon thee in the name of the Oakapple Clan,*" Marie Blanche called, clattering and shrieking into the thinning darkness.

The birds around her stilled, then began their chatter again. The sky would begin to lighten soon, and how far now were they behind Bella, on her magic steed? The thought made Marie Blanche's stomach clench. She might wish to shake Bella until she rattled, but to condemn her to marriage to a man like Charming, a man who would immediately abandon her again once the glamour wore off or—worse—stay, bitter and rotten with resentment... No, that she would wish on no one.

A shriek in the sky. *What, what, who calls?*

Marie Blanche called out again. "*Noble bird, in time of need I stand, I summon thee in the name of the Oakapple Clan.*"

Silent as a flake of snow, the peregrine flickered through the air, its pale breast just visible. Marie Blanche instinctively held up her wrist, but the peregrine took a nearby branch instead.

Embarrassed, Marie Blanche lowered her arm. This was no tame bird. She bowed. *"Noble bird, I need a message taken to the nearest dwarven clan, as swiftly as you may fly. Will you do me this great favour?"*

The bird tilted its head and stared at her with its bright gold eyes. *Yes.*

"Thank you."

Marie Blanche handed it the note she had written, on a tiny roll of paper. The bird took it carefully in its foot, and flew into the darkness, swift and silent as a thought.

"HOOO," THE DEMON Elathiel said. *"You are playing with the big girls."*

Rapunzel allowed nothing to show on her face, though beneath the table, her hands were trembling.

Elathiel looked through the mirror to where the doves blinked sleepily in their cage. *"I'll need more'n that."*

"I know."

"You're going to have a target the size of an arena on your back, you know that?"

"Perhaps."

"So will I, if anyone guesses where you got it."

"I think your protections will be more than sufficient."

"That's all you know." Elathiel scratched something that was probably an ear. *"Things down here can change. Not often,"* it admitted, *"but they can. Right. Blood,"* he said. *"Yours. Three drops. On white linen."*

"Don't be ridiculous," Rapunzel said.

"Me, ridiculous? You're asking for a ridiculous thing," Elathiel snorted.

"So you can't get it?"

"*Of course I can get it. Never said I couldn't get it. Want a reasonable price, that's all.*"

"In no world is that a reasonable price."

"*In no world is what you want reasonable, doctor.*"

"Then I shall go elsewhere."

"*Yeah? Where? You're not in your house, are you? You're already elsewhere, and something's up, I can smell it. You really want this. And within an hour. You're desperate.*"

"Not enough to give you my blood. I can, however, get hold of a white peacock."

"*A...*" Greed and a kind of unadulterated longing swept over Elathiel's features, making it look, for a moment, almost childlike. "*Really?*"

"Really."

A gamble. She hadn't been sure about the peacock, but Elathiel's reaction proved her right.

Then the demon's face collapsed back into its usual sullen unpleasantness. "*Don't believe you. Don't care. Blood.*"

Doctor Rapunzel leaned back in her chair and examined the nails of her right hand. "Well, maybe I shall give my recipient something else, instead. A small thing. A trifle, indeed. But they might find it amusing enough."

"*What can you possibly have that even comes close?*"

This was the real gamble. Developing a relationship with a demon took patience, and caution, and time—in this case, a good seven years—and this might destroy it. But it was the last card she had to play.

Doctor Rapunzel smiled. "The Thousand-Eyed is currently... the nine-hundred-and-ninety-nine-eyed, is it not? I might, perhaps, know what happened to their missing eye. And who was responsible. I'm sure my... client... would be delighted to have that kind of information, though I can't guarantee she'd keep it to herself."

Elathiel went a peculiar shade somewhere between green, puce and grey, only possible to a demon.

"*How...? When...?*"

"Does it matter?"

Elathiel called her a series of names so demonically obscene that some of them took shape in the air around it, glowing and stinking. Doctor Rapunzel, ever aware of the threat of dawn edging up the sky, kept her gaze firmly on the mirror.

"Now, Elathiel," she said. "There's no need for that. If you get the name to me in time, I will get you the peacock."

Greed, longing, hatred, and a kind of greasy admiration fought a slippery battle on the uneven terrain of Elathiel's face. "*All right,*" it said. "*Bitch.*" And disappeared.

Doctor Rapunzel covered the mirror, collapsed back in her chair and rubbed her eyes. Then she made more tea, and sat down to wait.

MARIE BLANCHE WAS used to waiting. As a hunter, still and silent, waiting for the movement or the sound that would betray her target. But this was a different sort of waiting, an itchy, edgy, tension between the time that must yet pass and the time that was passing far too swiftly.

She paced, and chewed her nails, and swore, and tried to remember all the names for the south wind in every language of birds that she knew, and gave up, and paced again.

Every now and then she glanced up at the window where Doctor Rapunzel worked, seeing shifting red glows and hearing sounds that made the hair on her neck crawl.

The tops of the trees were beginning to show against the sky when finally there was a flash of bright copper, and a fox the size of a wild boar appeared out of the trees as silent as a dream.

Hethotain was on its back.

"Hethotain!"

The clan leader jumped down, put her fists on her hips and looked Marie Blanche over. "Well, Your Highness, what sort of trouble have you got yourself into this time?"

Marie Blanche laughed a little, out of sheer relief. "I can't believe you're here."

"You think your mother'd forgive me if I found out you were dealing with the Good Folk and I didn't come check you weren't down a shaft with no rope?" Hethotain glanced up at the window and sniffed. "And not just the Good Folk, by the smell of it."

"How did you get here so quickly?"

Hethotain smiled. "We've ways, beneath the ground, that are a deal faster than your roads. And the Fox Queen can run, if she's a mind."

"Can she run again, carrying two, and then three?"

The dwarf cocked an eyebrow. "*If* she's a mind."

"Would you ask her for me, please?"

The door of the lodge opened, and Doctor Rapunzel looked at the Fox Queen, and at Hethotain, and bowed to both, and then sat down abruptly on the steps.

Marie Blanche hurried over to her. Rapunzel's face was pale as moonlight, so that the shadows under her eyes seemed deeper than before. She smelled faintly of sulphur. "Are you well?" Marie Blanche said. "No, that is a stupid question, obviously you are not well."

"I will do," the doctor said. "Forgive me," she said to Hethotain and the Fox Queen, "it has been a long night."

"Seems like it," Hethotain said. "You're Doctor Emilia Rapunzel, yes? So. If I help you, you going to look after my girl here?"

Marie Blanche gave her a sideways look. *My girl?* That was no way to speak of a princess who had been as good as running a country since before she was fully grown! And yet... *my girl.* Why did she suddenly want to cry? She would not cry; how ridiculous to cry at such a thing.

"I will do my best," Doctor Rapunzel said. "If *you* can get us there, *I* have something I can offer Ione, in exchange for not getting her story."

"What?" Marie Blanche said.

Doctor Rapunzel sighed. "Best you don't know until you must. This is the sort of information that gets people... Well, 'killed' might be the least of it."

Hethotain raised her glittering brows, took out a beautifully inlaid flask, and said, "If I'm right about where you got it from, I hope you know what you're doing." She took a drink, and offered the flask to Doctor Rapunzel.

"So do I," the sorceress said, and drank.

Hethotain led them to an opening in the rocks, deep in the woods.

Doctor Rapunzel showed the Fox Queen the map. She sniffed at it, gave a short sharp bark, and lay down with her feet tucked under her.

"How will you get back?" Marie Blanche said.

"Don't fret, I'll manage." Hethotain gave them leather water bottles and dried meat. "Hold on well. If you fall off, there's no guarantee someone'll be finding you. She'll wait for you, and bring you back."

"Thank you," Marie Blanche said, and Rapunzel echoed her.

"Just hold on, and keep my clan's name out of your dealings, if you please," Hethotain said.

"We will."

DOCTOR RAPUNZEL AND Princess Marie Blanche climbed on the Fox Queen's back, and she trotted into what looked at first like no more than a simple tumble of rock. Then the darkness opened before them.

They had no need of potions. The Fox Queen bore them both easily, and ran more swiftly than the wind, through deep and ancient ways.

Dark, pitch dark, but the Fox Queen ran sure-footed while her riders clutched the rough silk of her fur, feeling her muscles beneath them bunch and flow, and stared blindly into blackness.

Dark, pitch dark, with water trickling and chuckling and sometimes roaring, and air sighing and whistling through unseen ways, and the scatterfall of earth and creaking of rock and their own breathing and the panting of the Fox Queen, but the feet of the Fox Queen made no sound at all.

Dark, pitch dark, with the graveyard aroma of cold earth, the flinty clarity of running water and a sudden brief reek of stagnant filth, the bite of metal and dusty whiff of broken rock, the dark green must of moss and mould and—over it all—the constant, acrid, unmistakable tang of fox.

After a time which was impossible to measure, they

felt sweet forest air on their skin, and shapes began to declare themselves in the darkness. A grey scramble of rocks. Stalactites, gleaming and wet, like teeth. A deer, sketched in thin and flowing lines of red on a rock wall, so vital and graceful it seemed to leap into their view and out again.

"Did you see...?" Marie Blanche gasped, and her voice felt strange, like something unused for years.

"Yes. So beautiful. I wonder who would paint such a thing down here?"

Finally, sunlight through leaves, flooding into the mouth of the tunnel, shifting and dappled.

An Interlude

OOD FOLK MY poor, sore backside," Roland muttered as he drove the Mostly Donkey in Charming's wake. It should not have been able to almost keep up with a horse, but, being only *mostly* donkey, it managed, though it complained loudly whenever it could find the breath.

"Can smell 'em all over this," the little manservant grizzled. "How'm I supposed to keep the idiot safe when *they* stick their excessively jewelled fingers in the stinking pie, eh? But I don't *know* for certain, do I? So I still got to chase after him, like it or not, *and* on an empty stomach. Could ruin my digestion, this—it's *already* ruining my digestion, got acid like you wouldn't believe. That's anxiety and no breakfast, that is. I could end up with an ulcer, great big hole in my insides, not that *he'd* care. Why can't *he* get an ulcer? Probably not possible, for him. Probably charm it right out of there, got a gut like a pink silk stocking, I 'spect. Never even gets a toothache, him. You'd think he'd get one just from

252

the number of people who've wanted to punch him in the mouth.

"And who's going to have to deal with him if he wakes up married, eh? Who's going to have to handle *that* little tantrum, and still have to keep him out of jail and off the scaffold? Me, that's who. And I don't even *like* him.

"I tell you what," Roland announced to the night air, "there ain't no justice."

The Fairy Wedding

HE Fox Queen stepped out, delicately, her ears pricking, and moved slowly through the trees, sniffing the air.

A flicker of bright colour, figures visible between the trees.

The Fox Queen stopped. Her riders dismounted. The Fox Queen sat and panted, her tongue hanging out.

They thanked her, bowing.

She rose to her paws, shook herself all over, and trotted away.

"Do you speak her tongue too?" Doctor Rapunzel whispered. "I hope she remembers to come back for us."

"No. But if Hethotain said she'll wait, she'll wait. She's probably gone for water."

They crept towards the clearing, envying the Fox Queen's silent tread.

There was Bella, in a moss-green silk gown with a surcoat of magenta brocade, half her hair braided around her head and woven with pearls, like a crown, the rest tumbling down her back.

There was someone who could only be the Lilac Fairy, dressed in a cloud of pearlescent gauze that descended from a vast, elaborate ruff of gold lace. Her moonlight hair was piled into an intricate series of braids, woven with gold ribbons.

There was, as yet, no sign of Charming.

Though it was autumn, the trees around the clearing were laden with pink and white blossom, and flowers glowed in the grass. Birds crowded every branch, singing. An archway of woven willow stood in the clearing, with wild roses growing all over it, the blooms pink and fragile.

Beneath the archway there was a priest, standing with a pleasant, unmoving smile on his face, his eyes unfocussed.

Rapunzel suppressed a shudder. "Everything is blooming out of season," she whispered.

"The birds, too," Marie Blanche whispered back. "They're not making their proper songs, and half of them shouldn't even be here at this time of year. They sound like clockwork, a few nonsense phrases over and over, it's horrible."

"Fear not, pretty child," Ione said, as Bella paced. "Soon he will be here."

"How do we do this?" Marie Blanche whispered.

Doctor Rapunzel bit her lip, frowning. "I..."

"Your friends are here," Ione said. "Let them not whisper and hide, but come forth and be witnesses to the triumph of love."

The two women looked at each other, shrugged, and stepped into the clearing.

Surprise, and happiness, and guilt chased each other across Bella's face. Then she raised her chin, proudly. "I'm glad you're here," she said. "I hope you haven't come to try and... do anything foolish."

"So do I," Rapunzel said. "But I do have a proposition."

"And what is that?" asked Ione.

"Lift the glamour from the Prince, as soon as he arrives, and then let things fall as they will."

"And why would I do that?".

"A glamour?" Bella said. "He's under a glamour?"

"Hush, child," soothed the fairy. "It was only to bring him to you the quickest way, that is all." She stroked a strand of Bella's hair, twining the curls around her fingers. "Don't you believe in love, my little one?"

"Yes, but..."

"Then trust your heart." Ione turned back to Doctor Rapunzel. "Come, *doctor*, tell me why I should do anything you ask?"

"In return for something I have for you. Will you hear what it is?"

Ione lifted one white, slender hand, and covered a delicate yawn. "If you must."

"A story. A *better* story."

"What story could possibly be better than true love triumphant over the wickedness of a petty, jealous creature like Carabosse?"

"*Tragic* love," Doctor Rapunzel said, looking directly at Maleficent and avoiding Bella's shocked gaze. "True love nobly sacrificed for a higher cause."

"Hmm." Ione tilted her head. "Go on."

So Doctor Rapunzel put her hands together and began, "Once upon a time...

The Hazel Tree

NCE UPON A time, there was a beautiful princess who lived in a castle. She was of an age to be married, and her parents had found for her a handsome prince.

But when the news came to the Prince that it was time for him to be married, he looked sad and turned away his face.

For the Prince had a secret.

Seven years beforehand, he had been out hunting, and had heard cries of distress. He looked about to see what was making such sorrowful sounds, and found a hazel tree being gnawed upon by a deer. "Oh, oh, that hurts me," said the hazel tree. "Oh, oh, I will die of it."

The Prince was very startled to hear the tree speak, but he chased away the deer, and tore off the sleeve of his shirt to bind the tree's wounded bark.

"Thank you," said the tree. "My mistress will be most grateful, for I am her favourite tree, and she prefers my fruit to all others."

"I can see that you are indeed a rare and precious tree," said the Prince. Then he rode away, but could not stop thinking of the hazel tree, and worried that the deer, or another, would return. So he came back with wood and nails, and with his own hands he built a fence of stakes around the tree, to stop any deer or other beast that might cause it harm.

As he hammered in the last stake, a woman appeared before him. She was beautiful beyond mortal beauty, with hair like moonlight and eyes of lilac.

The Prince, recognising that she was a great Lady of the Good Folk, dropped to one knee.

"You are the saviour of my favourite hazel tree," said the Lady. "My name is Ione, and I thank you for your kindness. Ask of me a favour, and I will do it."

"Why, what other favour could I ask, but the chance to look upon your beauty?" said the Prince.

And Ione laughed, and said that he was most charming, but that was not favour enough.

"Then may I have a nut of the hazel tree, to plant in the garden of my palace?" said the Prince. "I will take good care of it, and it will always remind me of you."

So Ione agreed, and took a nut from the hazel tree, and gave it to the Prince.

He took it home and planted it, and let none of his gardeners care for it but tended it himself. Soon it grew into a strong tree, which gave most sweet fruit, though it was only an ordinary tree, and could not talk.

But the Prince would come and talk to it, when the gardeners were all done for the day and no one was about. And he would tell it of how he had met Ione, and how she had taken his heart in a single moment, so that he could never love another.

But the Prince knew that the fairy Lady would never wed a mere mortal, and so he put on his finest clothes and made his face pleasant, and invited the Princess who had been chosen for him to visit his palace so that they might become acquainted.

And the Princess saw how handsome and kind he was, and fell immediately in love. So preparations for the wedding went forward.

But one night the Princess could not sleep for excitement, and so went walking in the palace gardens. She heard the Prince's voice, and in great curiosity to know who he could be speaking to, she crept up, and saw him leaning his head against the bark of a little hazel tree.

"Oh, little hazel tree," he said. "Seven years ago I met the fairy Ione, and she took my heart in a single moment. The Princess is beautiful and good, but I cannot give her my heart. What shall I do, little hazel tree?"

And the Princess, who had also lost her heart in a single moment, was stricken with sorrow, and crept away.

The Princess returned home. She told her parents that she could not marry the Prince, nor indeed any man, and she had a tower built in the forest, and retreated to it and dwelled all alone, weeping and sorrowful.

After her departure, the Prince went once more to the hazel tree, and wept upon its bark, saying, "Ah, the Princess must have seen that my heart is given to another, and so my parents will have no grandchildren to comfort their age, and I am fated to be always alone."

Then Ione appeared before him once again. "O handsome prince, why do you weep?" she asked. "I thought you were to be married, to one who is beautiful and good. Should you not be happy?"

"My heart is forever given to another," said the Prince.

"Perhaps the Princess saw that there is nothing where my heart should be. In any case, she has gone away."

"I am sorry for it," said Ione. "Can you not wed the one who has your heart?"

And the Prince cast himself to his knees before her. "She is a great Lady of the Good Folk," he said, "and I would never dare to ask her."

And Ione realised that it was she that the Prince loved.

But Ione knew what the Prince did not: that if a human weds a Lady of the Good Folk, he will lose his soul, and she thought too well of him to condemn him to such a dreadful fate.

So she told him this.

"What do I care for my soul, when my heart is lost?" the Prince said recklessly.

"But I must care for your soul, even if you do not," Ione said. "Dear Prince, I will not wed you."

"Then it is my fate to be alone," said the Prince. So he withdrew to a cave in the forest, and gave up his kingdom, and lived as a hermit.

And one winter, the cold was very great, and the Prince died of it. And the cold in the Princess's country was also very great, and living alone in her stone tower, she too died of it.

So each was buried, to the great sorrow of all.

And when those who cared for them next visited their graves, they found growing upon each a hazel tree. And a story was told, that a beautiful lady with hair like moonlight could be sometimes seen, weeping over the graves, and tending to the hazel trees so that they grew strong and tall.

And still, in both those countries, it is the custom of the people to tell their troubles to a hazel tree.

The Fairy's Secret

HERE WAS SILENCE in the clearing when she had finished, apart from the birds singing their single string of notes, over and over again.

"But it isn't true, none of it's true," said Bella. "And I don't want to die alone in a tower."

"You do not have to," said Doctor Rapunzel. "All stories are what is *told* about what happened, not what *actually* happened. You retire from public life for some years. That should be more than enough."

"Hmm." Ione said. "I like it. But is it enough? Is it enough? I have spent a great deal of time on this, and trouble, to make it a perfect tale."

"But this tale puts you at the centre of it all," Rapunzel said. "The heart, as it were."

"I am sure you think you are very clever," said Ione. "But do not try me, mortal. No, I think I prefer my story. A wedding! What could be more perfect?"

"But I don't want to marry him if he's under a glamour!" Bella burst out. "How will I know if he really loves me?"

"Foolish girl," Ione said. "Of course he does."

"Then why did he leave?"

"Enough! He will be here any moment, and you will be married."

Doctor Rapunzel took a deep breath. "Then I have one more thing to offer," she said. "A piece of information that I think you would very much like to have."

"Information? How dry. How dull. Information instead of love!" Ione looked Rapunzel up and down. "Perhaps it is only to be expected."

"I have Carabosse's true name."

The birds stopped singing. Ione's lilac eyes fixed on Doctor Rapunzel's face.

Marie Blanche thought of the hawks in the mews when a mouse came in.

"Why, *that* is interesting," Ione said. "And of course, it is her *true* name? Because it would be very, very foolish to try and give me something that was not, wouldn't it? You are terribly arrogant, doctor, but you are not quite that much of a fool, are you?"

"You will know immediately if it is or is not," the sorceress said. "As I did, when it was told to me. It tastes of iron."

"Give it to me." The greed was unmistakable, sounding through the clearing like chalk on a slate.

"Lift the glamour when the Prince arrives, and promise to leave Bella, and myself, and Marie Blanche, to live out our lives without your meddling, and I will give you the name."

"Meddling!" Ione actually looked hurt. "I am taking an interest! You should be *grateful*."

The birds started to sing again. And now there were hoofbeats, coming closer and closer, and the strained panting of an overdriven horse.

Charming burst into the clearing, saw Bella, and flung himself from his horse. "My love! My only darling!"

Bella looked at him with her whole heart in her eyes, a smile trembling on her lips.

"See?" Ione said. "This is a happy ending, it's what everyone wants."

"It *doesn't* end there, that's the trouble," said Marie Blanche.

Bella looked from Charming, his face wreathed in a doting grin, holding her hand in his and stroking it like a kitten, to Ione, her head tilted to one side, her beautiful face showing nothing but smiling concern.

"But... but this isn't real," Bella said. "Not if he's glamoured." Her eyes glittered with tears. "Dear Lady," she said. "I don't wish to be ungrateful. But... it doesn't mean anything if it isn't real. Please, take off the glamour."

The fairy looked at her. "Such a *pretty* child," she said. "Very well then, if you will waste all our gifts locked up in a tower of your own making, so be it."

Ione snapped her fingers.

Charming blinked, dropping Bella's hand as though the kitten had suddenly turned into a toad. He looked around and saw the other women, and the priest, and Ione.

There was that wonderful smile... but not before the step backwards, the groping for his horse's reins, the look of utter, hunted panic—and the jab of contempt when he looked at Bella, sliding into her ribs as cold and venomous as a poisoned dagger.

Which was worse—the contempt, or the speed at which he wiped it away and fixed that devastating smile on his face—would be hard to say.

He turned to Ione and bowed.

"And you, too, so *very* pretty," she said. "What a picture you would have made. Come, doctor, give me what you promised before I change my mind."

Rapunzel walked up to her and whispered in her ear.

Ione shaped the name, silently. A look of utter, predatory satisfaction spread over her face, and she licked her lips, and laughed. "Oh, *yes*," she said.

Then she was gone, leaving nothing in her wake but the echo of her laughter.

The birds burst up from the trees in a flurry of distress calls and flew away.

A sudden breeze whisked all the untimely blossom from the branches, a blizzard of pink and white petals, already browning as they flew.

The priest, standing suddenly forlorn in the archway of dying roses, blinked and stared. "What...?" he tried. "Who...?"

Bella held out her hands. "I didn't mean... I thought..."

Charming, the smile still in place, swept a bow, and leapt on his horse in a single smooth motion, and was gone without a word.

"Bugger," Marie Blanche said. "I should have held the horse."

Bella stood, her hands clasped in front of her, looking at the place where Charming had been.

Roland saw Charming pelting towards him, mud spattering up from the horse's hooves.

He looked at Charming's face.

"There's an inn, not far," he said. "We can get a new horse before that one drops dead under you."

Charming gave a curt nod, and they rode on in silence.

*   *   *

MARIE BLANCHE HANDED the priest her flask and he grabbed for it like a drowning man.

"We should make sure he gets home," Bella said.

The Fox Queen stepped delicately out of the trees. The priest took her in, whimpered, picked up his skirts and fled down a path still scattered with blossom.

"I think he knows the way," Marie Blanche said. "He could have left the flask, though."

The Fox Queen gave a sharp metallic bark that sounded a great deal like laughter, and sat down with her tail neatly folded over her paws.

"Bella," Doctor Rapunzel said gently.

"Yes."

"We need to decide what to do. If you wish to go home, we can arrange that, I think?" She looked at Marie Blanche, who nodded.

"I'm sure Hethotain would help. We can get you part of the way, at least."

Bella stared at her hands, then sighed and shook her head.

"Then we carry on?" Rapunzel said.

"What about the horses at the lodge?" asked Marie Blanche. "And all your equipment?"

"We can send for them when we know we will be in one place for a few days. I have enough on me to keep tracking the necklace; apart from that we must make do. Bella? Bella, can you hear me?"

Bella looked up, blinking. "I'm sorry. Yes?"

"We are going to continue. Are you with us?"

Bella rose elegantly to her feet, and shook dead petals from her skirts. "Yes," she said.

"You're sure?" Rapunzel said. "I have played all but one of the cards I have."

"What in the name of all that's unholy did you have to do to get the true name of one of the Good Folk, anyway?" said Marie Blanche.

"I don't understand," Bella said. "Why would she want that?"

"You've *seven* fairy godmothers and you don't *know?*" Marie Blanche said. "The Good Folk guard their true names like a bear her cubs. True names are power. A lot of it. And if Carabosse ever finds out where her rival got it..." She shuddered and glared at the doctor. "You took a huge risk."

"Perhaps not," Doctor Rapunzel said. "I doubt Ione will wish to admit that she got such a thing from a mere mortal."

"And you're sure about that?" Marie Blanche said.

The doctor shrugged. "Well, no, but what choice did I have?"

"What exactly did you have to offer for it?"

"Threats," the doctor said. "Which means I may have burned a particular bridge beyond repair." She shrugged. "But one can always build more bridges."

"Assuming one is not imprisoned in a cave of ice or turned into a beetle or some such thing," said Marie Blanche. "Dammit, doctor, you could have *told* me what you were planning."

"Yes, I could. I'm sorry."

"Well, it's done now," Marie Blanche said.

Bella said, "I'm sorry. I'm so *sorry*." Tears began to slip down her face. "You did all this, for me, and I've been such an *idiot*."

"Ah, well," Rapunzel said. "He has fooled all of us,

and more than us, at one time or another, has he not?"

"But you put yourself in danger for me! And you barely even *know* me! And he... he doesn't..." The sobs began to catch up with her. "He doesn't... love me at all! That *smile!* He put it on like a... a hat! It was all just an *act*, every bit of it!" She gave herself up to tears.

Doctor Rapunzel and Marie Blanche each put an arm around her, feeling the sobs rack her small frame like a tree in a storm.

The Fox Queen came over and thrust her nose into Bella's chest, almost knocking all three of them over, making Bella choke out a laugh. She patted the Fox Queen's muzzle. "Thank you," she said. "You all care for me much more than I deserve. Does anyone have a handkerchief?"

"There," Marie Blanche said, handing her a slightly grubby square of linen. "How you contrive to look so pretty still when anyone else would be scarlet and puffy is simply infuriating."

"Oh, pooh," Bella said, and blew her nose, loudly. "As though my looks made any difference. They weren't even what he was after! That... that..."

"Blackguard?" Marie Blanche said. "Scoundrel?"

"Treacherous scum?" offered Rapunzel.

"Lying, thieving, conniving bastard?" said Marie Blanche.

"That subtle, perjured, false, disloyal... *toad*," said Bella. "He's a *toad,* and I want to *smack* him in the *head*."

"Finally," said Marie Blanche. "Unfair to toads, though."

"So are we going after him, then?" Bella said, blowing her nose one final time and screwing up the handkerchief with unnecessary force.

"We still have the means to track him, so, yes. It is time we brought our final card into play," Doctor Rapunzel said.

The Two Duellists

HE CROOKED SPOON tavern doesn't look like much from the outside. It's low and rambling and not particularly well lit. However, it does smell very appealing indeed. Especially if you're hungry, and Roland is always hungry. It's also the only halfway decent place for miles around.

Charming has said he doesn't care where they stay. Roland knows Charming *always* cares. Though he's perfectly capable of surviving a night in a less than salubrious tavern or on the ground in the woods, and has done so on more than one occasion—he'll invariably grumble about it for *days*. Mainly because he likes to wash. Frequently. With soap. And hot water. And fancy stuff for his hair, when he can get it. Roland sometimes wonders how his skin stays on, with all that scrubbing.

At the moment, though, it's possible Charming may do more than grumble. Roland, never having seen him in quite this mood, is treating him like a snarling dog on a fraying leash.

Fortunately the tavern not only has a good cook, but decent beds, deep wooden baths and an actual sauna for the use of guests. (Even Roland doesn't object to a good steam, though he tends to wait until there are no other occupants. All that choking, staring and running away isn't conducive to relaxation.) In the main room a double handful of other guests are chatting happily among themselves and devouring wild boar sausage and pizokel. A few small children skitter among the tables.

The presence of baths and a sauna seems, finally, to be lifting Charming's mood, as does the barmaid. She is a delicate, large-eyed little creature, with something of the faun in her looks but none of the shyness. The large, vigorously-bearded, broad-shouldered landlord, on the other hand, shrinks and bobs around her as though she could turn him to stone with one glance from those lustrous eyes.

Roland, personally, would prefer a barmaid who wore a bit less perfume, but drenching oneself in the stuff seems to be a thing around here, judging by the guards back at Eingeten. Roland rubs his notable nose, and twitches the ends of his fingers, and keeps his counsel.

"I EXPECT YOU hear this all the time, but what in the name of the Goose is a lovely creature like you doing serving in a tavern?" Charming smiled. If his smile had a slightly more cynical curl to it than usual, only Roland noticed.

"Thought it'd be a change from kitchen work," said the barmaid. "More fool me. Dull as ditch water, this place. In *fact,* I bet there's ditches with more going on." She ran a cloth languorously over the bar. "Might ask you the same question." It is not actually possible to look up at someone through your eyelashes, however long they may be—biology forbids it. But she made a valiant attempt nonetheless. "Not often we get a proper *gentleman* in here."

"Now, how do you know I'm a proper gentleman? I might be a very *im*proper one. A positive rogue."

"Might you really?" She giggled. "Well that'd be a change, too. Bet you don't talk about sheep all the time, if you're a rogue. Bet you've done all *sorts* of interesting things."

"One or two. Why don't you let me buy you a drink, and I'll tell you about them? But only if you tell me your name."

"Nell."

"Nell," Charming rolled the word on his tongue. "Nelllle. What a rich sound it has."

"Rich sound!" She gave a delicate snort. "Rich pockets'd be better."

"Well, maybe we can do something about that, hmm?"

The landlord crept up, as best as such a large man could creep, and muttered in Nell's ear.

"Well, if the barrel's finished, they'll have to drink the other," she said.

The landlord blinked, nodded, and moved away.

The outer door swung open and smacked against the wall.

"Oi!" the landlord shouted. "Mind that frame, will you?"

"I *do* apologise." The new arrival strolled up to the bar, and dropped a shiny gold coin onto it. "I hope this will cover any damages. The wind, you know." The voice was educated, clear, and courteous; the voice of a young man whose background and education would render him arrogant if he were any less polite.

"Of course, yeronner," the landlord said, eyeing the gold and, with slightly more reservation, its bearer.

The stranger turned and surveyed the other occupants of the tavern. The occupants surveyed the stranger back.

What they saw was a slight, graceful figure all in black: boots, breeches, shirt, a black leather waistcoat, and a short cape. The cape, it could be seen by the knowing eye, was weighted in the hem, so that it would swing away from the sword arm. A black silk mask covered the upper part of the stranger's face, and a black, wide-brimmed hat covered the stranger's hair; only a full mouth and a pair of sharp brown eyes could be seen. They too wore scent, though it was a darker, mossier one than the floral perfume Nell preferred.

Those brown eyes scanned Charming up and down. "Well, well, it seems I am in luck," the stranger said. "I follow a rumour on a whim, and what do I find?"

"What *do* you find?" Charming said.

"I believe I find the most famous—or perhaps *notorious*—Prince Charming," said the stranger.

Roland's eyes narrowed, and he and Charming exchanged a glance.

"A prince!" Nell gasped, clasping her hands to her chest. "No. Really?"

Charming sighed. "Now, what makes you believe that I'm this Charming fellow, hmm?"

"You *talk* like a prince," Nell said. "And your hair... Oh, tell me you're a prince, do!"

"Well, perhaps," Charming said. "That still doesn't mean I'm the Prince this person's looking for."

"And exactly how *many* people of royal descent are likely to be in this tavern at any given time?" the masked stranger drawled.

Nell's snort of laughter, this time, was a bit less delicate. "Got a point," she said. "Not a lot of 'em around here, as a rule."

The stranger bowed. "What remains to be seen is if you are indeed a noble man, or merely a nobleman."

Charming laughed. "And how do you intend to prove such a subtle point?"

"A duel, of course," said the stranger.

"How is a duel expected to prove my nobility?"

"One may tell a great deal about a person in a fight, if one has experience."

"You, I may assume," Charming said, having taken note of the cloak, and the stance, and the quiet but confident carriage of the stranger, "have a great deal of experience."

"You might say so, yes."

"Well, I am settled for the evening, I am enjoying my conversation with this delightful young lady, and I have no desire to exert myself so that you may prove some obscure point to your own satisfaction. So, in a word, no."

"You refuse my challenge?"

"I do." Charming took a swig of beer and winked at Nell, who was gazing wide-eyed from one to the other as though this was quite the most exciting thing ever to happen in the Crooked Spoon, or indeed for some miles around. Which, to be fair, with the exception of the standard sorts of births, deaths, injuries and tragedies of any community—and the time Eggen Buhler's pigs got into Orel Schlappi's brewhouse—it probably was.

"But you have a reputation as a swordsman, and I have an inclination to prove my worth, even if you do not," said the stranger.

"I'm afraid, then, you must find someone else to test your mettle on," said Charming. "Really, you seem a perfectly nice, if persistent, fellow; why don't you go to the nearest town that has a fencing school or some such and try and persuade their best into battle? I'm sure *someone* would be willing to accommodate you."

The stranger sighed. "If you won't do it to prove yourself"—they freed a pouch from their belt and jingled it—"will you do it for a wager?"

Charming held out his hand. The stranger dropped the pouch into it. It was heavy, and when Charming opened it, the mellow gleam of gold was visible in the lamplight. "A substantial wager, I see," Charming said. "I never wager without knowing the bet. In the unlikely event that you win, what do you want? Merely to carry my reputation away over your shoulder like a slain deer? Assuming I am, in fact, this Charming fellow."

The stranger looked him up and down. "For a man *of* such reputation, you don't seem to have gained much by it. Your breeches appear scorched—did you sit too close to the fire? Your shirt wouldn't fit me and is not in the least to my taste. I am not such a low creature as to deprive a man of his sword. Hmm. Even your boots are despicably scruffy. But I can't help feeling that leaving you barefoot would have a certain, shall we say, symbolic appeal to it. So. The boots."

"You want my boots."

The stranger shrugged. "*Want* is too strong a word, but I will accept them, since you seem to have little else of value."

Charming upended the bag, and the coins spilled onto the bar in a glimmering heap. Nell's eyes widened even further. "Coo," she said. "That's a big wager."

"Oh, well, if you must," Charming said, "at least there's enough here to buy me a new pair of boots." He winked at Nell again. "And leave a decent tip."

"That'd be a first," Roland muttered.

"Did you say something, Roland? You have an opinion you wish to share?" Charming said.

"Well, since you asked, *Yer Allegedly-Princeship,* can I have a *word?*"

"Excuse me," Charming said to Nell, "it seems my man has need of me." He strolled over to the table. "Well?"

"This is hinky as a ferret's wedding," Roland grated. "You're not seriously going to do this, are you?"

Charming raised an eyebrow. "You doubt my ability to defeat this arrogant sprig?"

"I doubt the effing *coincidence* of someone just happening to turn up here to challenge you to a duel. How'd they know you were here? How'd they know you were *you?* What if it's one of your father's men?"

"My father's men are generally muscular, brutish and unblessed with either education or subtlety. And the accent's wrong. Whoever this is, they aren't from home."

"And a bounty hunter?"

"They wouldn't challenge me to a duel, they'd simply knock me on the head and drag me back."

"But it'll be as good as stating that you are who they say you are! Leaving a great big marker saying 'Charming Woz Ere'!" Why are you so determined...?" Roland looked at Charming, looked at the masked stranger, then slumped back in his chair. "Oh, I get it." He said. "Fine, I've done me best!"

"And exactly what do you get?" Charming said, showing his teeth. "What subtle insight do you have to offer, Roland?"

"You're in a stinking temper and you want to hit something. And nothing I can say will make any difference until you've worked it off. Fine. Go ahead. I tried to persuade you," Roland said. "Did my best."

"I'm sure that will be sufficient," Charming said. "No blame will fall on you, Roland, should I fail. Which I won't," he said, slipping his sword from his sheath and giving it a flashy twirl.

The sound of tables being hastily dragged to the sides of the room drowned Roland's response. He shook his head, calmly tipped Charming's unfinished supper onto his own plate and perched cross-legged on a table by the wall, fork in his hand.

The landlord opened his mouth to object, but Nell pulled him aside and hissed a few intense words in his ear, accompanied by vigorous hand gestures. The landlord gave in. "All right, everyone into the other room!" he said. "Give the gents some space! Come on, move, all of you!"

"Aw..."

"Boo!"

"I wanna see!"

"*I* don't object to an audience," Charming said.

"Please, good people, give us the room," said the stranger. "I am sure the winner will buy at least one round."

"Do you fear they'll witness your defeat?" Charming said, as the would-be audience filed grumpily through the inner door.

"I'm not the one with a reputation to protect," the stranger said. "No one here has any idea who I am."

"I don't suppose you're inclined to tell me?"

"Not in the least."

The landlord, having tucked all the more fragile objects below the bar, followed the other customers, clutching a large bottle of brandy to his chest.

Roland continued eating. Nell was the only other person who remained.

"I'm glad you're staying," Charming said. "I'm sure you'll bring me luck."

"Well, you *might* get lucky," Nell said, pouring herself a tankard of beer. "*If* you win."

"I'd better win, then."

"Please stay behind the bar," the stranger said. "I don't wish you to be hurt."

Nell rolled her eyes, but perched on a stool out of harm's way, and raised her tankard in a toast.

Charming and the stranger faced each other, drew, and made the salute.

THE STRANGER MADE a lunge so swift and close that Charming felt the breeze of it, and blocked it only just in time.

"Your sword is better than I expected," the stranger said. "Maybe I should have wagered for that instead of the boots. But if you thought it was from Passau, I'm afraid you were deceived." Another lunge.

"Oh?" Charming said, keeping his eyes on the stranger but avoiding their point by less than he'd have liked. "If you thought I was going to glance at the wolf on the blade, I'm afraid *you* were deceived. I'm well aware that the smiths of Solingen have begun to copy it. This, however, is from Passau." He lunged, to meet only air.

"If you say so." The stranger thrust and Charming skipped aside.

Charming was a head taller than his opponent, with longer reach, but this advantage was swiftly proving less than he had hoped. The stranger was preternaturally quick, and irritatingly stylish with it.

Forward, back. A thrust, a retreat, a lunge, a block. The blades glimmering in the lamplight like flames.

"I see you know your Liechtenauer," the stranger said. To Charming's annoyance, they did not even appear to be breathing hard. He, on the other hand, was beginning to.

"A superb swordsman," he said, "but the Zettel is... such dreadful poetry. So... preachy, too."

"You don't believe ethics have a place in swordsmanship?"

"I consider them beside"—Charming lunged, convinced he had the wretch—"the point."

"So am I," said the stranger, eluding the blow. They jabbed forward, and Charming heard the tear as the blade caught his shirt. "Oh, dear, more work for your tailor," they added. "Tell me, do you ever pay them?"

"Does yours... ever get tired... of working in black?"

"Oh, surely you can do better than that," the stranger chided. Charming was no longer certain whether they were referring to his technique or his patter.

He was beginning to feel distinctly hard-pressed. He skidded in a patch of beer and went down on one knee, and bounced back up to see that his foe, instead of attempting the killing strike, had stood back, to allow Charming to get to his feet.

For some reason this made Charming utterly furious. He leapt forward with a flurry of blows.

Losing one's temper in a duel is seldom wise, and frequently fatal. The stranger shook their head, danced easily out of the way, and raised their arm for what should have been a humiliating—and disabling—blow to Charming's right shoulder with the hilt of their sword.

Nell, who had dragged her stool to the end of the bar and been leaning further and further forward in fascination, overbalanced and fell to the floor almost at the stranger's feet. The stranger pulled the blow for fear of hitting her, and wavered off-balance. Charming darted in and struck. The stranger only just recovered in time to block. Nell dived back behind the bar.

Now the stranger's stance shifted. That easy grace became something else, something utterly focused and predatory. Charming realised he had run out of time, as with one attack after another the stranger drove him back across the room, towards the bar.

He managed to turn the fight just enough that his back was to the room, and the stranger's to the bar, but he was tiring; his sword arm burned with effort, his reactions were slowing, he would have to *run*...

Then there was a *clonk*, a shower of beer, and the stranger dropped to the ground.

Nell held the empty tankard in her hand, then leaned over the bar to look wide-eyed at the fallen stranger as though not sure what had just happened.

Charming stared at his fallen opponent. Then at Nell.

He reached down, took the stranger's sword from the limp hand, shoved the point between two floorboards and bent the blade until it snapped.

Roland shook his head. "Dreadful waste, that."

"Shut up, come on." Charming snatched up the pouch, scooped the gold back into it, and ran for the door, glancing back briefly at the bar, but Nell had disappeared.

Roland sighed, grabbed the remaining sausage from his plate and went after him.

"I WOULDN'T TAKE that horse, if I were you."

Charming turned to see Nell leaning in the doorway of the stables.

"What?"

"That's Petri Kauffman's mare. Mouth like a carthorse and temper like a mule, and he doesn't look after her hooves properly; she'll be lame before you're past the town limits. You want that brown gelding and the grey. And me."

"While I'm flattered—" Charming began.

"Flattered? Bloody grateful is what you should be, mister. I just lost my job for you."

"Well, but—"

"Oh, go on," she said. "Even if it's just to the next town. I want to see a bit of life, and I did just save yours." She edged up to Charming and looked up at him with those large brown eyes, grinning and nudging him with her shoulder. "Be worth your while, promise."

Perhaps it was the contrast between the doe-eyed innocence of her appearance and her adventurous outlook. Perhaps it was because she had seen him at less than his best, and still seemed to like him.

"To the next town, then," Charming said.

"Yay!" She helped saddle the horses with nimble fingers, and leapt up behind Charming. With the Mostly Donkey in tow, they headed into the night.

LATER, IN AN upstairs room of the Crooked Spoon, Doctor Rapunzel dabbed ointment on the bump rising

Charming

on Bella Lucia's skull. The black mask lay discarded on the floor.

Bella submitted quietly to the sorceress's ministrations. She had barely said a word since the other two had found her sitting against the bar, holding her head.

"Look at the light," Rapunzel said, and held a lantern close to her face. Bella winced away.

"No," the doctor repeated. "Look at the light." She peered for a moment, then put the lantern down. "Good. Now. What is my name?"

"What? Oh, stop it, she didn't hit me that hard."

"What is my name?"

"You are Doctor Emilia Rapunzel, she is Her Royal Highness Princess Marie Blanche de Neige, and I am Lady Bella Lucia dei' Sogni and a *terrible person*."

Rapunzel looked at Bella thoughtfully. "Why do you say that?"

"Because I wanted to kill him! I really really *wanted* to kill him! And because I fell in love with that... that... *gah! And* he broke my sword and it was a gift from the Marquise d'Epigne!" Bella's voice cracked.

"Oh," said Doctor Rapunzel. "Well, I don't think any of those make you a terrible person. I have frequently wanted to kill people. It was not you who broke the sword, that is a very great shame, but I'm sure the Marquise would understand. And Charming is very, very good at making people fall in love with him. It is, in fact, his greatest skill."

Bella sniffed. "I need a handkerchief. Again."

Marie Blanche provided one. Again. "I wanted to kill him, too," she said. "I've thought about it a lot. I also wanted to kill my stepmother. And several other people over the years. It doesn't matter unless you actually *do* it, you know."

"You did kill your stepmother," the doctor pointed out.

"No, I did not," Marie Blanche said calmly. "She was executed by a skilled swordsman, under the rule of law. Had it been left to me, she might not have died so swiftly. There," she said to Bella. "I did not just want to kill her, I wanted to make her suffer. Now you know that I am a much more terrible person than you."

"You don't understand," Bella wailed. "*If I could have, I would*. I'm still angry that he got away!"

"We knew that was a possibility," Marie Blanche said.

"My dear," Doctor Rapunzel said, "bemoaning a deed you did not, in fact, do, is wearing on the soul and ultimately pointless."

"Also, you are still unaccustomed to losing," Marie Blanche said. "Your life will become a great deal less upsetting if you learn that losing is something that happens, even to those born to great fortune."

"You think I'm upset because I *lost the duel?*"

"Aren't you?" Marie Blanche said.

Lady Bella hunched her shoulders and scowled. "Yes, all right. Maybe. A bit."

"If it's any comfort, he looked worried, towards the end," Doctor Rapunzel said. "Even *with* his unfair advantages, he wasn't sure he was going to get away."

"He has, though, hasn't he?" Bella said.

"For now."

The House in the Forest

EAVY GREY CLOUDS bring the night early, rolling in thick with rain over a clearing that has long since been overrun by the forest. Here stands what was once a pleasant, sturdy house, the sort of place that might once have belonged to a successful merchant or craftsman.

Now the garden is nothing but brambles and wild roses, and one ancient, crooked apple tree. The wind hisses and howls through the broken panes and cracked shutters, and the first few rain drops fall into upper rooms.

The main lower room, however, has solid walls. The thick doors boast a great deal of fancy ironwork that looks somewhat newer than the rest of the décor, and the barred windows are tightly secured behind oak shutters.

Within, crates, ironbound chests, and similar items are piled up around the walls.

And there one may also observe Prince Charming, pacing the thick, handwoven rug before the fire, restless as a cat in a storm.

* * *

ROLAND PERCHED CROSS-LEGGED on a stool as close to the fire as he could get without setting himself alight. He looked as though he should perhaps be sewing something, but instead, as usual, he was eating (where he *put* all that food was a mystery for the ages).

"Who *was* that?" Charming said.

"Your guess is as good as mine," said Roland, around a mouthful of cold sausage appropriated from the Crooked Spoon.

"Oh, don't be so damned *helpful*."

"What do you want from me, Your Highness? I don't know who the masked stranger was. I don't know how they found you or why they challenged you. I mean, I've seen plenty of fights picked in taverns, and I've seen plenty of duels, whether for 'honour' or 'a lady's name' or the relative merits of rather mediocre racehorses. But that one felt... strange. Started off almost like playacting, then it got serious."

"I knew it! I *knew* they weren't really..." Charming, unusually, fought for words.

"Really what? Wanting to find out if you had a sense of honour? Well they found *that* out, didn't they?"

"Shut up."

Roland smirked.

Charming stood over him, large, muscular, and a little wild-eyed in the firelight. "We *had* a *deal*."

Roland looked up at him, his face stony. "If you can call it that, yes."

"Have you betrayed it?"

"I abide by the terms. It's not as though I have a *choice*, is it?"

Charming scowled and turned away. "You really do hate me."

"You know who I'd hate, if I could be bothered?" Roland said. "Me. For being an idiot. But I don't do hate, as a rule. Not unless I'm prepared to put in a *lot* of effort."

"Fine. Everyone *else* hates me."

"Oh, here we go."

"I'm doing what I have to."

"Yeah, yeah. Not like you *enjoy* it or anything. Not like you giggle with glee when we pull off a nice scam. Not like you—"

"I do not *giggle with glee*. For Goose's sake, you make me sound like a sixteen-year-old girl!"

"'Everyone hates me' doesn't sound like a sixteen-year-old girl, then?" Roland clapped a hand to his brow. "Everyone *hates* me and they're all *prettier* than I am... Nah, okay, you'd never say *that*."

Charming flung himself into one of the chairs. "Can you stop? For just a moment? And help me *think*? Whoever it was, they were *good*. A little old-fashioned in the fighting style, perhaps, but damn good. And the voice was educated. The clothes..." He scowled, this time in thought. "Well-made, but thinking back, the fit was loose. As though they'd been made for someone bigger. You didn't get anything from the smell?"

Roland shook his head. "Drenched in scent, like half of them 'round here. Can't wait to get somewhere where people smell like *people*. Look, I *was* suspicious, but they're not *here,* are they? What's the point worrying? Maybe it was just some local young buck trying his luck. Heard about a mysterious nobleman in the local tavern, heard about the dragon-slayage, put two and two together and decided to try and impress the barmaid. Speaking of which"—his eyes darted to the door into the kitchen—"you *sure* about that?"

"Sure about what?" said the barmaid in question, shouldering the door open and coming into the room with a tray of steaming dishes.

"Nothing," Charming said, the sulks disappearing from his face as though whisked away like a magician's silk handkerchief. He leapt to his feet. "Let me take that."

But Nell had already put it on the table. "That *kitchen!* If that stove's ever been cleaned—*ever*—I'd be amazed. I did what I could, but it'll probably all taste of smoke."

Roland was sniffing the air appreciatively. "Smells good to me."

"If we're staying here for long, I need stuff. Flour and soap. And some pans that aren't older than my grandma's best hat."

"I'm not planning on it," Charming said. "Besides, I thought you wanted to get to the city? See some life?"

"I do, but you're not planning on leaving in *this* weather, are you?" She pulled at one of the shutters, which groaned loudly at the indignity of being moved for (presumably) the first time in years, and peered into the dark. "It's pi—it's pelting down, out there."

"Well, not *tonight,*" Charming said. "Tonight, I thought we could make ourselves comfortable." He slid an arm around Nell's waist.

She stepped out of his grip and put the table in between them. "Not *that* comfortable, thank you. I want a lift to the city, and I don't want to arrive there with a bun baking in *my* oven." She patted the old but extremely well-sharpened knife she had tucked in her belt. "I'm no mysterious swordsman, but I can gut a pig faster'n you can blink, so don't do anything stupid."

Charming did, in fact, blink. "Sorry. I think I misunderstood."

"Yeah, you and every other chancer who turns up at the Crooked Spoon."

"I am not 'every chancer,'" he said, with some asperity.

"No, you're a prince, apparently. Don't seem to me like royalty's even one rasher's worth better behaved than my usual customers."

Now both Charming and Roland were blinking. Roland was looking at Nell with increased interest. "You," he said, "I could get to like."

"Well, I'm flattered, I'm sure," Nell said. "Now unless you want it cold as well as smoky, eat."

As they ate—the meal that was better than might have been expected, given the state of the kitchen—Nell looked around. "You don't *live* here, do you?"

"No," Charming said. "It's a... waystation. Place to rest the horses."

She waved at the boxes. "What *is* all that stuff?"

"Furnishings," Charming said. "For when I'm settled."

"And why exactly is a prince running around the place getting into fights in taverns anyway?" Nell asked.

"Well, the tavern fight was incidental," Charming said. "What I mostly do is rescue damsels in distress." He tipped his mug at her.

"Damsel, am I? I wasn't *distressed*. Mostly just bored."

"And to be fair, you pretty much rescued yourself," Roland said.

"To be *fair,*" said Charming, glaring at Roland, "it was much easier than slaying a dragon."

"Glad to hear it," Nell said. "So *you're* the one who got rid of the dragon in Eingeten? Very dashing, I must say. Wondered why your breeches were all scorchy."

"I had no idea it was that noticeable," Charming confessed. "I really must change before we leave." He fiddled with his fork. "So... you heard about that, then?"

"Whole duchy's heard about it."

"What are they saying, exactly?"

"That the dragon got murdered by a noble prince who then disappeared under mysterious circumstances. Some people were saying he left before he could be rewarded, so that he wouldn't be corr—corrup—get too up himself after his victory. Very worthy, eh?" She quirked her eyebrows at Roland, who sniggered.

"Well, that's a new one on me," he said. "Funny how some people just seem to have a way of getting the right stories told about them."

Nell pushed her plate away and cupped her chin in her hands. "Bit too virtuous, was she? The lady?"

"She was an exceptional person," Charming said, standing up abruptly. "Now, if you'll excuse me, I'm going to find some legwear more up to your standards." He bowed and left the room.

"What'd I say?" Nell said.

"Don't worry about it," Roland said. "He's got a bug up his bottom about the Lady Ysoude. And... another lady. Several ladies, actually."

"Well blow me over, I'd never have guessed," Nell said. "What a huge surprise that is."

Roland pointed his fork at her. "I *do* like you. Any of that stew left?"

BY EARLY EVENING, the pummelling rain finally eased off, leaving only water dripping from the eaves and into the attics, and widening damp stains on the ceiling of the one habitable room.

Here, worn out by the day's excitement and full of stew, the three travellers had fallen asleep. Charming had insisted on giving up the comfortable sofa to Nell, to Roland's loudly expressed surprise. Charming himself sprawled in an armchair. He had changed into old but slightly less singed breeches, and taken off his boots. Roland was curled up on the hearthrug, by the banked remains of the fire.

There was a faint crackling noise by one of the windows, like a twig breaking. There was a smell of bacon grease. Nell had opened one shutter earlier; now it shifted slightly, the latch rose as though by itself, and the shutter swung open, without any hint of the tortured creak that had accompanied its earlier movement.

A hand appeared through the window now inexplicably devoid of glass. The hand held a vial, which it cast on the floor.

The vial smashed with a tinkle no louder than a pixie's fart.

Vapour slunk out of the remains, glowing silver for a moment in the darkness of the room, then dissipating, invisible, into the air.

Charming's posture slumped further into the cushions. Nell's breathing deepened and slowed. Roland rolled on his back and began to snore.

A moment later there was a soft *snick* and the ironbound door to the room opened.

A hooded, black-clad figure moved silently across the floor towards Charming in a cloud of dark, foresty perfume.

It reached out and grabbed his boots.

The next moment the figure was flailing and stumbling backwards.

"Sleep begone, charm be done!" Roland yelled, seated on the figure's shoulders and pulling the hood tight about its face and neck. "Wakey wakey eggs and bakey!"

Charming bolted to his feet, Nell sat up rubbing her eyes.

Charming snatched the boots from the figure's grip, and levelled his sword at their throat. "Now let's see who you are!"

Roland yanked off the hood.

And Doctor Emilia Rapunzel stood glaring at Charming. Roland jumped down and pulled her arms behind her, wrapping the hood around her wrists.

"Wait..." Charming said. "Oh. *Oh*. The Rotterturm, yes? Emilia? Well, this is a surprise." He didn't lower his sword.

"*Doctor* Rapunzel, thank you very much. And I want what's mine," Doctor Rapunzel said.

"Congratulations on the doctorate; I *knew* you were clever. But the boots? Technically, they never belonged to you, but to Doctor Hilda von Riesentor, who—so far as anyone knows—is still alive. They *would* be yours, if you could take them. Which I am afraid you have signally failed to do." He looked her up and down. "Somehow I don't think it was you who accosted me in the Crooked Spoon. Exactly how many black-clad strangers should I expect?"

"Wait, there's *more* of 'em?" Nell said.

"Exactly how many people have you robbed, deceived, and defrauded?" the doctor asked.

Charming sighed. "Roland, be a good fellow and tie her up. And make sure she hasn't any other nasty little surprises about her person."

"Will do."

Emilia remained silent as Roland whipped a rope out of his ever-present backpack and bound her wrists and ankles, leaving enough loose rope between her feet to allow her to walk, and briskly searched her. "Not a thing," he said.

"You relied on a single potion for this?" Charming said. "Oh, dear, I think you should ask for your doctorate back."

"My doctorate was in the arcane arts, not in confidence trickery," the doctor said. "Perhaps you should set up a school. Professor Charming's College of Crooked Dealings. Your conscience surgically removed upon entry. Classes in robbery, heart-breaking..."

"Oh, now, you can't tell me I broke *your* heart," Charming protested.

"Mine? No. It had already been hardened beyond such fragility, by one only a little worse than you."

Charming put up his sword and turned away. "Take her away, Roland. Anywhere, so long as it isn't here."

"Shall I bung her in the spare stable?" Roland said. "It's pretty watertight still, and the door's mostly solid."

Charming waved his hand. "Fine, fine."

Nell watched this exchange silently, and slipped away to the kitchen, to pull the kettle over the fire.

NO ONE WENT back to sleep.

Charming slammed the open shutter, and paced about searching for something to wedge under the latch. Roland returned from the stables and inspected the door, nodded to himself, and when Charming asked, snappishly, how the doctor had managed to get in, said: "Not sure. I mean, probably a crowbar? And a charm of silence? If she only had enough stuff on her for one, I understand why she used bacon grease on the shutter..."

"I don't actually care," Charming said. "What I want to know is, can you make it secure?"

"If you don't care, why'd you ask? I can shove a couple of those chests in front of it," Roland said. "Or, you know, you could. If it's not too much trouble. Having something to push around, other than me, might calm you down."

Charming's hands curled into fists. Roland grinned at him.

Charming walked over to one of the mounds of chests and looked them over, pulling at one, then shaking his head and pushing it back against the wall. "What about some of the stuff from upstairs?"

"Well, we could, if we could get it down here, but most of it's rotten. Like this stuff will be if you don't get that roof seen to." Roland eyed the spreading damp stain on the ceiling. "Or you could get up there with a hammer and nails, eh, Your Highness?"

"Why don't I send you up there, instead, hmm?" Charming said.

Nell shook her head. "I need a cup of something. *If* there's anything in that kitchen that still tastes of anything."

A moment later there was a loud *clang* and Roland rushed into the kitchen to see Nell standing over a spilled, dented kettle, cursing.

"What happened?" Charming said, hopping into view shortly after Roland, pulling his boot up.

"Heard something grunt. Right outside, like it was just under the window. Scared the life out of me. And the horses..."

They could hear the whickering and thuds from the stable as the horses apparently tried to kick their way through the walls. The Mostly Donkey let out a long, shrieking bray.

Roland sniffed the air. "Oh. That's... interesting."

"What?" Charming said.

Roland raised a finger in the air, quelling him.

A deep, resonant grunt, a sound so massive it was almost solid, reverberated through the cracks in the walls, the splintered boards, the missing tiles and straight into the back of the brain. The sort of sound that tells you something in your vicinity is large and annoyed and about to do something about it.

Grunt... grunt... grunt.

"Bear?" Charming said.

"Bear. *Bears,* plural." Roland was frowning to himself.

"Why would they be here? We ate what we brought, there's no food here to pull 'em," Nell said.

"Strictly speaking, yes, there is," Roland said, waving at her and the Prince.

"Oh."

Nell and Charming backed towards the kitchen table, as though a bit of wood between them and what was out there might make a difference.

Roland jumped up on the sink and peered through a knothole in one of the shutters.

Charming gathered himself. "How many?"

"I can see better in the dark than you, Your Highness, but I'm not a frickin owl. But judging by the eyes I can see—a lot. Twenty, maybe? And they're not all local, neither."

"What... how?" Nell said.

"Roland knows things," Charming said, tightly. "Useful, but he gets very full of himself."

"If you're going to be like that," Roland said, "I shan't tell you what else is out there."

Then there was another sound. This one was a strange, creaking groan, a drawn out yawp, with a threatening urgency.

"Stag," all three of them said.

"What the *Goose*...?" said Nell. "It's not even rutting season for another month!"

Arooo! Aroooo! Arooooo!

This sound bypassed the brain altogether and went straight to the bowels and the knees.

It said, *Run, ape.*

Charming found himself, much to his annoyance, pressed against the rear wall of the kitchen. Nell was next to him, holding up a frying pan, her teeth bared in a grimace. Charming had the brief and extremely irrelevant thought that they were very good teeth, white and well-kept.

"But *why?*" Nell wailed. "They don't... they shouldn't..."

"That's the worrying bit," Roland said. "No reason for any of 'em, except the wolves, to be moving around at night. Less reason for 'em to be yelling their heads off, and no reason at all for them to all be here together, unless someone's brought them. And is whipping them up to make all that noise."

"So they're just trying to scare us," Nell said. "I mean, that's not so bad, is it? If they're just trying to scare us?"

"It's not so bad if that's where it stops," Charming said, looking grim, "Because *someone* out there has the power to get a lot of wild beasts to do what they want."

"Make me feel better, why don't you?" Nell muttered, gripping her frying pan harder.

The noises stopped. Water dripped. The kitchen clock, which Nell had wound out of habit, went *clonk—clonk—*

clonk. A few whickers and thuds and a hoarse bray came from the stables.

"We should get that woman out of the stables," Nell said.

"Are you joking? She's part of it!" Charming said.

"Well, what about the horses? And your pack beast?"

"If they were after the horses, we wouldn't still be hearing the horses," Roland said. "The house is pretty tight, but you could get in those stables with a bent teaspoon."

"I thought you said the door was solid? What if she escapes?" Charming snapped.

"*Mostly* solid, I said. Told you you should keep this place up better."

Nell sat down on the kitchen settle and dropped the frying pan on the table with a *clang*. "All I wanted was a bit of life," she said. "And now look. What did you *do?*"

"Is that really the important question right now?" Charming snapped.

"If I'm going to get torn apart by enchanted wild beasts I'd at least like to know *why*. I mean, you stole someone's boots. So what? Is this really about *boots?*"

Charming slumped on the other settle. "Is there anything to drink in this place?"

"Three barrels of Morgensen's Vastly Peculiar Rum and that bottle of wine from Uparal," Roland said.

"That bottle is worth a king's ransom!" Charming said.

"Oh, please. That seneschal was a lush and the Duke had about as delicate a palate as your average dog. Anything decent had been drunk and replaced with whatever came to hand well before we got there."

"What? So why in the name of the Goose did we take the stuff?"

"Well, I wasn't going to tell whoever you *flogged* it to, was I?"

"If there's rum," Nell declared, "I want some. And you *still* haven't told me what you did. Except you stole some rubbish wine from someone. And boots."

"You don't want the rum," Roland said. "Trust me. Not if you want to wake up knowing your own name and without any mysterious new tattoos."

"Who's going to give me a tattoo?" said Nell. "We're at least two days' journey from the sea here!"

"With Morgensen's Vastly Peculiar, that's not really a problem. Whyn't you tell her the history of your noble deeds, Your Highness, and I'll have a look and see if there's anything more drinkable in the place?"

"I don't—" But before Charming could finish, the grunting and the howling and the roaring rattled the shutters in their frames.

Silence fell again, broken only by the scratch of branches (or claws, or antlers) against the windows and the brush of the wind (or perhaps of thick, rough fur) against the corners of the walls.

"Well, *I* need a drink," Roland said, and left.

"Go on, tell me of a noble deed," Nell said. "Or a not-so-noble one, so long as it's a good story. I could do with something to listen to."

"Would you care? If it's not a noble deed?"

"Look." Nell leant forward. "I wanted to leave that village because it was *boring*. I wanted to go with you because you *weren't* boring. I already know you're not *nice*. Neither am I, I s'pose, or I wouldn't have hit that duellist. *And* I would have tried to stop you stealing those horses instead of telling you which one to take."

Charming was looking at her with curiosity and

something that might almost have been admiration. "You're very straightforward, aren't you?"

"My nan always said if my tongue were any blunter I'd beat myself to death with it."

He gave a bark of laughter. "Fine turn with a metaphor, your nan."

"A what now?"

"Never mind. All right, why don't I tell you about how I tricked the Doge of Penisilia out of his sacral robes?"

"Now, that's an interesting choice," Roland said, re-entering the room. "Wonder why you want to tell that story. Instead of, you know, one of the others."

"Did you find any drink, or have you just returned to make snarky remarks?"

"Ta-da!" Roland held up a small, murky bottle.

Charming peered at it suspiciously. "What *is* that?"

"It's *not* Morgensen's Vastly Peculiar, is what it is."

"Fair point."

Roland poured small measures of deep purple-red liquid into three battered tankards. "Cheers."

Nell sniffed, sipped and looked thoughtful. "Had worse. Had better, too."

Roland sniffed, sipped and sighed. "Yep."

Clonk, went the clock.

Charming tossed his liquor back in a single gulp and said, "Right. I shall tell the tale of The Doge of Penisilia and his sacral robes."

He sat up, and his slightly sullen demeanour visibly changed. His eyes sparkled. His voice became light, rhythmic, a voice you wanted to lean towards.

"Fair Penisilia! City of many rivers, great pillared halls, birthplace of artists and fine duellists. Ruled—in name at least—by its Doge, though in truth the actual running of the place was done by an army of scribes and stewards and bureaucrats.

"The Doge of Penisilia was a man of vast wealth, vast girth, and a sense of self-importance greater than either. He lived in a fine palace full of servants and splendour, adorned with very many self-portraits and three separate kitchens, each headed by one of the Doge's personal cooks.

"When he inherited the position of Doge, he declared that the splendid sacral robes that went with the post were too shabby for a man of his importance. If anyone realised that the real reason he wanted them replaced was that he was simply too wide to get into them, they were far too afraid of the Doge to mention it. For as well as his vast wealth, vast girth, and vast self-importance, the Doge was possessed of vast vanity, and a temper so hot it could have cooked the six meals he got through each and every day."

Nell giggled.

(It is worth remembering who is telling this tale. The Doge might, indeed, have been a man of generous appetites. He might also have been a man of genial and persuadable nature, whose new friend, the mysterious Prince Affascinare, induced him to commission his excessive new robes in order to impress the city's rivals with his prestige and power and thus improve Penisilia's standing and economic status. Unfortunately, the Doge disappeared when his suddenly impoverished city, lacking the money to pay its troops, was overrun by its neighbours, so no one can ask him.)

"So he ordered new robes be made, more splendid than any before them. The inner robe was to be of the finest silk, all the way from Madilanar, sewn with the iridescent blue wings of twenty thousand tiny butterflies. These must be captured alive, and fed upon lavender honey for a month, and soothed to death with the vapour of sacred incense from the mountains of Dhirr, or their wings would lose their lustre.

"The outer robe was to be of finest brocade, made by the weavers of Tentrini, known all the world over for the exquisite beauty of their work and the astonishing amount of gold they charged for every single foot of it. This brocade would have the Doge's symbol worked into the weave, where it would shimmer as a constant reminder of his position to anyone who might be in danger of forgetting it. And in case this was not enough, the symbol would be embroidered in gold thread on the cuffs, and the collar, and the hem, interwoven with the symbol of his natal house—a red rose adorned with a single drop of dew—which would be embroidered in rubies, with diamonds for the dewdrops.

"But though the Doge had created the designs himself, and so of course was entirely satisfied that they were of the most perfect pattern and exquisite taste, he feared that any ordinary tailor would be simply incapable of rendering his vision as he desired. So he sent out messengers throughout the land, seeking a tailor skilled enough to fulfil his desires—"

Grunt. Graahh! Arooooo!

Nell, who had been listening intently, yelped and knocked her tankard onto the floor.

Roland cocked his head. "Well, that's it, they're all around now," he shouted over the racket.

"Dammit!" Charming jumped to his feet and started pacing. The noise eventually quieted, leaving only the quiet dripping of Nell's spilled tankard, the tick of the clock edging towards midnight, and the rap of Charming's boots on the stone floor.

"Don't know what *you're* worried about," Roland said.

"What do you mean?" Nell said. She turned to Charming "What does he mean?"

"He's got a way of, shall we say, avoiding getting caught in situations other people can't get out of," Roland said.

"What? So he'd just *leave* us here?"

Roland shrugged. "He's done it before."

"I'm not leaving anyone," Charming snapped. "More to the point, I'm not leaving the... furniture."

"Hmm," Roland said.

"I do wish one of you would tell me what the Goose is really going on," Nell said. "Boots, furniture... I just don't *understand*. Why...?"

"What do you need to understand?" Charming said. "Unless you can think of a way for us to get out *with* everything..."

"What am I, a wizard? If you mean everything in those boxes, you need a train of packhorses not one measly sort of a donkey and a pair of farm horses! Especially since they'll all bolt the minute they get the chance, and so would I!" Nell jumped to her feet. "I wish I'd never met you," she said, with a depth of feeling that silenced even Roland for a moment.

The clock struck midnight with a *bong*.

A tidal wave of noise broke over them: howls, grunts, shrieks, crashing and thudding and *boom* and *crack,* the hollow pounding of hooves into wood, the splintering of shutters, the crunch of glass.

Nell grabbed the frying pan and scooted under the table.

Charming bolted for the main room, followed by Roland.

The outer door was beginning to splinter and smoke around its iron bindings. As they watched, one of the shutters cracked completely across, and the bottom half fell to the floor, accompanied by a shower of glass splinters. A hot animal reek filled the room, and yellow eyes glowed through the gap in the window bars.

Charming snatched up his bow, nocked, aimed, shot through the gap. There was a thud.

"The door, Roland," he yelled over the racket.

"I'm trying!" Roland said, dragging a chest almost his own height towards the door.

"Not that one!" Charming shouted.

"It's the heaviest!"

"But—" Charming's protests were interrupted as two great clawed paws gripped one of the window bars. A glimpse of a muzzle, teeth the length of his hand, a *grunt*.

He nocked and loosed, and the bear shrieked in rage as the arrow pierced its paw, stuck there for a moment, then fell to the floor. It had hit the window bar instead of going all the way through.

Charming swore.

The bear, bleeding and extremely annoyed, pulled even harder.

The bar began to bend.

Charming scrabbled for another arrow. There was a deep, hollow *whock* against the door, such as may have been made by a large set of antlers hitting it hard.

The metal plate around the lock did not bend, but the wood around it creaked, and an inch-long splinter shot out. A crack streaked across first one plank, then another.

"It won't hold!" Roland yelled.

The plate popped free of the wood, letting off more splinters. One stabbed Roland through the earlobe, and he yelled in protest.

The door began to inch open. Roland, his hands on the trunk and his feet braced against the floor, slid slowly backwards.

A black-clad figure dropped from the ceiling, in a rain of disintegrating plaster.

Charming spun around, dropped his arrow and had his sword in hand in a movement almost too fast for the eye to follow. "You *again?* Didn't you have enough last time?" He lunged.

The figure danced out of his way. "Perhaps I prefer an honest fight."

"Oh, how virtuous. Wondering where your friend is? She's out in the stable. It's not very safe out there."

"Safer than with you," the figure said. "And where's *your* little friend?"

Charming knew better than to glance behind him, although he did briefly wonder if Nell was still under the kitchen table. She'd been very helpful the last time, but that was against one duellist, not a forest full of magic-driven wildlife. He was conscious of a fleeting regret at the thought of Nell, but was immediately distracted by his opponent's blade whistling uncomfortably close to his neck. He avoided it by the barest breath, and started edging around the room, keeping the stranger at bay. They pressed hard, the blades clanging and sparking. A seething mass of fur and teeth showed through the widening gap in the door, and the broken window was all bent bars and snarl and claws.

Charming gained a brief advantage, and drove his opponent back, towards the piled trunks. He took the risk of glancing up, at the rain-dripping hole in the ceiling.

The gap in the doorway was suddenly empty. Charming made a dive for it, and was almost impaled on the sword held by the second figure who had suddenly filled it. Charming sidestepped with unnatural speed. The second fighter did not have quite the superlative grace and agility of the first, but was worryingly competent—little style, but a lot of *stab*.

The two converged on him.

Roland leaped from his perch on the trunks and grabbed at the newcomer, catching a sleeve, spinning them off balance.

The first advanced relentlessly, pushing Charming back step by step.

The second attacker shook Roland off, flinging him back towards the trunks. Roland hit, rolled, dove for their legs, and brought them down. They cried out, the sword spinning from their hand across the floor, and Roland pressed the edge of his knife to their throat. "Gotcha," he said. "Now I suggest you stay very, very still, eh?"

Charming smiled at the first fighter. "Your friend is in trouble," he said, as calmly as he could for how fast he was breathing.

"Let her go." Irritatingly, his opponent was barely out of breath, but their voice was tight, and higher than he remembered.

"Oh, I don't think I want that. You two have given me a great deal of trouble. Why don't you drop your sword?"

"You'd best do it," Nell said, leaning in the kitchen doorway, wiping her hands on her skirt.

"Do you know who he is? What he's *done*?" the prone figure cried, showing little fear of Roland's blade.

"He's not the one broke in someone's *house* in the middle of the *night,* with a bunch of savage *animals,*" Nell said.

Roland shifted his weight, and the figure on the floor gasped.

The first fighter put up their sword. "I see you have as much honour as I suspected," they said. "Very well. Don't hurt her."

Charming took their sword.

"'Her,' is it?" Roland snatched off the second fighter's mask.

Princess Marie Blanche de Neige glared up at Charming, who tapped his chin thoughtfully with his left hand for a moment (sword still raised in his right), then said, "The apple! Of course."

In a fashion not generally approved of in princesses, Marie Blanche spat. "Am I supposed to be grateful that you remember me?"

Charming ignored her. "And you?" He turned to the black-clad fencer. "I wonder if I can guess."

Bella sighed and pulled off her mask. "I shan't put you to the trouble," she said.

"Oh, dear. You *really* don't know when to give up, do you?" Charming said.

"Don't worry, I don't want to *marry* you," Bella snapped. "Not anymore."

"Trying to force my hand like that. I wouldn't have thought it of you," Charming said, shaking his head. "I really wouldn't."

"You mean you actually thought of me at all?" Bella said. "Am *I* supposed to be flattered now?"

"I should have guessed who my challenger was from your skill," Charming said. "And your grace, of course.

As for you..." He looked down at Marie Blanche. "I must say your ability with beasts is astonishing. I do hope none of them are going to do anything foolish, at this point—out of misplaced loyalty, or anything like that."

"No," Marie Blanche said. "I do not wish any more of them to be hurt needlessly."

"Quite prepared for *me* to be hurt, weren't you?"

"Are you surprised?"

Charming shrugged. "I *did* actually rescue you, after all. I rescued all of you."

"You also robbed all of us. You destroyed my father."

"Oh, come now. I did nothing of the sort."

Marie Blanche's look was so murderous that despite her being on the floor with a knife at her throat, Charming took a step backwards.

"No, really," he protested. "I *liked* your father."

"You liked him so well you were prepared to deceive him and rob him, and in doing so destroy the last of his confidence in his own judgement. He has never been the same. You are despicable."

Charming's mouth tightened. "Your confidence in *your* own judgement remains unimpaired, I see," he said. "Well, delightful as this reunion is, I think it's time we called it to a close. Roland, help me get them to the stable. I'm sure such enterprising women can work out how to break out. If not, no doubt some wandering woodcutter or the like will find them. And perhaps they'll be a little more *grateful* for being rescued, this time."

Roland sighed and got up, and helped Marie Blanche to her feet. Then he turned to Charming.

"No," he said.

Charming simply blinked. "What do you mean, no?"

"I mean, *no,* Your Highness." Roland put his knife away.

Marie Blanche brushed herself down.

The door to the kitchen opened. Doctor Rapunzel walked in.

Charming said, "Roland?" He looked around. Bella blocked the door, and Marie Blanche the window. Nell was nowhere to be seen.

"Guess Nell decided buggering off was the better part of valour," Roland said. "Which is what I'd have done as soon as I saw you, if I'd had any sense."

A few moments earlier...

ORRY ABOUT THIS," Roland said, leading Doctor Rapunzel into the stable. "It is *sort of* watertight in here..."

Any further conversation was rendered briefly impossible by the Mostly Donkey, which let forth a series of shrieking brays until Roland pointed at it and said, "*Shut up.*"

It stopped as though its mouth had been sewn together, then hunched its back. "No kicking, neither," Roland said, "Just *be quiet.*"

The Mostly Donkey turned its back to them.

"Actually, I'm most sorry about leaving you with her," Roland said. "But she'll keep shut for a bit. She'll probably fart, though. Haven't worked out a way to stop that, yet. I have to say, you've got further than most. The potion was a good idea."

"Oh, I knew it wouldn't work," the doctor said. "Not on you. The one that works on demons is *much* harder."

Roland froze, then slowly turned. "Wha—?"

"You must have recognised me, once my mask was off. Did you really think I wouldn't know who *you* were... Rumplestiltskin?"

"Oh, *Goose*." The small man—or imp—slumped against the stable door. "So *that's* what all the stinky perfume was about. Didn't think that was your style."

"I remembered the accuracy of your nose."

"How'd you find out?"

"Charming's other victims described his manservant in some detail. I began to suspect that perhaps you hadn't returned to the Infernal Regions when Mother Hilda died. A little further research, and a considerable amount of bribery, eventually provided me with your real name. So why did you stay?"

Rumplestiltskin rubbed his accurate nose and sighed. "Look. The cuisine in the Infernal Regions isn't exactly what you might call *gourmet*. Or even what you might call edible, most of the time. And it gets dull as a plank, down there. I fancied having a few more decent meals, kicking around a bit, having some fun, now *she* wasn't in control anymore.

"So I got chatting with ol' Prince Smarming, didn't I? Reminisced about a few places I'd eaten—I didn't *know* he'd knocked you out, by the way, thought you'd just fallen asleep from, you know, being tired. It had been quite a day. Anyway, I mentioned this really good fish supper I'd had, at this place which just happens to be in his hometown, of all the stinky luck. I mean, I've been around, I can't remember *everywhere*. And he remembered me."

"Because you ate in a tavern in his hometown?" Doctor Rapunzel said. "That was all? So how did he know your *name*? Come, I know there's more to it than that. Please don't take me for a fool. I might have been one when we first met, but that was some time ago."

Rumplestiltskin grinned. "Oh, you were never a fool. Inexperienced, yes. But I could tell you were going places. All right. There might have been some, you know, local trouble. With his dad, who holds a grudge, and went and had an artist do a picture of me in case I came back. I mean who *does* that? So it turns out there's been a picture of me hanging up in the royal treasury ever since—and as it happened I was using the same body. I mention his hometown, Charming goes, *Ah, now I know where I've seen you before,* and says my name, right then and there. He must have been keeping it in his head all this time, just in case he found me. Bastard. So then of course I'm *bound* to the annoying arsehole."

"Surely he didn't have the power to make you his familiar?"

Roland shuddered. "He didn't have *her* abilities. But he knew enough to bind me for one specific service."

"Hmm. I thought as much." Doctor Rapunzel smiled, and picked a bit of straw from her jacket. "Explain to me the *specific* wording of your agreement with him, and perhaps we can work something out."

Prince in Boots

OU'RE STILL BOUND!" Charming protested, as Roland (let's continue to call him Roland, since that's what we've called him up to this point) took the Prince's sword from his slackening grasp. "You're bound to help me stay free!" He shoved his hands in his pockets and glared.

"I'm bound to help you stay free from anyone *sent by your father*," Roland said. "These ladies came after you entirely of their own accord. It's all in the wording, Your Highness."

"You little *wretch*."

Roland aimed a finger at him like a dagger. "I'd just got out of *years* of being bound as familiar to that witch, strung like a puppet, hardly able to move or speak without her say-so. And you snatch me into another binding before I have a moment to breathe. What did you expect? Lifelong loyalty?" He grabbed for Charming's arms, but Charming twisted out of his grasp, pulled something from his pocket, and crushed it against Roland's forehead.

Roland shrieked and staggered backwards. A coil of greasy smoke and a smell of scorched imp, like someone setting light to a rotten egg, rose into the air.

"Rowan berries!" he wailed. "It burns! It burns!"

Doctor Rapunzel grabbed him. "Hold still! Let me help!"

Marie Blanche and Bella lunged for Charming, but he jumped.

It was not a jump any human should have been able to make. But the boots—the precious, scruffy boots, enchanted to always carry their wearer away from danger—propelled him up into the hole in the ceiling. He caught a rafter, swung himself up, and disappeared.

CHARMING LEAPT ACROSS the upper room, floorboards crumbling behind him, the boots finding the few solid beams with their usual uncanny accuracy. He yelped and folded his arms across his face as his feet propelled him towards a window with a few panes of glass still left in it, felt the shattering *crunch* and the rainy night air, spun, dropped and landed in something soft.

It turned out to be the midden.

It was a well-developed midden, of long standing. Or, since the house had been mostly unused for some time, perhaps 'of long oozing' would be more apt.

Charming spent some moments struggling out of the mire, trying desperately not to breathe through his nose.

"Need a hand?"

He looked up to see Nell, seated on one horse and holding the other by the reins.

"I thought you'd gone!"

"I probably should have; seems like you're a much worse person than I thought."

"It's not what it sounds like. I promise I'll explain."

"Hmm. You'd better." She reached down a hand to help him up, wrinkling her nose. "Ew. Come on, then, quickly."

Charming swung himself onto the other horse, which snorted and kicked.

"Sorry, horse," Nell said. "Let's hope the rain gets worse and washes him off a bit."

They urged the horses into a canter and disappeared into the night.

The Imp and the Mostly Donkey

OCTOR RAPUNZEL FINISHED wiping the last trace of rowan from Roland's head, as he swore steadily, calling down (or up) imprecations on rowan trees, sneaky bastard so-and-sos in general and Charming in particular.

The doctor told him to hold still, dipped a cloth in a vial of green murk, and dabbed it on the burn. "There. That should help. How do you feel?"

Roland shifted his shoulders, then stared at a spot somewhere in midair. "You know what? I'm free." He jumped up, and did a little jig. "Free!"

"Would someone please explain what's going on?" said Bella.

"Rowan destroys magic," Doctor Rapunzel said. "It burned him, but it also broke Charming's binding." She looked at Roland. "I still don't know how in the name of *Goose* you persuaded him to use it on you."

"Oh, well, bloody stuff grows everywhere," Roland said. "Pretended to get it on me a couple of times, made a big fuss. He got curious." He shrugged. "Didn't really think he'd ever use it, I was taking anything I could get. And listen... I'm sorry, right? I wouldn't have done you over if I'd had a choice."

Rapunzel gave her cool smile. "Are you *sure* you're an imp?"

"Oh, eff off. Look, you always treated me decent, insofar as you were allowed. I got *standards*. I got loyalties, when I get to choose 'em."

"Well, likewise," Rapunzel said, sealing the vial and rising to her feet. "And I will fulfil my part of the bargain, and ensure your name is wiped from Mother Hilda's books. And I, of course, will hold my tongue, and do my best to discourage any of your compatriots from revealing it. Assuming I still have any influence."

"Oh, don't you worry about that," Roland said. "Next time I'm down there, I can do my own discouraging." He cracked his knuckles and grinned. "I'm looking forward to it." But the grin fell away almost immediately. "Much good it does me, since that bastard Charming knows it. And that bloody picture's probably still up in the palace. Well, I'll make well and damn sure to never go near *him* again! I know his smell by now, whatever he douses himself with, no matter how he scrubs—and he does, I swear; never met anyone that vain. Not even in the Infernal, and we're *known* for it." He bounced up and down a few more times, then stopped, and smirked at the three women.

"Well, ladies, it's been an *interesting* experience. Good luck with the slippery Prince. I think he'll live to regret taking you on. I'd hang around and watch, but I got places to be that aren't here." He swept a bow that was only slightly mocking, and disappeared in a puff of sulphurous smoke.

"I hoped he might stay," Bella said.

"Really?" said Marie Blanche. "Why?"

"He helped, didn't he?" said Bella. "And I thought he liked us."

"He helped because it was of use to him," Marie Blanche said. "You—Oh, never mind."

"I know, I know, you think I'm naïve," Bella said. "But he *does* like the doctor. And he was sorry. He said."

"A capacity to see the best in people is a good quality to have," Rapunzel said. "I hope you may never lose it."

"I would rather see people exactly as they are," said Marie Blanche. "It would save a great deal of grief."

"Since most people struggle to even see themselves as they are, I think that power is exceptionally rare," said the sorceress. She looked around at the piled trunks, and boxes, and bottles, and rolled carpets, and raised her eyebrows. "Does anyone recognise anything, or shall we just start opening them?"

MEANWHILE, IN THE stables, Roland (as he shall, if he's lucky, henceforth be known), appeared in front of the Mostly Donkey. "Come on," he said. "We've got a portrait to hunt down and burn."

The beast blared.

"It's no good yelling," Roland said. "Even if she hears you, she hasn't guessed. And *I* certainly wasn't going to tell her. Just in case she gets some silly ideas."

He took the Mostly Donkey's headrope in his hand, and pulled its face close to his, staring into one of its red-rimmed eyes. Deep down, there might have been a flicker of something, a smear of cold grey. "Thirty-years-and-three you kept me captive," Roland said, "and three times thirty-years-and-three I'll keep you. Should have picked another imp, Hilda my dear."

He tugged on the headrope, and the Mostly Donkey, unable to resist, followed him out of the stable.

The Kitchen Maid, the King, the Curse—and the Cat

ND LO, WE see before us another tavern: The Stag. Snug and firelit, weathertight and warm. It is morning, and the birds are singing up the sun. Steam curls from the nearby fields as they warm, and berries glow in the hedgerows.

The tavern cat has, in the way of cats, found the best guest room with the best fire, and lies on the hearthrug stretching its belly to the heat.

CHARMING SAT IN the chair closest to the fire, where he slept, and stretched not his belly but his stockinged feet to the flames, leant back, stared at the door to the other room, and shook his head ruefully.

"I wish *I* was a cat," he said idly to the beast. "Bring in a few mice now and then and everyone pets you and thinks you're wonderful. No one expects much, do they?"

The cat half-opened an eye at him, then sat up and began to wash itself lazily.

"*And* no one calls you vain, just because you look after yourself," the Prince continued.

"What was that?" Nell called from the other room.

"Nothing." Charming got to his feet and began tucking things into his pack. "Talking to the cat. I wish I'd managed to grab a *few* things. And I shall miss Roland."

"I thought you were furious at him?" Nell said, still rummaging about in the next room. "Oh, arse, there's a great tear in this skirt. And I haven't got a needle."

"We'll be at the city soon; you can buy a new one." Charming sniffed dubiously at a pair of hose. "And Roland was irritating, impudent, inclined to moralise—the damn hypocrite—and smelly. But he was bloody useful."

"I'm sure you can find another servant."

"Not one like him, I'm afraid. Still, you're pretty useful too, and you smell a lot nicer."

"I'm not your servant," Nell called. "And if you're offering me the position, no thank you."

"Not even if I find *lots* more treasure and give you some?"

"'Find'?"

"Don't you start."

Nell poked her head around the door. "Start what? Moralising? Hah. We're both thieves now, remember; we took those horses. And where d'you think I got the money to pay for our rooms? I'm carrying a week's takings from the Crooked Spoon. Didn't take 'em on purpose, I was supposed to be putting them in the lockbox when the fight kicked off. But I've got 'em, and I'm not going back, so I guess it's stealing."

"I'll pay you back."

"I'll believe that when it happens." She disappeared again.

Charming gave a reluctant smile, shaking his head. "Almost seems a shame," he said to the cat. "But you know how it is. Anyway, she *wants* to part ways. She said."

The cat paused, with its tongue partly out and its eyes half shut. To most people it might have looked adorably dim. To Charming, at that moment, it looked distinctly cynical.

"I don't need to be worrying about someone else," he said. "Just want to get back to being footloose and fancy free. New worlds to conquer, new treasuries to loot... I'm going to have to get a move on, though, the way I've been set back." He looked worried for a moment, but shrugged. "Still, I think I might get out of the romance game. Been there, done that." He tossed his head casually. "Shame to waste these looks, but..."

The cat turned its back on him, flicking its tail disdainfully.

"Be like that, then."

Charming looked around. Everything was packed. He turned to the window to check the weather. "Rain's stopped, Nell," he called over his shoulder. "Bring my boots through, will you?"

Behind him, there was a hard *clunk* and a clatter.

He turned around.

There on the floor, instead of the boots, were a pair of dancing shoes. Very heavy, very *shiny* dancing shoes, blazing sunlight and firelight from every gleaming glass facet.

Charming looked at the shoes. Then he looked at Nell, who stood with her hands on her hips, one eyebrow raised. The boots were nowhere to be seen.

"Wait—" he said. "Who—?" Then, "Ella."

"And to think I thought you were in love with me. *Oh, my most precious and beautiful darling, one glimpse of your face was enough to haunt me forever...* Five miles down the road and you couldn't have picked me out of a crowd, could you?"

"You were wearing a mask when we met!"

"Not for that bit."

"And you sound—you didn't sound..."

"I sound like I work in a kitchen. Which I did for half my childhood, remember? Oh, no, of course you don't."

"All right, all right, you needn't go on! I'm sorry, all right?"

"Bit late for that," she said. "Just think yourself lucky it was *me* caught up with you, and not my godmother."

Charming threw up his hands and slumped back into the chair.

The door opened. Doctor Rapunzel, Princess Marie Blanche, and Lady Bella dei' Sogni walked in. They all stood looking down at him.

He glared. "I suppose she was with you all along," he said.

"No, she just happened to have up and left her throne and her country to take a summer job in the Crooked Spoon," Marie Blanche said. "Idiot."

"Well, *you* did."

"Yes, and for the same reason as her. To bring you to justice."

Nell (shall we stick with Nell?) grinned. "I didn't think it would work, you know. When I heard what they had planned..."

"You mean what Doctor Rapunzel had planned," Marie Blanche said. "I'm sorry I distrusted you, doctor."

"Sometimes distrust is merely caution," the doctor said.

"I do not blame you for it."

"None of us should be blaming anyone except *him*," Bella Lucia said. "Look at us! Look at *him*, sulking, as though he'd been caught stealing jam tarts, instead of..." She glared. "I could run you through right now," she said, her hand hovering near the hilt of a new, and very good, sword. "For everything you've done."

Charming swallowed. The phrase *You're beautiful when you're angry* trembled towards his lips, then, sensibly, retreated to the depths of his brain. She *was* extremely beautiful. She was also furious, hurt, and armed.

And he didn't have his boots.

"Fine by me if you do run him through," said Nell. "We've got the loot. I can tell the innkeeper he left already, play the abandoned maiden... I'm *good* at that, I've had practice..."

"Bodies are easily disposed of," Marie Blanche said. "Especially if one knows where there are wild boar."

"Er..." Charming said. "Look."

"At what?" Rapunzel said. "A liar and a thief?"

"Yes, I know!" Charming said. "Fine! I'm both! And I wronged all of you, I admit it! I'm sorry! But before you spit me on your sword and throw me to the wild boar, can I just explain? It wasn't for me!"

"Oh, here we go," Nell said. "I've been waiting for this. 'It wasn't for me I robbed that coach, it was for my poor old mother, yer honour, she's crippled with the rheumatiz...'"

"I think his mother would be ashamed of him," said Bella.

"Bah, enough of this," said Marie Blanche. "His father's men are less than a day's ride away. Let us hand him over and be done with him."

Doctor Rapunzel raised her hand. "One moment," she said, and pulled a vial from her bag. The liquid within was purple, and thick, and moved with syrupy slowness against the glass. "This is a truth potion," she said. "Take it, and we will listen to you talk, Your Highness."

"Truth potion," he said, staring at the vial. "Really?"

"Really. Call it morbid curiosity, or whatever you like, but I really would like to hear your explanation."

"Am I going to start saying incredibly embarrassing things?"

"Only if you find the truth embarrassing. This will not force you to reveal what is irrelevant, it will merely silence lies. Will you take it?"

"*Fine,*" he said. "Give it here."

He grabbed the vial, pulled the cork, and tossed the contents down his throat, shuddering, then opening his mouth to show his purple-stained tongue. "Satisfied? *Goose,* that tastes vile. Ugh."

"Talk," the sorceress said. "But keep any self-justifications and flourishes to a minimum, if you please. We are all bored of them."

"You've spoken to my father's men, then?" Charming said. "You know he's ill. What else did they tell you?"

"That his illness is the result of a pact you made with a demon," the Doctor said.

"Honestly, people hear one thing, and they get *everything* wrong," Charming said. "Yes, I made a pact with a demon. It was to *cure* the old fart, not make him sick!"

"You made a pact. With a demon. To *cure* someone." Doctor Rapunzel ran her hand down her face, shaking her head. "I hardly dare ask *which* demon."

"Said his name was Mephistopheles," Charming muttered.

"Oh, dear *Goose*," the Doctor said. "And I thought you were *clever!*"

"We're not all educated in the ways of the Infernal," Charming snapped. "And I was frantic! I didn't want the old bastard dying on me!"

Both Marie Blanche and Bella Lucia were staring at him in something like horror.

"What?" he said.

"For someone who made a pact with a demon to save him," Marie Blanche said, "you seem to have very little respect for your father."

"We don't get on," Charming said stiffly. "But I didn't want him to *die*. I don't *want* to take the throne and have to listen to people boring on about border security, and *taxes*, and *farming*, and marry some..." He stopped abruptly and coughed. "Anyway. He didn't want me on the throne either; it was supposed to be my older brother—but *he* had to go off on some stupid quest, didn't he? And after three years, and being sent his signet ring which someone found in a bear's stomach, it was fairly clear he wasn't coming back. So I get dumped with the position of heir to the wretched throne. Which I don't want and never did and the idea that I'd kill to get it is just *ridiculous*, all right? Only the family's never bred well, and there *was* no one else. Which my father pointed out frequently, at length and with obvious regret. Thing is, there's *always* some cousin-by-marriage or *something*, he just didn't *want* them, he wanted *me*. Even though he made it entirely clear he didn't think I was up to the job. I mean, I don't want to be King, he doesn't think I can *do* being King, but he still insists I'm the only one for the job. What sense does that make?"

"It's called succession, and *sense* has never been part of it," said the doctor. "Go on."

"So he's sick and getting worse, we've dragged every healer, herbalist, alchemist, apothecary and barber-surgeon from every corner of the land and half the neighbouring countries, and none of them can do a thing. And I can *feel* the damn crown hanging over my head like a thundercloud that'll never stop raining again once it starts, and so I send for one of *your* lot." He glared at Rapunzel. "A doctor in the arcane arts."

"Oh? Who?"

"Wintering. Wittering. Some name like that. Fussy little fellow, all snuff and spectacles."

"Von Witherham." Doctor Rapunzel made a choking sound. "He showed you his certification, yes?"

"Yes! With the college seal! Doctor whatever von whatsit, doctor in the arcane arts, first class. It was on his certificate. Big swirly letter F."

"The F does not stand for 'first class,'" Doctor Rapunzel said in an oddly tight voice. "It stands for 'failed.' Which was why there would be a very large and obvious line through the seal, if you had bothered to look. I can't *believe* he's actually using it to prove his bona fides."

"Oh *no*," Bella's eyes widened. She gave a choke of laughter, which rapidly dissolved into giggles so utterly delightful and entirely infectious that soon the whole room was laughing, with the exception of Charming and, of course, the cat. Though even the cat appeared to be grinning.

"Well, how was I to know?" Charming snapped. "And I was desperate!"

"Well, desperation makes fools of the best of us," Doctor Rapunzel said, all laughter gone, looking Charming straight in the eye.

He dropped his gaze.

"So you took Von Witherham's advice, and summoned a demon," she said. "The nature of your pact?"

"He said that what was wrong with my father was a curse. He'd lift it in return for a pile of gold as high as I am tall, to be paid seven years and one day after the pact was made, by me, in person, at the top of a mountain in my country. It's called Devil's Head, and now I know why, I suppose."

"A pile of gold as high as you are tall. Specifically gold," Doctor Rapunzel said.

"Yes."

"So why the rest? The crowns, the necklaces, the mechanical bird? You had no need of them. To sell them?"

"Because they were pretty and I wanted them. And because I could." The Prince glowered. "I really *hate* this truth potion," he said.

"And if you fail to fulfil the bargain?"

"Not only does Daddy Dearest kick the bucket, but *I* then get sick, and die in seven years. The due date's in about six months. And now, thanks to you lot—"

"Whatever the next words were that were about to leave your mouth," Marie Blanche said, "I *strongly* suggest you swallow them."

Her voice was so utterly cold it did, in fact, shut him up.

"This mess is your doing," Marie Blanche went on. "No one else's. In order to avoid your responsibilities, you behaved in a most stupid and dangerous fashion."

"I was trying to save his *life*."

"Only because you wished to continue acting like a child," Marie Blanche said. "Running about and playing while others do the work. Had your brother still been around, would you have taken so much trouble to save your father?"

Charming's shoulders slumped, and he sighed. "I don't know," he said. "It was a while ago. I was scared and, yes, probably stupid. And my father is not a nice man. He's a pretty competent king, all things considered, but he's not nice. So maybe not. Anyway. Are you going to turn me over to the guard? Because they *did* finally find that cousin-by-marriage to take the throne."

"They did?" Doctor Rapunzel looked irritated. "My sources were inaccurate. How annoying."

"In *any case*," Charming went on, "I've been cast from the succession, and I'm going to be executed for treason as soon as I get home, and I'd much rather not, if you don't mind."

The women looked at each other.

"We can't, can we?" said Bella Lucia. "I mean, not without making sure the demon gets paid. Otherwise, the King is going to die."

"Indeed. The Prince cannot make the payment if he is dead," said Marie Blanche. "And I doubt the King will believe his story. Unless, doctor, you can persuade His Majesty as to the worth of your truth potion."

"Oh, she wouldn't even be allowed in the country," Charming said. "After what happened, every single doctor of the arcane was banned from setting foot there. Bit of a tendency to overreact, has my dear old dad. Especially when he doesn't know all the facts. Rather like some other people I can think of."

"Oh, *bugger*," said Nell.

Doctor Rapunzel flung up her hands. "After all this!"

Charming eyed the flickering glow at the ends of her fingers uneasily.

Marie Blanche frowned. "Unless someone else can make the payment…"

Doctor Rapunzel shook her head. "The bargain specifically requires the Prince to make the payment. You may trust me that Mephistopheles had a very good reason for that." She looked at Charming again and shook her head. "Probably so that he may continue to toy with you in whatever way gives him pleasure."

"Oh, lovely," Charming said. "Thanks for that."

"So what now?" said Bella.

"Now," said the doctor, "I suggest we go through the rest of the treasure and work out how to return most of it to its original owners. I am prepared to sacrifice a portion of what was stolen from me, to save the King's life, if necessary. However." She fixed Charming with a cold stare. "There will be a full accounting."

Charming pouted. "You're going to count every penny?"

"*I* am," said Marie Blanche. "I have been working with my father's accountants to try and rebalance the kingdom's books since a large portion of our treasury inexplicably disappeared. We will have either yourself or money. The money is of far more value."

Charming sunk his chin into his collar and muttered.

"What," said Bella, "do you feel humiliated, being treated as though you were worth less than gold?"

"Ouch," Charming said. "You've changed."

"I wonder why," Bella said.

"You're going to let me go, then?" Charming said.

"Once you have been measured," Doctor Rapunzel said, "yes. And we will each keep aside some of our portion of the gold, which you may retrieve in time to pay Mephistopheles—if everyone is in agreement?" She looked at the other women, who nodded. "If you try to slip out of it, we do know *exactly* where you'll be in six month's time. And the precise date, if you please?"

"September twenty-second. The first day of autumn," he told her, then tried to glare down at his own mouth. "Oh, shut *up*."

Bella stepped up to Charming and looked down at him. "You've got a chance," she said. "I'm not going to ask you to change, that's up to you, just... don't hurt anyone else like you did us. Please."

He chewed his lip and looked away. "Can I go, then?"

"I suppose we have no choice, do we?" said Marie Blanche. "I don't know about anyone else, but the thought of riding herd on *you* for half a year is more than I can bear."

"Rest assured that the feeling is entirely mutual." Charming heaved himself to his feet. "My boots?"

"Don't even think about it," said Nell. "If you want something to wear, you can take those damned glass shoes."

"Fine." Charming swept a bow. It was a very elegant bow for a man in ill-fitting breeches and stockinged feet. "It's been an experience, ladies."

None of them said anything, not even Bella. The cat yawned.

Prince Charming made a mundane exit, closing the door quietly behind him.

"Well," said Doctor Rapunzel, and clapped her hands together, as though ridding them of dust.

Bella sighed.

Marie Blanche stroked the cat, which purred and stretched.

"Do you think he'll come to get the gold?" said Nell.

"He will," said Rapunzel. "And if he doesn't, we can always find him."

"But the necklace is back with the other treasure," said Bella.

"The necklace is, yes. But the truth potion... well. There might have been a charm of finding in it, too."

"Of course there was," said Marie Blanche. "Always one step ahead, doctor."

"If only that were true."

"Is that...? That seems wrong," Bella said. "He only knew it was a truth potion, he didn't know about the charm."

"Had he known," the doctor said, "he would not have drunk it."

"He might," Bella said. "He really wanted us to believe him. And you could have *asked*."

"Oh, really," Marie Blanche said. "After everything he's done, this troubles you?"

"Well, yes, it does."

"Why is it different from the necklace?" Nell said.

Bella frowned. "Because... he *knew* he was stealing the necklace? That... comes with consequences?"

Marie Blanche made an exasperated sound and threw up her hands.

"No," Doctor Rapunzel said. "She has a point." She looked down at her own hands, turned them over, stared at the stained fingertips. "I have tried very hard not to become she who raised me," she said.

"You're not!" Bella said. "That's not what I meant at all!"

"You might not have meant it so, but you are right, nonetheless," said the Doctor. "Whatever gifts the Good

Folk gave you, you have one of your own: you have a sense of what is right, and that is all yours. Take pride in it, even though it is likely to make your life more difficult—and that of those around you," she added, with a wry twist to her mouth.

"Well," Nell said, "it's too late now, in any case. Don't regret what's done unless you can do something to remedy it, that's my motto. One of 'em, anyway. Which reminds me." She turned to Bella. "I never meant to hit you quite so hard. I'm sorry. I really wanted to hit *him,* and it sort of got misdirected."

"If you hadn't done it, I might have killed him," Bella said, "boots or no boots. So it's probably just as well."

"I'm still sorry. Forget my own strength, sometimes." Nell sighed and stretched her shoulders. "I suppose I should start for home. Funny, I never thought I'd miss kitchen work, but damn, it's been nice to do a little cooking again, make a decent dinner from scraps and not have to watch my mouth all the time in case the Queen disappears and Nell pops up."

"Maybe you should let Nell out now and again," Marie Blanche said. "Personally, I find her refreshing company."

"I spent a lot of time shoving her into hiding," Nell said. "Couldn't have a kitchen girl running things."

"If more rulers knew how to run a kitchen, they might be better at running countries," Marie Blanche said. "I suppose I should head back, too."

"And me," said Bella, rubbing her thumb over a mark on the table.

"Well, I will not—not just yet," Doctor Rapunzel said. "There is a great deal of property that must be returned to its original owners, if they can be found. I should have asked the Prince more questions while he was under the effects of the potion, but with everything else going on, it rather slipped my mind."

"You have been doing most of the thinking for all of us," Marie Blanche said. "You can hardly be blamed if you did not think of absolutely everything."

"So..." Nell said. "If you want some help... I don't absolutely *have* to go home just yet. I left good people in charge, and if they slip"—she gave a slightly malicious grin—"Godmother'll whip 'em into line."

"Can I ask...?" Bella said. "Is your godmother one of the Good Folk?"

"Not if you ask *her*," Nell said. "It's usually safer not to broach the subject. At all. Ever. Anyway, what do you say, doctor?"

"I would greatly appreciate the company," Rapunzel said.

"You know, my parents aren't expecting me back just yet, either," Bella said. "I mean, it's not as though I've found someone appropriate to marry..." She shuddered. "I'm not sure I want to get married at all, honestly. Not unless I know the person *really well* first. Anyway, I can always tell them I'm still looking."

"Your company, too, would be very welcome," Doctor Rapunzel said.

Now, they were all looking at Marie Blanche. "I *can't*," she said. "I have *responsibilities*."

"You have had more responsibilities than you were due since you were fourteen years old," the sorceress observed.

"You *want* to go back to all that lovely bureaucracy?" Nell said. "Those delightful endless meetings about a yard either way on a border? All that *fascinating* paperwork? All the people who need your attention and time and energy every minute of the day and half the night if they can get it?"

"If I were you," Bella said, casually, "I'd rather be going on a hunt. A treasure hunt in reverse, but still, a hunt."

"Oh, you *wretched* women," Marie Blanche said, throwing up her hands. "All right, all right. Papa can manage without me for a little longer. In fact, it may do him good. So long as we don't get involved with any more Good Folk, or Infernals, or..."

"Or dragons?"

"Dragons are all right, if you know what you're doing," Marie Blanche said.

"So're some of the Good Folk, under the right circumstances, not that my godmother's one of 'em in any way at all," said Nell.

"And Roland turned out alright in the end, sort of," Bella said, "and *he's* Infernal."

"Fine, fine, can everyone promise not to fall in love with terrible people? Is that too much to ask?" Marie Blanche said.

"No, don't," Nell said. "A promise like that is just asking for trouble."

"We can promise to look out for each other," Bella said. "That much, at least."

"Oh, yes, that goes without saying," said Rapunzel.

"Doesn't hurt to say it, all the same," said Nell. "So. Where do we start?"

"We start with going through the loot in more detail, I suppose," said the doctor.

"I can remember most of what the other... the other *victims* told me," Bella said. "I know who some of the magical things belong to."

"I need to do more research on Mephistopheles,"

Rapunzel said. "I should see if that fool Von Witherham is still undeservedly alive and in human shape, for a start."

"I just thought of something," said Bella. "Who do you think *put* the curse on Charming's father in the first place? And why?"

"Now that," Doctor Rapunzel said, "is a *very* good question. As is the nature of the quest Charming's brother went on, and whether he is actually gone, or merely... missing."

"Oh, dear. So many questions," Marie Blanche said. "This is all going to take quite some time, isn't it?"

Nell grinned. "You never know your luck," she said.

EVENTUALLY THE ROOM was empty.

The cat uncurled itself. The sun had moved. The cat wandered into the other room, and there the sunlight still fell through the window, making a pleasantly warm patch on the bed, coincidentally illuminating the cuff of a boot poking out from beneath it.

Some things just get forgotten. Some things, perhaps, have a knack for it.

The cat sniffed at the boot, then pawed at it, and eventually dragged it and its scruffy companion out into the light.

It sat down and looked at them, and an expression that was unusually thoughtful, for a cat, began to creep across its face.

(AND CHARMING? HE swiped a pair of quite ordinary boots from under a bench in the bar, and though they were a little small, they kept his feet out of the mud. He slumped and grumbled and sulked down the road, but the sun was out, and the birds were singing, and before many more miles had passed, the sound of a merry song with *extremely* rude lyrics—perhaps one he learned from Roland—began to echo through the trees...)

The End

About the Author

Jade Linwood was raised in Oxfordshire, with books, cats and apple trees.

Jade has lived in Dorset, Wiltshire, Wales, Cambridgeshire and London, and has travelled to Venice, Paris, Rome, Athens, Jordan, and Egypt's White Desert. Jade has competed in swordfighting competitions, been a member of a travelling theatre company, flown on military transport and was once offered a part in *The Bill*.

There are still books, cats, and apple trees. Everything else is mutable.

FIND US ONLINE!

www.rebellionpublishing.com

/solarisbooks   /solarisbks   /solarisbooks

SIGN UP TO OUR NEWSLETTER!

rebellionpublishing.com/newsletter

YOUR REVIEWS MATTER!

Enjoy this book? Got something to say?

Leave a review on Amazon, GoodReads or with your
favourite bookseller and let the world know!